He needed to kiss her.

He needed to feel her mouth against his—this insane pull toward her making him unaware of anything else.

He backed her toward the wall, then placed both hands on either side of her head, his mouth never breaking contact with hers. Her hands wrapped around his neck as her tongue teased his bottom lip, demanding entry. He felt himself grow thick in his jeans, and anticipation flowed through him, making his entire body sweat and his heart thunder in his chest.

He knew one thing—he wasn't stopping unless she told him to. In fact, he might never stop unless she asked him to. The thought only made him harder as his hands fell away from the wall and landed on her hips.

A long, breathless moment later, she pulled away. Her gaze flittered from his lips to his eyes and back again.

The moment of truth. Did they cross yet another line? Or would her common sense tell her to run from this, from him?

Maybe
THIS
LOVE

JENNIFER
SNOW

FOREVER

NEW YORK   BOSTON

Copyright © 2017 by Jennifer Snow
Preview of *Maybe This Christmas* copyright © 2017 by Jennifer Snow
Preview of *Maybe This Summer* copyright © 2017 by Jennifer Snow

Cover design by Elizabeth Turner. Cover photography by Claudio Marinesco. Cover images © Mitchell Funk/GettyImages. Cover copyright © 2017 by Hachette Book Group, Inc.

Forever
Hachette Book Group
1290 Avenue of the Americas
New York, NY 10104
forever-romance.com
twitter.com/foreverromance

First Edition: May 2017
Forever is an imprint of Grand Central Publishing. The Forever name and logo are trademarks of Hachette Book Group, Inc.
The publisher is not responsible for websites (or their content) that are not owned by the publisher.
The Hachette Speakers Bureau provides a wide range of authors for speaking events. To find out more, go to www.hachettespeakersbureau.com or call (866) 376-6591.

ISBNs: 978-1-4555-9487-0 (mass market), 978-1-4555-9489-4 (ebook)

Printed in the United States of America
OPM
10 9 8 7 6 5 4 3 2 1

To my son, Jacob—thank you for convincing me that trampoline parks are a better way to spend an afternoon. The four a.m. writing sessions will always be worth it.

Acknowledgments

Thank you as always to my agent, Stephany Evans, who continues to be a cheerleader through bad synopses and half-assed plot outlines. You always believe I'll get there eventually. Thank you, Madeleine Colavita, for helping me get there. With each and every book, I learn from you, and I value your feedback and notes. The entire team at Grand Central is amazing—Michelle Cashman and the art department—thank you for all the work you do to promote my books and help them find good homes ;)

And a special thank you again to Brijet and Ray Whitney for your hockey research help. I learned so much from you both about the sport I love.

To my husband, my son, my family, my writing tribe, and my amazing readers—you all keep me sane and your support and love mean everything.

And Rachel Lacey—you rock! I appreciate all the ways you help me navigate the promotion world! XO

Maybe
THIS
LOVE

CHAPTER 1

❧

I guess there are worse things than finding out you're married."

Ben Westmore nearly choked on his beer. "Do you not hear something wrong with that sentence?"

His brother Asher drained the contents of his own glass and set it on the table. "Look, man, I think you're sweating this whole thing for nothing. There's no way that marriage certificate is real." He flagged their waitress and put his baseball cap on as the final boarding call for his flight was announced. Airways, the restaurant inside the Colorado airport, was quiet that afternoon, and the brothers had enjoyed a rare meal where they weren't interrupted by hockey fans.

"You think it's a joke?" Ben studied the blurry image on his iPhone. The spirally signature at the bottom looked a lot like his.

"Of course it's a joke. This is *you* we're talking about." Asher reached for his jacket.

"Asher's right. It would take a gun to your head to get

you down the aisle," Mia, their waitress, said, leaning over Ben's shoulder to take a peek at the marriage certificate. She handed him their bill with a grin. "Besides, you wouldn't break my heart like that."

Ben ignored the teasing and waved the bill at Asher. "I'm paying?"

"It's the least you can do after taking me out of the play-offs."

He reached for his wallet, but Mia shook her head. "It's been taken care of." She rolled her eyes as she nodded toward several women sitting at the bar.

The ladies had been smiling at him since he'd walked in with Asher. Captain of the Colorado Avalanche and MVP in the league that season, he was one of the more recognizable hockey players, and his reputation as a playboy was one he didn't even try to dispute. Getting a pretty woman's attention was easier than winning a game of pick-up hockey against eight-year-olds.

He glanced back at the phone. Had he inadvertently, unknowingly gotten married? This copy of a marriage certificate, forwarded to his personal email from the team's fan mail site, seemed to indicate as much. December 31 was listed as the nuptial date, and unfortunately New Year's Eve wasn't ringing so clearly in his memory. He'd been in a bad place at the time. And far too much alcohol had gone into easing his pain.

Enough to make him lose his mind and get married? Impossible.

He handed Mia several bills anyway. "Cover their tab, please."

She shook her head. "This could cover the tab for every-one in here." She tried to hand him back the money, but he refused it. He knew she worked three jobs to support herself and her two kids. One of whom had a birthday in a few days and was a huge hockey fan. "And I'll have those game tickets at will call for you next week."

The look of appreciation in her eyes made him uncomfortable. "Thanks, Ben. You know, if you were going to marry someone..."

He grinned, kissed her cheek, and followed Asher out of the restaurant, before the women at the bar delayed their exit.

"Sure you can't stick around for a few days?" Ben asked.

Now that the New Jersey Devils were officially done with their season, his brother was free, unless he got an invitation to play in the World Championships scheduled to start the following week. Which Ben suspected he would. Out of the three hockey-obsessed Westmore brothers, Asher was arguably the best. Not that Ben would ever admit it.

"I'll be back in a couple of days. I just need to wrap up some things in Jersey," he said, slinging his hockey bag over his shoulder.

"Like getting rid of that crap on your face?" His brother looked more like a bushman than a hockey player the further his team had advanced and his playoff beard grew longer.

Asher ran a hand over it. "Don't shit on me just because I can actually grow one."

Ben laughed. It was true. A thin covering of stubble was all he could hope for, even though he hadn't shaved since the start of the playoffs four weeks ago. "Anyway, clean yourself up before Mom sees you."

His brother shot him a look. "When she finds out the mess you're in, I'll be able to do no wrong. Later, man," he said with a wave as he headed toward security. "Make sure to bring home the cup."

That was the plan. After successfully taking his own

brother out of the running for the Stanley Cup, no one else stood a chance of getting in the way.

At thirty-four years old, he'd been in the NHL playoffs twice before. This was his year to win. The Colorado Avalanche's year to win. This year, nothing was going to keep him from reaching the goal.

His cell phone rang as he headed out of the airport. "Call from Kevin Sanders..." the tone revealed. The team's lawyer. Finally. He'd forwarded the marriage certificate email to him earlier that week and had left several voice-mails. He needed to know if this thing was joke...or something to worry about.

"Hey, Sanders."

"How the hell did you get yourself into shit this deep, Ben?" Kevin said.

Obviously he needed to worry. "Fucked if I know, man. I would have had to be unconscious or drugged to get married." Full stop. He didn't mean just to get married to a stranger or to get married drunk in a chapel in Vegas. He meant to get married. Period. The cool, early spring mountain air made him shiver as he stepped through the revolving doors, and he raised the collar of his leather jacket higher around his neck.

"Well, you look conscious in the video."

"What video?"

"The one I just received from Happy Ever After."

Ben's gut tightened. There was footage of him in a chapel in Vegas?

"And unfortunately, if you were drugged, the evidence would be out of your system, so we will be submitting a drunk and stupid plea and filing for divorce right away," Kevin said.

He thought he was going to throw up.

"Unless, of course, you want to stay married," the lawyer said in his silence.

"Like hell," Ben grumbled. Crossing the airport parking lot, he unlocked his Hummer, climbed in, and slammed the door. "What do we do?"

He sat quietly as Kevin took him through the divorce filing procedure step by step, making sure he was aware of the predicament he found himself in. For four months, this Ms. Kristina Sullivan—the woman's name didn't even sound familiar—had remained quiet; now she'd resurfaced to ruin his life, claiming she wanted a relationship with her "husband."

"This is bullshit. I don't even know this woman."

"Since when has that ever mattered to you?" Kevin asked.

Ben ran a hand through his hair. It was true; he liked the company of women, but marriage? No. Right? Damn, he wished he could remember that night clearly—or *at all*.

"Ben, this is not going to just go away," Kevin said when he didn't respond. "I'll file the required paperwork to start the divorce process, and we'll pray that this Kristina Sullivan chick doesn't contest it. In the meantime, we should find out who her legal representation is and request a mediation session. Find out what her angle is. If we can keep it out of the courts, we have a better chance of keeping things quiet."

Fantastic. He wouldn't have been able to pick out his new "wife"—he cringed—from a police line-up if his life depended on it, and now he would have to sit across from her and ask that she be reasonable enough to let him out of this mess without too much headache? He had his doubts the meeting would go smoothly. "Fine. Let me know when and where." He stabbed the button to start the vehicle. He didn't have time for this. In four days, he planned to lead his team to a four-game, shut-out victory in the semifinal round of the playoffs; he couldn't afford stupid distractions.

Ms. Sullivan better prepare herself for a battle, because he was pissed. He didn't know what kind of game she was playing, but he wanted nothing to do with it.

"Hang in there. Keep breathing and we'll figure this out," his lawyer said through the speakerphone.

Where was that note of optimism two minutes ago when the man was explaining in fine detail the shit-storm Ben's life was about to become. "Can we figure it out quickly? Like before the next playoff round?"

"I can't work miracles, Ben. Talk to you soon."

Disconnecting the call, he swore under his breath. This was the last complication he needed right now. But one thing was for certain: there was no way he would let a little thing like marrying a woman he didn't know in a ceremony he couldn't remember prevent him from hoisting the Stanley Cup that season.

No way in hell.

* * *

She had good eggs. Not perfect eggs. Not young, ideal eggs, but not bad eggs for her thirty-six years, according to the evaluation of her ovarian reserve at the Glenwood Falls Fertility Treatment Center, and for now Olivia Davis would count that as a win.

Of course, if she'd gotten the nerve to make the appointment earlier and hadn't had to sit on a waiting list to see fertility god Dr. Mark Chelsey for over a year, the eggs might have been three to six percent better...

She shook her head and lowered the visor. She retrieved her sunglasses, sliding them on as the sun broke through the clouds. She wouldn't do that. She wouldn't play the what-if game. It only led to more indecision and doubt. What mattered was that at thirty-six, she was starting the process of having a family.

The family *she* wanted.

The mid-April sun warmed her face and the mild, cool breeze whispered a promise of summer as she exited the highway. She hated to raise the top on her BMW convertible as she pulled into her office parking lot.

Life was good. She had good eggs.

She was going to have a family. She bit her lip.

Nope. No more second-guessing. This was what she wanted.

Or at least the next best thing. Her passion for her career as a top divorce attorney had left little time for her to have one the traditional way. But these days, a single career woman had choices.

She'd made hers.

She took several deep breaths, letting thoughts of that morning's fertility clinic appointment take a backseat and switching gears. She had a one o'clock with Kevin Sanders and his hockey player client, and she needed to be on her game. She'd only gone up against him in a divorce case once before and he was tough. It didn't help that she couldn't fully wrap her mind around this particular case. A playboy getting married in Vegas to a woman he claims not to know? Really?

Her client swore they'd known one another for years. Someone was lying, and Olivia would bet her fertility treatment down payment that it was Ben Westmore.

Representing the soon-to-be ex-wives of professional athletes for ten years, she'd seen her share of bullshit. She suspected this guy was regretting his impulsive decision and was desperate to get out without losing his shirt—or hockey jersey, as the case may be.

Well, he couldn't just skate away from his mistakes this time.

She sighed as she approached her reserved stall. Parked next to her was the biggest cobalt blue eyesore she'd ever seen. The tires on the right side of her tiny car scraped against the curb of the sidewalk as she carefully squeezed into the tight space made even smaller by the gas-guzzling, environment-destroying tank crossing the yellow line into her spot. Tinted black windows and silver rims completed the "I'm owned by a douchebag" look of the vehicle, and a Colorado Avalanche license plate that read MVP 1 confirmed the owner. Her opposition's client—Ben Westmore—had arrived.

She cut the engine and peered through the window, eyeing the distance between her door and the lift kit of the monstrosity blocking her in.

Her size eight hips wouldn't squeeze through there. She'd be lucky to open the door wide enough to push her overstuffed briefcase through.

Glancing toward the passenger side, she decided to take her chances with the cherry trees starting to bloom on the office building's lawn. Their bud-covered branches might scratch her when she opened the door, but they would be more forgiving than the tank.

Unbuckling her seatbelt, she slid the fabric of her pencil skirt a little higher over her thighs and then swung one leg over to the passenger side. The gearshift pressed into her butt and her hair caught static along the soft top. Sometimes, she wished she had a bigger car. Holding the passenger seat headrest, she awkwardly swung her other leg over, and the sound of tearing fabric made her cringe.

She glanced down, grateful to see just a tiny rip in the back of the skirt where it was slit to allow movement. Sighing, she collapsed onto the seat, pulling the skirt back into place. Then lowering the visor, she used the mirror to smooth her flyaway strands back into place and reapply a pale nude gloss to her lips.

She squared her shoulders and lifted her chin. "I am a successful, strong, confident woman," she told her reflection. The daily affirmation was part of her routine before every face-to-face with an opposing lawyer. "I can achieve greatness. I can be the best version of myself." She smiled, then added a new one. "I have good eggs."

CHAPTER 2

❧

$\mathcal{W}$as the woman talking to herself?

Ben had been about to enter the law offices when he saw the tiny convertible wedge itself into the space next to his Hummer. Before he could get the attention of the woman inside the car, she was already climbing over the gearshift. He waved as he approached and hesitated when she noticed him outside the passenger window.

The daggers coming from the woman's dark, coffee-colored eyes gave him a chill, despite the uncharacteristically mild weather. He'd seen pissed-off women before, but usually *after* he'd slept with them, not before. "Sorry about the parking. This thing is a little big," he yelled. He'd signed an endorsement deal with GM years before, and he was under contract obligation to drive the beast. He'd asked for a truck, but they'd insisted the Hummer better suited his image. "Just give me a second and I'll move it."

The woman opened the door, pushing through tree branches.

"Don't bother. You'll be leaving before me," she said climbing out, ducking to avoid the pointed twigs and leaves.

"Can I help you with your things?" he asked, as she bent to retrieve her briefcase and a stack of file folders. Out of habit, his eyes shifted to the long, shapely legs and sexy ankles, and he had to remind himself why he was there. His weakness for hot women had landed him in enough trouble.

"I got it, thanks," she said, tightly, avoiding his gaze as she struggled to close the door. She was taller than he'd expected, her three-inch heels putting her head just below the line of his jaw.

The perfect height to kiss. The perfect lips, too. The full, pale nude glossed mouth would be incredibly tempting... under different circumstances.

She cleared her throat loudly and his stare snapped back to hers. "Excuse me," she said, moving past him.

As she did, her long, dark hair snagged on a tree branch, yanking her backward. Her eyes widened and her cheeks flamed with embarrassment.

"Hold on, just stay still. Don't make it worse," he said, stepping forward.

"Don't," she said quickly. "I got it."

He held his hands up. "Sorry, just trying to help."

"If you'd parked in a space that could accommodate your vehicle, I wouldn't be stuck in a tree in the first place," she said, readjusting her files in one arm as she reached back with her hand to free her hair.

"I offered to move it." He folded his arms and continued to watch her fumbling. "You're making it worse."

She shot him a look, then not having any success, she sighed. "Fine."

"Fine what?"

"You can help," she said through clenched teeth.

He was tempted to say his offer had expired, but this was technically his fault. "Okay, hold still." Trying to avoid the scratchy tree branches poking him, he stood in front of her and reached around. As predicted, the top of her head fit nicely under his chin. His chest brushed against hers, but he kept his focus on the tangled hair, relying on every ounce of gentlemanly manners not to sneak a peek down her blouse. The smell of her jasmine-scented shampoo competed with the cherry blossoms, and he held his breath as he untwisted the strands from the tree. Delicious, intoxicating-smelling women were another of his weaknesses.

Her hair was thick and soft and the natural golden high-lights reflected the sun. He resisted the urge to let the locks run through his fingers as he unwrapped them from their snag on the twigs. She was perfectly still, her eyes staring straight at his chest, her breath warm against his neck as he worked. He could hear the dull throbbing of a heartbeat, but he couldn't be sure if it was his or hers. The close proximity made him suddenly uncomfortable, and after freeing the last of her locks, he moved away quickly. "There."

"Thank you," she mumbled, but it sounded more be-grudging than grateful. Avoiding his gaze, she smoothed the hair back in place and stepped around him.

He rushed to match her pace as she headed toward the building. "Do we know each other?" She looked familiar, and the knot in his stomach had him questioning whether he'd had the pleasure of meeting her before. It might explain the way she was acting.

"Not yet," she said.

At the office doors, she reached for the handle, but he stepped quicker. Holding it open, he gestured for her to en-ter. "After you."

She sighed as she went inside.

"Look, I apologized about the Hummer."

"It's fine." She hit the button for the elevator. "If you like destroying the environment," she muttered.

"What was that?"

"Nothing." She checked her watch, as the elevator light lit up and the doors opened. Everything about her, from the dark gray charcoal suit jacket and pencil skirt to the red leather briefcase, screamed lawyer, and when she pressed the button for the ninth floor, he suspected they were headed to the same place.

"You work here?" he asked.

She turned to face him, and he remembered exactly where he'd seen her before—she'd represented his soon-to-be sister-in-law in her divorce case the year before. Shit. His palms started to sweat. "I'm Olivia Davis—the lawyer representing Ms. Sullivan, or should I say 'your wife'?"

His stomach dropped as he realized just how screwed he was. "If I'd known that, I would have left you stuck in that tree."

*   *   *

Did he have to be so gorgeous?

Embarrassing herself in front of the opposition's client wasn't the way she'd hoped to start this process. Especially not when the man had sent her pulse racing while he'd rescued her hair from that stupid tree. Tall and muscular, with dark brown hair and clear blue eyes, a chiseled jawline lightly covered in stubble—it was almost as if he'd stepped right off her wish list.

It figured that the same day she officially decided to take herself off the market—for at least nine months—she experienced an overwhelming pull toward a man she not only couldn't have, but shouldn't want.

Pro athletes were on her "no dating" list. She'd had one athlete-induced broken heart, and that was enough for one lifetime. Of course, that was high school, and by now she should have gotten over being dumped by the captain of the basketball team a week before prom, but her career choice suggested she was still holding a grudge. A tiny one.

There was just something about Ben that was irritatingly tempting. Despite his reputation. Despite his unconscientious preference of vehicles. And despite the way his gaze taking her in in the parking lot had made her knees feel slightly unsteady. It no doubt had everything to do with his unexpected friendliness as he'd apologized for the parking situation. Or more likely, it was the biceps straining against the navy suit jacket he wore and the glimpse of his muscular neck and chest beneath the open collar of his shirt, which should have been wasted hotness where she was concerned.

Hotter the man, deeper the cut.

She suspected her client's scar would take quite a long time to fade.

Her client who'd yet to show up. Olivia glanced at the clock on the meeting room wall. Eleven minutes after eleven. Her chest tightened in an involuntary twist.

Eleven eleven, make a wish. Her mother's voice echoed in her mind.

She swallowed hard. Right now, she wished Ben Westmore would stop staring at her. The look of nervousness on his face made her want to reassure him everything would be okay. What the hell was wrong with her? She cleared her throat. "Let's get started. I'm sure my client will be here shortly," she said, opening her briefcase and removing the paperwork.

Across from her, Kevin Sanders put his cell phone away and opened his laptop. "First of all"—he turned the screen to face her—"this footage of my client is inconclusive."

She stopped him with a cock of her head. "It might not be a clear shot of your client's face on the chapel's security cam footage, but any hockey fan would recognize the man in this video as Mr. Westmore." Westmore. Even his name rolled off her tongue like honey.

"It's inconclusive," Kevin repeated.

"It's him." She reached for her list of Ben's teammates. "But if you insist, I'm happy to subpoena the guys from the team who were with him that night. I'm sure someone can verify the footage."

"Not necessary—it's me," Ben said. "Don't drag the guys into it."

Admirable and honest. She really didn't need him adding any more to the "pro" column. Her job was much easier when the soon-to-be-ex-husband was an asshole.

"Ben, as your lawyer…"

The player turned to his counsel. "I don't want all of this affecting the team or getting back to Coach," he said. "Everyone is stressed enough with the semifinals starting."

If Ben thought he was going to be able to keep this divorce case private, he was delusional. She was surprised that the media hadn't grabbed hold of it already. They would. Especially now that the Avalanche had made it into the semifinal round of the playoffs. She didn't follow hockey, but her boss was a sports fanatic. Last week he'd shown up at the office wearing his Avalanche jersey and a big foam finger, not having made it home to change after a night celebrating the series win. He was going to be pissed when he found out who her opposition was in this case.

She'd applied for the position at the firm ten months ago, when her aunt got sick and she moved to Colorado to take care of her. Her boss, Lyle Kingsley, had hired her, expecting she'd develop her client list on the other side of the proceedings—representing the athletes. But so far, only their spouses were interested in her services. And he'd reluctantly agreed to allow her to accept the cases she knew how to win. But sliding this one past him would be a challenge.

"I admit that it is me in the video," Ben said, breaking into her thoughts. "But I'd like to keep this quiet."

"That's not my job nor my concern," she started.

"Please, Ms. Davis."

The gaze locked on hers was free of any pretense, any cockiness, of anything other than desperation. So unexpected, so different than most arrogant, cocky athletes she sat across from that it caused her to stumble slightly. Looking away quickly, she flipped through her file. "I won't leak information, but I can't promise my client will stay silent throughout this process."

He nodded. "Okay."

"So, moving on," Kevin said, oblivious to the slight ground shake she'd felt in that odd moment with his client.

It had to be the hormone injections the fertility clinic had given her. It was the only logical explanation for the unhealthy, unsafe attraction she was experiencing for a man completely off-limits for so many reasons.

"As per my client's statement, before the night of December thirty-first, he had never met Ms. Sullivan. Therefore, her statement that they have known each other for over twenty years is ridiculous."

Olivia reluctantly turned her attention to Ben. "So, you'd never met this woman until the night you married her?" She slid a photo of her client toward him, forcing her hand steady.

He glanced at it and shook his head. "Never."

Wow. That almost sounded truthful. But it had to be a lie. How drunk would a person have to be to marry someone they'd just met? The thought helped to dampen the intensity of her attraction. Good. Focus on his perceivable flaws—lacks good judgment and drinks too much. "She claims you two met in school years ago."

He repeated her name several times and shook his head. "We had a small class in Glenwood—maybe twelve students. I don't remember her because I'd never met her before." His voice took on more confidence now. "Obviously she recognized who I was, saw that I was shit-faced drunk, and took advantage of the situation."

"Exactly," Kevin jumped in. "And if she wanted a relationship with my client, why did she wait four months before coming forward?"

"That's not accurate. Ms. Sullivan"—who still hadn't shown up—"attempted to contact Mr. Westmore numerous times over the last few months." Pulling out her client's phone and email records, she slid them across the boardroom table.

Ben's eyes scanned quickly. "This email address is monitored by the team. It's screened for weirdos before legitimate fan mail is forwarded on to players or their fan club managers," he said, reading the emails supposedly for the first time. "I've never seen these before, and I'm pretty certain they wouldn't have been forwarded to me anyway."

Unfortunately, that all made sense. "What about the telephone calls and texts?"

He glanced at the phone record. "Shortly after Vegas, I had to change my phone number." He shifted in his seat.

"To avoid my client's calls?"

"No. Because an angry one-night stand tweeted my phone number."

Wow. "Can you prove that? Can your cell provider confirm the number was changed?"

Jennifer Snow

He nodded.

Next to him, Kevin made a note to get the evidence.

She sighed. This wasn't going exactly as she'd planned or hoped. Being able to validate his silence throughout her client's attempts at contact didn't go in her favor, but she still didn't believe they didn't have the shared history her client was so adamant about. She glanced toward the boardroom door again. Where the hell was Kristina? "Okay, so according to you, alcohol was to blame that night? You have no recollection of that evening's events, and you had no former connection to Ms. Sullivan other than a hook-up on December thirty-first of last year?" She was stalling, but until her client showed up she had little else to try to nail him with to further their case. Nail him. The choice of wording in her thoughts made her blush.

Ben's intense gaze locked with hers and made her cheeks feel like they were on fire. "I don't know this woman."

Damn. Had someone turned up the heat in there? She resisted the urge to remove her suit jacket. "Well…"

"Call from Rebecca, red head, long legs…Call from Rebecca…"

Ben quickly silenced the call coming in on his cell phone.

Obviously he'd dared to give out his new number. "As opposed to Rebecca with short legs?"

"What? He knows more than one Rebecca—hardly a crime," Sanders said.

Ben released a breath. "She put her number in my phone that way…It was joke."

The door opened and her assistant, Madison, poked her head inside. "Ms. Sullivan is here," she said.

Thank God.

She saw Ben sit straighter, clenching his hands together in front of him. "Let her in, please."

Kristina looked just as nervous as she entered the room and approached the table, clutching her purse strap. "I'm sorry I'm late," she said. "I had to drop my son off at school."

"You have a kid?" Kevin asked.

Ben's knuckles turned white.

Olivia usually loved the element of surprise, but today it made her stomach turn. Dragging a kid into this mess only made things more complicated. "Yes. Your client has a new stepson," she said, the words tasting sour on her lips.

"Fuck," Ben muttered, not quietly enough. Then leaning across the table, he glared at Kristina. "Look, I don't know what you want. But I don't know you. So whatever game you're playing needs to end."

Kristina's expression was slightly embarrassed as she retrieved an old elementary school class photo from her oversized purse. She slid it across the table toward him. "*Clueless* Kristina, *Tubby* Tina?"

Ben's mouth dropped at the mention of the nasty nicknames. A look of recognition registered on his face.

"Care to retract your last statement, Mr. Westmore?" Olivia asked.

CHAPTER 3

❧

Three hours later, Ben swung open the door to his family home in Glenwood Falls. The familiar smell of homemade bread, fresh from the oven, reached him, but today he found no comfort in it. Little had changed in the house over the years—from the lace curtains his grandmother had made hanging in the living room windows to the family pictures they had taken each fall lined up on the wall in the hallway. The hardwood floor still held the evidence of indoor hockey games played when their parents weren't home, and the furniture had been reupholstered so many times his mother could have refurnished the entire house for the amount she'd spent holding on to the old stuff. Coming home was usually a far too rare occurrence, and one he looked forward to, but today he was on a mission.

"Mom!" he called as he made his way toward the kitchen.

She collided with him rounding the corner. "Ben? What are you doing here?" She wiped damp hands on her apron and reached out to pull him in for a hug.

When she held on a little too long, he pried himself away. "Hi, Mom."

"I didn't think you were coming by until family dinner on…"

The last Sunday of the month. The one day he and Asher both made an effort to be in town, so the entire family could get together. "I know. I just needed to get something."

His mother's perceptive eyes bored a hole through his. "What's wrong?"

"Nothing." Too quick.

"Right. Because you always drive out here just to visit during playoff season."

"You're not happy to see me?" Okay, now he was stalling.

She swiped a dishtowel at him, zapping his arm.

"Ow! That'll leave a welt," he said, massaging the spot.

"I'll be happier to see you when you're carrying a big silver cup," she said with a look.

"That hurts even more," he grumbled. His family certainly kept him humble. Being so close to a cup win twice before and not hoisting it in victory, he'd never live it down if it happened a third time. Oddly enough, the family didn't put the same pressure on Ash. Curse of being the oldest son.

"You know I'd welcome a visit from my favorite son anytime…"

He scoffed. She gave each of his brothers the same story. To claim the title of favorite son, he just needed to be the one standing there.

"But I know you're supposed to be at practice right now, so what are you doing here?" She placed her hands on her hips and waited.

She still knew how to make him feel guilty for skipping practice with a simple look. The one that said, *I'm not mad, I'm disappointed.* Disappointed was always so much worse…and his latest antics were sure to earn another disapproving look. "I just wanted to take a look through some of the boxes in the attic." He knew his mother was the one person besides his lawyer he could trust with the knowledge about his current mess, but he also knew she was the one person on the planet who didn't believe his "I'm never settling down" story. The last thing he needed was his mother getting excited for absolutely nothing. He had no intentions of staying married to Kristina Sullivan.

He still couldn't believe the woman who had sat across from him in the boardroom hours before was Clueless Kristina, Tubby Tina, and countless other mean-spirited names he knew her as—a girl he'd gone to school with when his family still lived in Denver. He'd attended kindergarten through grade three at Red Oak Elementary, before his parents moved the family to Glenwood Falls and he'd switched schools.

When the lawyer said they'd been classmates years ago, he hadn't even considered that far back.

"So, who the hell is she?" his lawyer had asked as they'd left the law office.

"Some girl I went to elementary school with. She was quiet and shy and everyone teased her…"

"Let me guess—she struggled in class and was a little chubby?" Even his lawyer looked annoyed by the meanness of kids.

He'd nodded.

"So, what? It's a revenge thing?" Kevin had asked, coming to the same conclusion Ben had.

"I guess so."

And unfortunately, he wasn't sure he didn't deserve it.

Which was why he needed to find the boxes containing his old school memories to try to figure out just how much trouble he was actually in.

"The old boxes?" his mother asked now, raising an eye-brow. "Since when are *you* sentimental?"

Since never. This trip down memory lane was simply to save his ass. He was going to have to be straight with his mother. "Do you remember a girl I went to school with in Denver—Kristina Sullivan?"

The old-fashioned kettle whistled on the stove, and she waved a hand for him to follow her down the hall. "Kristina Sullivan from Denver," she repeated. "It doesn't sound familiar."

It hadn't to him at first, either, but as Kristina had re-counted stories of their past in the conference room, old images of schoolyard bullying had his stomach in knots. Kids hadn't been kind to Kristina. But he took comfort in the fact that he didn't recall participating in the teasing and taunting. Did she remember things differently?

She hadn't seemed angry or vengeful in the boardroom that morning, but that might be because she knew her lawyer would make sure he paid for any forgotten past mistakes—financially and with his reputation.

An image of Olivia Davis's piercing dark eyes flashed in his mind, followed by the same gut-twisting sensation he'd felt untangling her hair from the tree.

His mother snapped her fingers. "Was she the little girl who lived in the trailer park just outside of town?"

He nodded, a memory of her rundown home appearing in his mind. Every Christmas, their local church sponsored less fortunate families in the neighborhood, and most lived in Pine Oaks Trailer Park. Kristina's family always refused to accept the donated hampers of food and toys, so the family would leave them on the broken front step. He remembered looking in the side mirror as they drove away and seeing Kristina and her brother bringing the box inside once they left.

The lesson on kindness and giving back to the community hadn't been lost on him. The three children's charities he supported now were a testament to that.

"Why the sudden interest? Did you see her recently?" his mother asked, pouring a cup of chamomile tea. The soothing scent filling the kitchen did nothing to soothe his frazzled nerves.

"You could say that," he mumbled, lowering his gaze to the floor when she swung around to face him.

"Oh, Ben—what did you do?" she asked, shooting him her best I'm-your-mother-and-I-can-still-ground-you look.

"I might have married her."

Luckily his instincts were as sharp as his reflexes, otherwise he'd never have caught his fainting mother right before she hit the floor.

*   *   *

"Damn," Olivia muttered as the stack of folders the medical clinic had couriered over fell across the tiled office floor. She hoped nothing in them was loose. Mixing up the contents of these files could make the selection of a sperm donor a little trickier.

Setting her coffee on the reception desk, she readjusted her purse and bent to pick up the files.

Madison came to her aid.

"It's okay, I got this," Olivia said, quickly, gathering them. She'd only been working for the firm for ten months; she had no intentions of telling anyone about her plans until she could no longer hide a pregnant belly behind a banker's box.

Unfortunately, despite her scramble to reach the files farthest away, she wasn't fast enough.

She should have requested the files be sent to her home,

but she had a two-hour gap between appointments that afternoon, and she was eager to start the selection process.

Madison studied the files in her hands and shot Olivia a wide-eyed look.

Deep breath. There's no way the young, twentysomething paralegal would recognize the fertility clinic logo on the corner…

"You're planning to have a baby?"

Oh my God. "Shhhh…" She sighed, taking the folders from her and standing. "Please grab my coffee and follow me."

Inside her office, she set them near her purse on the floor and took her coffee from her. "Thank you. Um…when you were hired you signed a confidentiality agreement, right?"

Madison nodded, her asymmetrical pixie cut hair falling in front of her eyes. "Yes. And believe me, it's so hard to keep quiet about some of the…"

Olivia held up a hand. "Don't admit that to anyone." Though she got it. The high-profile clients and their often sensitive situations made for some pretty juicy gossip…not that she had many girlfriends to spill to anyway. Moving around a lot with her aunt as a child, after her parents died, Olivia had never bothered to make lasting friendships—a trait she'd carried into adulthood. And was starting to regret. With her aunt gone now, she was feeling the loneliness even more.

Was she hoping a baby would fill that gap?

Across from her, Madison's perfectly applied fake lashes met her thin penciled-in eyebrows. "Oh, I swear, I'd never say anything."

"Good. Well, this information needs to be kept to yourself as well, okay?"

She nodded again. "No one knows?"

"Not yet." And hopefully not for a while. She wanted to prove herself with a few more cases before requesting a maternity leave from the company. She wasn't even sure what she would do after the baby was born—the temptation to return to L.A. was strong now that her aunt was gone. In fact, she might have already, had she not discovered the fertility clinic in Glenwood Falls.

She sat and wiggled her computer mouse until the Hawaiian sunset screensaver disappeared. It was the default on the computer, and she'd never changed it to a personal picture, like most of her colleagues. No selfie shot with a significant other or recent vacation picture. Her dating history was laughable, her career demanded all of her time, and she couldn't remember the last vacation she'd taken. And even if she had a pet, she'd refuse to post pictures of it everywhere. She kept her professional life professional and her private life private, though lately she'd been wondering where that left her.

Instead of leaving, Madison sat. "Those were sperm donor files, right?"

How did she know so much? She simply nodded, opening her email.

"Have you chosen one yet?"

"Not yet," she said, scanning the 164 emails appearing in her inbox. By the look of all of the urgent flagged ones, she probably wouldn't get to the files itching to be read until midnight.

"Have they harvested the eggs?" Excitement was evident in Madison's voice. "When is the implantation?"

Wow. Did the girl specialize in this field? "I really need to get to these emails."

Madison looked disappointed as she nodded. "You're right, you're busy. Sorry. I just find it fascinating."

What was fascinating? That she'd let her window to conceive naturally slip by and was now feeling the desperation of a ticking biological clock? "It's okay," she said simply, then quickly added, "but this stays between us." Though it did feel oddly comforting to not be keeping the secret exclusively anymore.

Madison stood to leave. "I was conceived through in vitro."

Olivia's head snapped up. "You were?"

She nodded. "My parents were older when they decided to have a family."

Older. Right. At thirty-six, she wasn't exactly considered a geriatric mother, but she wasn't far off.

"I think it's really awesome. If you want to talk to someone about it."

She didn't. "I'm good. Thanks. Just remember not to say anything."

Madison made a zipping motion with her lips as she left the office and closed the door behind her.

Slumping back in her chair, Olivia sighed. Seeing the *Sullivan v. Westmore* file on her desk, an image of Ben appeared in her mind. That man would make gorgeous babies. If he'd marry a woman he barely knew, she couldn't help but wonder if he'd donate sperm to one.

* * *

The asthma-inducing layer of dust on the boxes in the attic made Ben hesitate. Did he really want to send all of that settled, heavy protective coating spiraling into the air around him? He was currently being haunted by one ghost from his past; he wasn't sure he could handle any more.

He scanned the small space above the garage. Christmas decorations, old quilts from their childhood, boxes of family photos up to three generations back, some of his father's old tools. He moved along the beams, and insulation immediately clung to his pants and shirt. He wasn't dressed for this.

He rolled the sleeves of his shirt. When he spotted boxes labeled with his name in the corner, his stomach tightened. The memories of his elementary school days were coming back slowly; though they were faded, they offered him no sense of peace.

Neither had his mother's words when she'd regained consciousness only to slap him on the side of the head. "What the hell were you thinking?" she asked now, joining him in the attic.

He *hadn't* been thinking. He'd been piss-ass drunk. Unfortunately, that didn't take much as he wasn't a heavy drinker. He treated his body with respect, knowing it was his greatest ally in prolonging his time on the ice. "I told you, I don't remember that night."

She eyed him. "Vegas…New Year's Eve?" Realization dawned on her still pale face. "Tell me this isn't about Janelle's engagement."

He should have known his mother would have heard. One of his brothers had probably mentioned it. More than likely Asher—the guy was glued to every sports news station app possible. And Ben's ex-girlfriend's public engagement had been splattered all over Sports News Vegas.

He glanced around. "Are those my only boxes?"

"Ben, honey, it's been years. It's time to move on."

He nodded. The thing was, he thought he had moved on, but seeing Janelle's surprised, glowing expression as her co-anchor had dropped to one knee on set had been like a bullet to his chest.

It had reminded him of another New Year's Eve, when their own three-year relationship had ended just before the countdown. Only shot after shot of Jose Cuervo had been enough to dull the ache.

"Well, you know I'd love nothing more than for you to settle down, but this isn't ideal, and I know you don't want to stay married, so what are you going to do?" his mother asked.

"My lawyer has filed for divorce, and we're trying to keep all of this out of the media."

She raised an eyebrow.

"*Trying* being the operative word. In the meantime, I need to remember the deal with this Kristina woman and figure out why the hell I married her. And why she'd want to marry me." The idea that this was a revenge thing made him shudder.

He grabbed a blanket and, turning his head away, shook it free of as much dust as possible before laying it across a box labeled with Asher's name. He sat and reached for the closest box of his own items.

"Good luck," his mother said, starting to descend the ladder.

"Not going to help?"

"Nope."

Great. He might get out of there by midnight. He blew the dust away before opening the flaps and looking inside.

Old hockey trophies and medals, team photos…He sorted through them quickly, not needing to see the items to conjure memories. Hockey had been his life for so long, every moment of his twenty-eight years on skates were etched in his mind.

As a kid growing up in Glenwood Falls, every day had been spent outside as much as possible. The only question was whether the lake was warm enough for swimming or frozen enough for ice hockey. For a young kid in love with the sport, there was no better experience than a game on an outdoor rink in the cold fresh mountain air. The large ice surface didn't restrict the number of players, and they'd play with the neighborhood kids until the last signs of daylight disappeared over the mountains, even forgetting to eat. Their parents' "Be back before dark" was often forgotten as well, resulting in their fathers' arrival at the lake long past curfew, where they'd stay and play just a little bit longer with his warning not to tell their mothers.

He closed the box and moved it to the side, noticing his first pro-scale hockey stick on the floor. He smiled as he reached for it, wiping it free of dust. He stood and flipped the stick over in his hands, still loving the feel of it, or rather the memories the feel of it evoked.

The stick had been a Christmas present from Jackson when he was twelve—the year they'd both made the AAA Junior league. His brother had wanted the high-scale pro-caliber stick, from the moment they'd seen it inside Rolling's Sports before the season started.

Of course their parents couldn't afford to buy one for each of them, so Jackson knew that if he wanted one, he'd have to get a job and save for it. And he did. Every morning for three months, his brother would climb down from the top bunk in the room they shared and head out to deliver the daily paper before the school bus picked them up. He saved every cent he made, kept it in a Mason jar under the mattress, where he thought it was hidden, but Ben could see it above his head through the metal bedsprings, filling up each week after collection.

Seeing the cash his brother was earning tempted Ben to get a part-time route as well, but he'd liked his sleep a little too much. Besides, it wasn't the stick that made the player, but what he could do with it.

Waking up Christmas morning to see the stick under

the tree with his name on the tag had surprised him, and now he wondered if Jackson had known even then that he lacked whatever special quality Ben and Asher seemed to possess—the drive or the determination or just sheer will to make it to the big leagues.

Ben sighed, playing with the edge of the fraying red tape. He still couldn't believe Jackson had turned away from the opportunity of a lifetime: a second chance to play in the NHL.

Ben liked his brother's fiancée well enough, and they seemed happy together, but he couldn't shake the feeling of disappointment that Jackson had chosen the quiet, simple life as Junior league coach over the dream.

He wondered if his brother would ever regret it.

Setting both the stick and the thoughts aside, he resumed his mission to find the old elementary school yearbook. Three boxes later, he found it.

The spine on the thin, forever-closed hardcover yearbook creaked as he flipped to the page of his third grade home-room class. His goofy, toothless grin and long, disheveled hair (hockey season playoff hair) smiled back at him, and he shook his head. Thank God, he'd filled out in his teenage years. At age nine, he'd had only his fast skating and puck handling to carry him through the various leagues.

His gaze scanned the page for Kristina and his chest ached when he saw the sad smile on the little girl's chubby face. Memories of the teasing chants he'd heard following her down the hallways of school and the way she'd eat lunch alone, or didn't eat lunch at all, which was far too often the case, made him close the book abruptly.

Damn. Kids were cruel sometimes, and he hated that he may have played a part in that little girl's pain.

And shit, if she was out for revenge now, who was he to stop her?

CHAPTER 4

*Ⲟ*livia leaned against her kitchen counter, her favorite coffee cup in her hand—the words NEVER TRUST A NON-COFFEE DRINKER fading after years of use—bit her lower lip, and stared at the pile of file folders on her round, glass-top table.

Oh, come on, she told the nagging, persistent nerves. This was just part of the process.

She'd known she'd have to select a donor, but until she was faced with rifling through profile after profile of potentials, the reality of the situation hadn't hit. Since starting the in vitro process, all talk had been about the procedure, and the focus had been on her—her ability to conceive through in vitro methods, her ability to carry a baby to term and deliver safely, and her readiness for a family.

Not until yesterday's appointment had she ever allowed herself to think about the other half of the equation—the part that made it all possible.

She shook off her apprehension, picked up the files, and

carried them onto her deck, which overlooked the backyard of the apartment complex. The snow was long gone, though it was still visible along the mountaintops in the distance, and the trees were starting to bud. She loved this time of year—new beginnings, new life...

She sat on her rocking swing chair and tucked her legs under her. Pulling her sweater closer to her body as the mild day gave way to a cooler spring evening, she reached for the first folder.

Just like reviewing potential cases.

The identities of the donors were kept anonymous, but the files listed everything from physical descriptions of height, weight, and eye, skin, and hair color to any family illnesses. They also provided a chart that listed any aptitudes or acknowledged weaknesses.

Not surprisingly, few weaknesses were admitted to.

As she scanned the first donor's medical history, she paused. The doctor had said to select the closest candidate to her idea of the perfect donor. But what was her idea of the perfect sperm? Smart, handsome, funny, driven, quiet determination...Seemed like a lot of expectations to put on a tiny swimmer you can't even see without a microscope.

Besides, selecting an astrophysicist as a donor didn't guarantee her a baby who would be a rocket scientist someday, but the odds were a little better, at least.

The testimonials from previous patients of the clinic had really emphasized the caliber of donors offered, but she'd been so preoccupied with whether or not she could hold up her end of the bargain with eggs that hadn't expired, she hadn't given the Y chromosome much thought. Now she had a week to find what normally took women years of searching for Mr. Right to discover.

How exactly did she choose the perfect father for her child?

Panic crept into her chest, and her grip tightened on the file folder on her lap.

Well, she wouldn't reach a decision by freaking out.

She took a gulp of hot coffee, burning the back of her throat, before setting the cup aside and returning her attention to the file.

This donor was Caucasian, five-foot-eleven, and 180 pounds…dark hair, brown eyes…So far so good. Profession: marketing manager for a hotel chain.

She paused. Marketing people were generally outgoing, personable, outside-of-the-box thinkers…She'd always been drawn to personalities like that, having been the complete opposite.

Or at least since her parents died.

Over the years, not much had changed. Career-focused and driven, she still didn't attract much friendliness in her life.

Was a baby to fill that gap?

It wasn't the first time she'd questioned her intentions of starting a family alone, and loneliness might be part of the reason she was doing this—the desire to have someone in her life she could care about, who would care about her. But another part of her knew she was hoping to recreate a part of her past she'd lost long ago. The part with her parents. The short, precious part where things were different. When she'd felt safe and loved and supported. Her aunt had been a great role model for her—a successful corporate law attorney, she'd taught Olivia the value of hard work and determination, but she'd never been the nurturing type…unlike Olivia's mother.

She pushed all thoughts of her past aside as she continued

to read. Heart issues on his maternal side and diabetes on his paternal side…Diabetes ran in her family as well. Too much of a risk.

She closed the folder and reached for another.

This guy was six-foot-two, two hundred pounds, blue eyes, and dark hair. A pro athlete.

An image of Ben Westmore flashed in her mind, and she almost set the file aside without reading further. Sure she'd thought about it the other day, but she hadn't been serious…

It was ridiculous. No doubt Ben Westmore had donated plenty of sperm in his lifetime. All wasted, of course. None at a fertility clinic, destined for greatness.

And while she wasn't thrilled by the idea of a pro athlete donor, the more she read, the more this one appealed. No medical history to be concerned about. Thirty-two and Catholic.

She put him in a maybe pile and sighed.

This wasn't exactly other women's idea of a fun Friday night, but at least she knew two things—she'd be going to bed alone and at the end of the evening she'd have a father for her unconceived child.

* * *

Ben stared at the financial statements in his hand as he rode the elevator to the Kingsley Family Law Offices. He refused to read too much into the fact that he'd decided to hand-deliver them to Ms. Davis instead of couriering them the way Sanders had told him to. His lawyer was out of town that week, and Ben didn't trust the time-sensitive and private documents to anyone else—that was all.

It had nothing to do with wanting to see Olivia Davis again. That would be stupid.

Entering the offices a moment later, he straightened his tie and cleared his throat. The young receptionist was on the phone, but her eyes widened when she glanced up. "Mom, I'll call you back," she said, standing. "Hi. What are you doing here?" Her cheeks flamed and she removed her glasses. "I mean, do you have an appointment?"

He smiled. "No, but I have some documents to drop off to Ms. Davis. Is she available?"

"Is she representing you?"

"No."

"Is she expecting you?"

"No."

"Well, I'm sorry…"

"Holy shit—it's Ben Westmore," a booming male voice said to his right.

Ben turned and extended a hand to an older man with thinning gray hair and coffee stains on his white dress shirt. "Nice to meet you…"

"Lyle Kingsley—senior partner at the firm." His smile faded slightly, and he lowered his voice. "Are you looking for representation?"

"Actually, I…"

"The firm is currently representing his wife," Olivia said, coming out of her own office.

Her expression as she approached was one of annoyance and slight apprehension. Unlike the day they'd met, today she was dressed more casually in a pair of tan dress pants and a figure-hugging black sweater that put her hourglass figure on full display. The boatneck design of the cashmere accentuated her collarbone, stealing his focus, and made her neck appear long and slender. Her dark hair was pulled back into a low ponytail, and the memory of its softness made him regret his decision to come. If possible, this polished casualness with a hint of sexy shook his confidence more than the power suit she'd worn.

"Why wasn't I aware of this?" Lyle asked her.

Watching Olivia squirm was actually fun. She was trying to maintain an outwardly calm and unfazed appearance, but she was failing miserably. Yet when she shot daggers at him from her gorgeous dark eyes, it was *his* mouth that went dry and his palms that sweat.

What the hell? Why was he feeling nauseous? She was the one in hot water with her boss.

"It's on this afternoon's meeting agenda," she said tightly.

"Can we talk over here for a sec?" Lyle said, moving away from the reception desk toward Olivia's office. "Just a second, Ben."

"Take your time."

Trying to appear as though he wasn't straining to hear every word, Ben picked up a magazine and flipped through it. She'd taken on a case without her boss's approval? Admittedly, she didn't strike him as a woman who would have even asked. Her stubborn independence was evident in the fact that she'd been ready to spend her day in the cherry blossom tree rather than accept his help.

"He's in the playoffs," he heard Lyle say.

"That's not my problem," Olivia said.

"This has to be affecting him, and we need him on his A game…"

A scoff from Olivia. "This isn't about hockey."

"Look around, Olivia! The Avalanche are closer to the cup than they have been in years. All of Denver is buzzing about hockey these days, and no one wants Westmore to choke again."

Ben almost choked at that moment. He'd led the team to the playoffs twice already; people had to get off his back.

He wasn't the only one on the team. Sure, the playoffs made him a little edgy and nervous, but the misconception that he suffered from playoff anxiety had to stop.

The not-so-private conversation behind him wasn't helping. "You know what, I just needed to drop these off, so…" He placed the envelope on the reception desk.

"Wait," Lyle said, but his office phone rang.

"That's the courthouse calling," the receptionist said.

"Shit…okay, I have to get that. Sorry about this." He shot a disapproving look Olivia's way before turning back to Ben. "Good luck with the semifinals."

"I'll try not to choke," he said as the guy disappeared into his office.

Olivia picked up the envelope from the receptionist's desk.

"Did I get you in trouble with your boss?"

"No. These your financials?" she asked.

"Yes."

"Could have couriered 'em."

So she *was* in trouble. He grinned. "Thought I should stop by to make sure you didn't need rescuing again. You know, a high heel caught in a sewer grate or skirt tucked into your pantyhose."

Her own quick, slightly embarrassed smile nearly put him on his ass. The way it transformed her features had him dazed. Gone was the serious, determined lawyer, and he was given a glimpse of a different woman. One he'd be tempted to get to know better, under different circumstances.

Shifting from one foot to the other, the smile faded and she looked uncomfortable, as though she regretted relaxing her guard—ever so briefly. "Thank you for these." She waved the envelope then checked her watch. "I need to get back to work."

He nodded. "Right…Yeah, I have to get to practice…"

She paused, studying him. "There's a lot riding on these playoffs, huh?"

"Just about everything," he said, surprising himself with his honesty.

Her brows furrowed. "It's only a game."

Spoken like someone who wasn't a sports enthusiast. It was true that he wasn't saving lives out there on the ice, but she couldn't possibly understand the pressure of thousands of fans depending on their idol to bring home the win. The pressure of being an idol. The pressure of proving to himself that he was as good at the sport as everyone believed—or hoped—before time ran out. He didn't want to retire with the regret of not having tried hard enough. "This could be my last chance to prove I can bring home the cup. I'm not getting any younger, you know?"

Her jaw dropped, but she quickly recovered. "Actually, I do," she said, her gaze locked on his, a look in her dark eyes that made him think she just might understand. He wondered what she might be chasing. From what he knew of her, she was successful in her career, but was there something else missing in Olivia Davis's life?

They fell into silence, and the unexplainable connection vibrating between them was something he hadn't been at all prepared for. He resisted the urge to invite her to coffee to continue the conversation, to dig deeper into the inappropriate yet undeniable attraction. The temptation to once again break the touch barrier was overwhelming—the soft sweater, the curves of her body, the scent of jasmine lingering on the air clouded his common sense, made him forget that she was off-limits.

Her expression was hesitant, as if she was waiting for him to say something to break the tension but also a little fearful of what her own response would be. For the first time around a beautiful woman, Ben was at a standstill—he couldn't pursue her, yet he couldn't turn and walk out of the office.

"Call from Isabelle…Call from Isabelle…" Damn. Reaching into his pocket, he hit Dismiss. He hadn't returned any of the calls from the women in his digital black book in weeks, but the timing of them was killing him. Returning his attention to Olivia, he saw the moment was gone.

She cleared her throat and took a deep breath. "Well, thanks again," she said before turning on her three-inch heels and disappearing into her office, where the door shut a little too loudly.

* * *

Shit, shit, shit.

Olivia dropped the envelope onto her desk and bit her lip as she paced her office.

What the hell was that? The electric tension between them had her pulse soaring and her knees slightly weak. The way his gaze had drifted over her had made her want to retreat to the safety of her office, but retreating wasn't something she did. The obvious interest in his expression had her feeling all kinds of uneasy, and she hoped she could get through this case with as little interaction with him as possible. He was far too tempting, and feeling something for the opposition was certain to mess with her ability to represent her own client's best interests.

But damn, it had been more than just a superficial attraction. She'd actually experienced a connection with Ben Westmore. The first real connection she'd had with anyone in a very long time.

That cell phone had impeccable timing. But thank God.

She'd needed the reality check. Ben Westmore was a player, and she wouldn't be played.

Unfortunately, the uneasiness in the pit of her stomach remained. There had been an obvious attraction when they met—the man was gorgeous, and she'd have had to be dead not to feel one—but the momentary connection a few minutes before had been different. His vulnerability had struck a chord in her.

Last chance…Not getting any younger.

She knew exactly how he felt.

She forced several deep breaths, the list of reasons he was off-limits replaying on a loop in her mind. Rebecca the redhead with long legs, Isabelle, and no doubt countless other women quickly rising to the top.

She needed to pull it together.

Yet the brief glimpse he'd given her of a man running out a timer had been too real, too familiar.

For that split second, it had almost felt like Ben Westmore might be the only person who would understand her own ticking clock.

CHAPTER 5

~∞~

$\mathcal{M}$ an, when you fuck things up, you fuck them up good."
Telling his buddy Owen about his latest disaster may not have been the best idea, but Ben was going crazy. "It's not funny." Since the dropoff at Olivia's office two days before, he hadn't been able to shake thoughts of her from his mind. She was a beautiful woman, but he'd had beautiful women before. There was something else about her...a quiet vulnerability under the strong exterior that he'd caught a glimpse of. The way her expression had softened for just a moment, resulting in a heated spark between them. Emotions were things he reserved for family and maybe a handful of close friends, yet his momentary lapse of judgment in lowering his guard had exposed him, and he didn't like it. "I've never been this...conflicted over a woman before." And it was driving him insane.

"Relax. It's just because she's the first woman you've been attracted to since puberty that you weren't able to get in the sack within three hours of meeting."

"Maybe you're right. It's the pent-up sexual energy messing with my brain." That had to be it. Usually he exhausted that energy, and then the woman was a beautiful but distant memory. The more distant the better.

Unfortunately, this attraction felt different, like it came with a new set of rules—ones his body and mind didn't understand.

"Well, obviously you can't deal with it in your usual way, so what are you going to do? It's not just affecting your brain, it's affecting your game…again."

"Said the team's mascot," he said grumpily, readjusting his hockey bag on his shoulder. He knew it was true—he'd had a shit practice—but he didn't like hearing it.

"Hey! I used to play, remember. And in fact, my points in my last season were…"

"Better than mine this season, I know. But that was six years ago." Owen had once been an offenseman for Colorado before he'd decided serving his country as a Marine was a better purpose in life. But his second tour overseas had taken the sight in his left eye when an undetected land mine had exploded. His sniper career over, he'd returned to Denver with a Congressional Medal of Honor for bravery, but no future in either the military or the NHL. Except as the Avalanche's mascot—a big, furry, Saint Bernard. Yet, his friend never complained about what might have been had he continued playing…just reminded everyone how awesome he'd been at one time. "How long are you going to use that pick-up line to get dates?" Ben asked.

"As long as it will work." Owen switched the bag containing the mascot costume to his other shoulder as they left the locker room. "Unlike you, I wasn't born a walking aphrodisiac."

"True enough." Seeing the Major Junior signups posted to the stadium announcement pegboard, he stopped. "Hey, do you know any of these kids?"

"If you're looking for me to take out your future competition for MVP, my sniper days are over my friend," Owen joked, checking the list.

Ben's gaze zeroed in on one name. Brandon Sullivan…Kristina's kid?

"What's up?"

"This kid here. I think he might be the reason I'm in this situation." It would explain a lot. But if Kristina thought staying married to him would help her son make it to the major leagues, she was wrong. This sport didn't give a shit about who you knew—it all came down to talent.

"Who is it?"

"The kid of the woman I…you know…"

"Shit, man. She has a kid?" Owen shook his head.

As Ben turned away from the board, his cell phone chimed in his pocket. A text from Sanders.

Have you seen this?

Clicking the link, he saw the cover of *Sports Now* magazine. Apparently four months after the fact, someone had released a photo of him and Kristina leaving the Vegas chapel. "That's convenient," he mumbled, tossing the phone to Owen.

Owen squinted. "She's beautiful even blurry," he said.

Ben snatched the phone back. "Whose side are you on, man?" Had Kristina leaked the photo to the press? Not exactly the way to get him to help out her kid, if that was her angle.

"No real sports fan reads that garbage. It's like the soap opera daily for sports."

His friend was right. Still, it was on every newsstand

in America with the big bold caption—MOST VALUABLE PLAYER WEDS UNKNOWN IN VEGAS.

Kristina wouldn't remain an unknown for long.

* * *

So much for keeping things quiet. Olivia studied the picture of Ben and Kristina in *Sports Now* magazine as she sat in the examination room at the medical clinic. The blurry snapshot showed the two leaving the Vegas chapel. They were laughing, and if she didn't know better, she'd actually believe the two of them were in love and happily married as the image depicted.

Pulling the paper closer, she peered at Ben.

His genuine smile and deep-set dimples on the cover of the magazine brought back thoughts of how he'd looked at her in her office, and her stomach knotted.

"It's just the hormone injections," she told herself as she tossed the magazine aside. This shot, this publicity was a good thing for her client. Drunk or not, Ben Westmore looked happy in that photo.

Which irrationally irritated the shit out of her.

She released a sigh and checked her watch. How much longer would they keep her waiting? She was a hundred percent certain of her decision to go through with the egg extraction, but her nervousness grew the longer she waited. The doctor had explained the process, and while she wasn't thrilled about the idea of an IV and being sedated for the fifteen-minute procedure, she'd feel no pain, and in an hour she'd be on her way. And it wasn't as though it would be too late to back out even after today's procedure. Until the implantation process, she could still change her mind. Which she wouldn't.

Her gaze landed on the picture of Ben. Had they met under different circumstances...She shook her head.

Had they met under different circumstances, she might be stupid enough to fall prey to his appeal like so many other women. Pregnancy or not, divorce case or not, Ben Westmore would be a bad decision, a huge mistake.

Sticking to her no-athlete rule had served her heart well so far.

The door opened and Dr. Chelsey entered. "Sorry to keep you waiting. How are you feeling?" He snapped on new examining gloves and sat on the stool at the end of the bed.

"I'm good." She was. So why didn't that sound convincing?

He smiled. "It's natural to feel nervous. Do you have any other questions for me before we begin?"

Yeah, compared to fish and guinea pigs, how hard were children to raise?

She shook her head as a nurse entered the room to start the IV. "I'm ready." Her body trembled slightly and tiny goose bumps surfaced on her bare legs and arms.

Damn, why was she so nervous?

"Wait," she said quickly as the nurse approached with the anesthesia meds strong enough to knock her out. For what, she still wasn't sure. She wasn't afraid of needles. She didn't fear the sedation. So why was she still hesitating?

"What are we waiting for?" the doctor asked gently, and she caught his meaning. She'd already told him how much she wanted this. She'd given it more than enough thought, and it still wasn't the last opportunity to back out.

So, what were they waiting for? Her gaze flew to the magazine on the chair once again and the image of the happy, newly married couple—however fake—made her stomach knot. Was it really too late to have a child a different way?

She was only thirty-six…she could meet someone. She could be as happy as that couple in the magazine.

A couple that was in the middle of a divorce. A *man* who was in the middle of a divorce.

She shook off any lingering trace of longing as she lay back against the pillow and extended her arm toward the nurse. "Nothing. I'm ready."

* * *

Low profile was out the window now that his face was plastered all over the tabloids, so it was time to move on to plan B. Social appearances that might help save his image and keep the team managers as happy as possible. Everyone was already on edge with the semifinals starting in a few days. Negative attention focused on the team or its players was the last thing anyone wanted.

"How about the wives charity signing on Saturday? They're still looking for a few extra players to attend," the team's PR rep, Ashley, suggested, flipping through a file on her desk.

Ben flinched as he sat back in the leather chair across from her and extended his legs. On a normal day, those women made him cringe with their attempts to set him up with everyone they knew. They saw a single player and made it their mission to change his Facebook status from "No strings, no complications, and I like it that way" to "Blissfully wed and miserable." Now, seeing them would be even worse. They'd either hate the fact he'd gotten married without their approval or hate him for trying to get a record-breaking divorce. "Pass."

"We're running out of options, Ben," Peter Aisley, his long-time agent and manager, said. Peter had been guiding his career for more than fifteen years, and the poor man looked more stressed than Ben was. Taking a handkerchief from his jacket pocket, Peter wiped at the beads of sweat forming on his balding head and his left knee bounced.

"Hey, don't sweat it. Ashley's the world's greatest PR manager—she'll have my reputation back on track in no time." He tapped his agent's arm.

They spoke in unison. "That's what I'm afraid of…"

"I'm not a miracle worker, Ben…"

He leaned forward, resting his elbows on his knees. "Okay, let's get serious. Do we have anything with kids? A hospital visit or school career day?" He liked the more hands-on events with the children, where he would have little contact with women—tempting, angry, or otherwise. Kids he could handle.

"Nothing like that," Ashley said, "but what about that children's hospital charity event—I received the invitation last month."

One of the charities his foundation supported yearly.

"We weren't sure about your availability with the pending playoff schedule. But it's tomorrow night. You're in town, right?"

He nodded. Not ideal, but at least he'd get it over with quickly and before the first game of the next round. "I should be able to get out of practice in time to attend." He paused. "Actually, check the guest list." There were a few nurses at the Colorado Center for Children he'd rather avoid if possible.

Ashley and Peter exchanged looks.

"Neither of you are touching the cup when I win it," he mumbled.

Ashley's long gel nails, painted in the team's blue and silver, clicked against the mahogany desk surface as she did a quick scan for the names he called out. "You're in the clear," she said. Then she hesitated, readjusting her purple-rimmed cat-eye glasses as she peered at the computer. "Actually, maybe this one isn't such a great idea. Kingsley Law Firm is a platinum level sponsor of the event, and Olivia Davis is on the guest list."

Ben sat straighter. "Olivia will be there?"

"She's on the list. Not sure she RSVP'd yes…Let me keep looking."

"No!"

Peter sent him a narrowed-eyed, knowing look.

"I mean, that's fine. She's probably too busy boiling balls to attend, right?"

"Damn, Ben," Peter muttered under his breath.

Ashley looked between the two of them. "So, you're sure? Tomorrow night, at the Daniels and Fisher Clock Tower. The event starts at seven thirty, and they asked if you'd be willing to offer up your time as a silent auction prize like you did last year."

Ben nodded. "Sure, of course. Got it." He stood. "I have to get my suit to the cleaners. Great seeing you, Ash. Peter, always a pleasure."

"Be prepared to write a big check," Peter said.

"I'm on it."

"Oh, and Ben—do not bring a date," Ashley said.

Ben smiled. "Don't worry—I got this."

CHAPTER 6

A skating lesson with NHL star Ben Westmore.
Ha! As if.

Unbelievably, the silent auction bid sheet was nearly full already, with the highest bid sitting at five thousand dollars, and the charity event had only started half an hour ago. A skating lesson from him was worth that much?

Hopefully Ben's silent auction donation would be his only contribution, and he wouldn't feel the need to make an appearance. Just the thought of being in the same room with him made Olivia's stomach do an involuntary flip.

Though if he did show, the event venue's five floors made it easy to hide. Each floor offered its own breathtaking panoramic view of the city and an opportunity to explore behind the magnificent clock faces. The décor was elegant and modern, with its black-and-white theme accented with white leather sofas and chairs positioned near the clock faces to barstool seating along the windows. It was a beautiful place to hold any sort of event.

She took the stairs up to another floor and accepted a glass of nonalcoholic Champagne from a waiter tray as he passed. Looking around, she saw most of the casual seating areas were occupied, leaving only the dinner tables, and she didn't feel like sitting at one alone. Guests mingled in little black and white groups in various areas of the room, chatting and laughing, looking comfortable and having fun. Not for the first time did she regret not having a go-to male best friend—preferably gay with impeccable style—to call on to attend these events with her. She was too socially awkward to approach a group already in mid-discussion and introduce herself. In the courtroom, she possessed all the confidence in the world. Outside the courtroom was a different story. The law firm being a major sponsor of the event, she knew she'd be asked to say a few words later that evening, and she was already having a mild anxiety attack.

Standing near the railing, with a bird's-eye view of the four floors beneath, she took a sip of her drink and willed the event to officially start. The sooner she could get home and out of this tight dress and into her pajamas, the better.

Noise from below made her lean slightly to get a better view of the entryway on the seventeenth floor. She sighed. So much for avoiding the sight of him.

Accepting another glass of virgin Champagne from a passing waiter, Olivia watched as Ben entered the elegantly decorated ballroom and was immediately swarmed by adoring fans.

What was it about these athletes that people treated them like gods? She didn't see anyone swarming the pediatric physicians who performed life-saving surgeries every day. Those men deserved to be showered with praise and adoration.

Ben Westmore played with a puck for a living. She took a

healthy gulp of her drink, the bubbles in the dry liquid making her cough.

She couldn't see the short woman on Ben's arm through the crowd, but she caught the tail of an off-white, crochet-style floor-length gown, between the legs of suits crowded around them.

Unbelievable. Wasn't he the one who wanted to keep a low profile? News of his marriage was all over the tabloids, yet he brought a date to this event?

Jealousy she refused to acknowledge had her on edge. Since that day in the office, she hadn't been able to shake off the unsettling connection she'd felt to him—ever briefly. He was the last man on Earth that she would have expected to feel anything for—arrogant athletes weren't her thing—but she had to admit that she could understand how women fell for him. Besides the gorgeous exterior, he had a magnetic pull to him, drawing people in…Obviously the woman on his arm didn't care about his reputation or the fact that he was married.

Well, if Ben wanted to give her more ammunition to use against him in court, Olivia would gladly take it. She shrugged, taking another sip of her drink, which really did need alcohol, before setting the glass down.

The host of the evening—Emelia Michelin, the hospital's director—took the stage at the front of the room on the first floor, and a silence fell over the venue. Olivia moved along the railing as several others joined her for a better view.

"Thank you all for coming out this evening. On behalf of the Colorado Center for Children, I want to thank our event sponsors for making tonight possible and all of our donors whose continued support ensures the hospital can provide the best level of care for our patients. We have some amazing items on the silent auction tables upstairs…"

Ben glanced up as the woman motioned, and grabbing the arm of the man next to her, Olivia hid.

The man shot her a look, then smiled. "Hi…Have we met?"

Shit. Now she'd have someone else to avoid for the rest of the evening. "No…I apologize, I thought you were my date."

"I could be," he said, holding her hand on his arm.

She yanked it away as politely as possible. "Excuse me," she said as she moved toward the stairs.

The man's eyes followed her, as though waiting to see if she'd been lying about the date, and she was relieved when she heard Emelia announce it was time for everyone to take a seat at their designated tables for dinner. As she descended the stairs carefully in her three-inch strappy silver sandals, she retrieved her table number from her purse.

She scanned the room for table six. Near the window in the far corner. Perfect. She could hide away and skip out unnoticed after the final presentation and speeches. Finding her place card, she set her clutch on the chair next to hers and reached for her chair.

"Looks like we have similar taste in charities," Ben's voice said behind her. Her hand missed the chair as she turned, and he moved it away from the table for her.

He wore a black tuxedo better than any other man in the room. He'd looked great from afar, but up close, he just wasn't fair. The way the perfectly tailored jacket fit across his shoulders and chest made her mouth water. The smell of his cologne made her slightly dizzy as the masculine yet soft musky scent tempted her to lean closer. Instead, she held her breath as she sat. "You're at this table?" she asked through clenched teeth.

"As fate would have it."

"Where's your date?" she asked pointedly when he sat two seats away.

He looked around and a smile spread across his face. One that sucked the air from her lungs. Those dimples should be illegal. They were obviously the secret weapon he used to lure unsuspecting women like her client. His dark hair, which had been a spiky, controlled mess that day in her office, was now neatly slicked back, the slightly longer top pieces brushed to the side. She couldn't decide which look was sexier...before she remembered she wasn't supposed to be contemplating that anyway.

"There she is," he said, as the woman's dress came into her peripheral vision.

She turned and Ben stood to hold the chair next to her for his date.

Fantastic. She was content in knowing he was making her case easier by appearing at public events with another woman on his arm, but she didn't exactly feel like watching the two of them together all evening.

And she absolutely refused to read anything into that.

She sat straighter as the woman's chair inched closer to the table and plastered on her best fake smile as she turned for introductions. But the smile faded fast.

"Olivia Davis, this is Beverly Westmore," Ben said. "Mom, this is the lawyer trying to ruin my life."

* * *

The oh-shit-is-it-too-late-to-change-tables flush of color on Olivia's cheeks brought the woman's hotness to a whole new level. One he hadn't thought possible.

He'd noticed her leaning over the railing above them almost immediately, and the sight of her had nearly knocked the wind from his lungs. The white dress, with its low-cut neckline, exposing her beautiful neck and collarbone, and the high slit up the left side, revealing legs that seemingly went on forever, had him practically salivating. With her dark hair pinned back from her face, the thick curls dancing on her shoulders when she moved, she was stunning. But it was her expression that got to him. The wistful, slightly longing look as she'd surveyed the crowd, then the flicker of panic when their gazes met.

She'd felt their connection that day in her office as much as he had.

Pulling out her chair had been a mistake. The faint scent of her perfume had tempted him to draw her closer.

He didn't know what was wrong with him. It wasn't as though he'd never seen a beautiful woman before. Hell, he usually had three or four beautiful women on the go at any given time. Not exactly noble, but in his defense, he was always straightforward about what he was looking for.

More specifically, what he wasn't looking for.

So, why this woman had such an effect on him, he didn't know. But he didn't like it. He didn't do complicated relationships. And anything with Olivia was sure to be complicated.

He glanced around, expecting to see her date arrive at the table, but the seat on the other side of her remained empty.

Had she come alone? Was it possible that a woman this appealing was unattached? He knew so little about her, and yet she knew so much about him. Private, confidential information that she planned to use against him. That should be enough to cool his attraction to her, but it didn't. Though he'd prefer to even the field a little.

"Hello," his mother said, extending a hand to Olivia. Her presence was a reminder to keep his actions in check.

That didn't mean his thoughts had to behave.

"Hi. It's a pleasure to meet you, Mrs. Westmore," Olivia said politely.

His mother laughed. "I'm sorry if my son is being a pain in the ass," she said.

His eyes widened. Where was his ally?

Olivia's eyes met his, and her I-like-your-mom expression made him shift uncomfortably in his seat. "Mom, would you like some wine?" he asked, reaching for the bottle of Merlot on the table.

"Yes, please."

He poured. "Ms. Davis?"

"Olivia," she corrected. "And no, thank you."

"You don't drink?"

She shook her head.

"Neither does Ben," his mother said, taking a sip of her wine. "Which is why the alcohol hit him so hard in Vegas that he lost his mind and married someone."

Well, there would be no avoiding this conversation tonight. *Thanks, Mom.*

Olivia eyed him. "For someone who doesn't drink to get that drunk, there must have been a reason. Celebrating?"

He cleared his throat. "Yes, celebrating. It was New Year's Eve."

"More like trying to avoid New Year's Eve," his mom said.

He shot her a look, but not before Olivia—interest obviously piqued—shuffled her chair closer. "What do you mean?"

"Nothing," Ben said quickly. "She meant nothing." He stood and wiggled the back of his mom's chair.

She frowned, glancing up at him. "What are you doing?"

"Switching chairs before you can say something to land

me in more trouble," he said. Maybe requesting the same table from the event organizer had been a bad idea. He'd wanted to make Olivia squirm, sitting next to his mom, but that plan had backfired in record time.

Olivia smirked and his mother laughed as she stood and moved over to his abandoned seat.

He sat and instantly regretted the switch.

The slit in Olivia's dress left her shapely thigh exposed almost all the way to the hip, and the sight made his mouth go dry. Combined with the tantalizing scent of her soft jasmine perfume, that tempted him to both move closer and run for his life. He knew making it through dinner would be a challenge.

Luckily, the hospital director saved him.

"Once again this year we are going to hold the food ransom as we ask several of the organization's supporters to come forward to present their generous donations. First, we'd like to invite Olivia Davis from Kingsley Family Law to present the company's donation of twenty thousand dollars." Emelia smiled and everyone clapped as Olivia stood.

"A little better than a free skating lesson," she whispered as she passed his chair.

His body sparked to life at the challenge mixed with unexpected flirtation in her tone. Resisting the urge to pull her down onto his lap to teach her a different kind of lesson, he simply winked at her, then reached into his coat pocket for his checkbook as she walked away. He quickly ripped off the check on top for twenty thousand and wrote a new one for twenty-five.

His mother raised an eyebrow. "Competitive much?" she asked, draining the contents of her wine glass.

"It's for children," he said, putting the checkbook back and returning his gaze to the woman at the podium.

"Good evening, everyone. Kingsley Family Law is honored to sponsor such an amazing organization. The tremendous work the physicians do at the Colorado Center for Children is commendable, and we are happy to support such a great place for children and their families. We hope to be involved in partnership with this organization for many years to come, and I encourage all of you to open your hearts and your wallets this evening. Don't forget there are a lot of great silent auction items up for grabs," she said, grinning at him.

She thought his item contribution was a joke? He smiled. Let's see how she feels about it when she's the highest bidder.

* * *

It was time to go.

In fact, time to go had come and gone hours ago.

She collected her clutch from the empty seat next to her. Olivia's new mission in life was to get as far away from Ben Westmore as possible. Being one of the best-looking men she'd ever had to tear apart in court was one thing. There, his easy, charming demeanor was inconvenient…but out on the dance floor, spinning his mother around was entirely too much.

Damn.

This case would be so much easier if Ben had been an asshole, or at least not the adoring, fun-loving son he appeared to be at that moment.

Her common sense reminded her this could be just a fantastic show to prevent his name from being dragged through the mud, but her gut told her this was exactly who he was—a good guy beneath the ego. Quite possibly a great guy. One currently married to her client.

And therefore she was in trouble.

From now on, she'd deal directly with his lawyer. The way it was supposed to be.

Chatting up his mom at a charity event and learning more about her opposing client's adorable childhood antics than was safe hadn't been professional. In two hours her attraction to him had grown exponentially, and she was out and out in love with his mother. Who could resist the woman? Funny, sweet, a hard-ass on her children when she had to be. Exactly like the mother Olivia had had and lost. Exactly the kind she hoped to be. Beverly Westmore's priority was her family. And the jealousy she felt for Ben was outweighed only by the urge to be part of such a close-knit, supportive family.

She had to get out of there.

Ben's gaze landed on her from the dance floor and her mouth went dry when he winked. God, that simple gesture had her common sense abandoning her. Staying a second longer was not a good idea.

"Leaving already?" Ben said behind her as she reached for her wrap.

His forehead glistened with sweat, and at his side, his mother was smiling as though she were having the time of her life.

Her current oversensitive maternal instinct kicked into high gear. The possibility that someday she too could have a son or daughter to be so obviously proud of made her chest tighten. "I have an early morning." Turning to his mother, she said, "Pleasure meeting you, Mrs. Westmore. You have a talented son."

Ben grinned. "Was that a compliment from the enemy?"

"On your reputation on the ice only," she said, hating that she was being drawn in by his flirty tone and banter. *Leave. Now. Walk. Away.*

"You two should dance," his mother said. "I need a break."

Her eyes widened and she shook her head. "Oh no, I can't. I really should go." Dance with Ben Westmore? No chance in hell. He couldn't possibly think that was a good idea either...

Yet there it was, his hand extended to her expectantly.

He had to be out of his mind.

Surely, he felt this weird, completely inappropriate attraction between them.

Her eyes narrowed. Or did he have an ulterior motive?

Was all his charming flirtation an act to soften her up? A hope that those crystal baby blues would have her swooning too much to do her job?

Without thinking, she said, "Sure, why not?" She refused to let him believe that he'd had his desired effect on her. Setting her clutch and wrap on her chair, she took his hand and followed him to the dance floor.

Thank God the sound of her heels clicking against the tiled floor helped to drown out the steady, loud thumping of her heart.

She wasn't a great dancer, and if he was as graceful on the ice as he was on the dance floor, then no wonder he was the team's MVP player three years running. Okay, so she'd done her research on him; it was part of the job.

She hoped she could hold her own for one song...Wait, what happened to the fast-tempoed music they'd been playing for an hour?

Gone.

The slow, soft chords of an Ed Sheeran song began instead.

Shit.

Ben didn't seem to have an issue with it as he spun her

once slowly, before capturing her other hand in his and pulling her into his chest. She stiffened at the closeness and straightened her spine in an effort to create a gap between their bodies, as he started to sway.

"Relax," he said smoothly, his gaze locked on hers, his expression soft, unfazed—the look of a man not dancing with the lawyer who could ruin his life or at least playoff season. She had to learn this guy's secret, because there was no way he was this unaffected. Yet, his hands weren't sweating the way hers threatened to, and the only heartbeat she could hear thundering was her own.

She forced a slow and what she hoped was unobvious breath. "I *am* relaxed. I'm not the one who should be worried."

The palm of his hand spread across the exposed flesh of her back and she prayed the tingling sensation in her spine didn't result in goose bumps. "So you're saying *I* should be?" he asked, turning them in rotation to the steady beat. Despite her resistance to this dance, her hips betrayed her by swaying in sync with his, and her feet kept time with his every step. He led with a silent authority that she was forced to follow. And for the first time in her life, she wasn't hating giving up control.

"I think so, yes. My client is…"

He brought their joined hands between them and placed a finger to her lips.

Her heart all but stopped.

"Why don't we save the shop talk for the courtroom? Let's just enjoy this dance."

She swallowed hard, but nodded. Dancing in silence, she could do that.

Unfortunately, Ben seemed eager to chat. "How long have you been practicing law?"

He expected her to remember stats as his hand on her back dipped slightly lower, his hold drawing her even closer? It had been far too long since she'd been enveloped in the arms of a man who felt and smelled so strong, so confident...How long would it be again if she went ahead with her plans for a baby? She pushed the thought aside when he stared at her, still waiting for an answer. "Twelve years," she said, cutting out her time as a junior lawyer and intern, so as not to age herself. She knew from his online Wikipedia page that he was thirty-four, two years younger than she.

"Do you love what you do?" he asked.

"If I say no will I get the inspirational 'do what you love and it will never feel like work' speech?"

"*Is* that a no?"

She shook her head. "Actually, I really do enjoy my job." She couldn't say watching families get ripped apart by bitter divorces was something she loved without sounding like a sociopath, but she enjoyed her career.

"Can I ask why only professional athlete divorces?"

"I was dumped by a jock," she said.

Ben laughed. "So one guy ruined it for us all, huh?"

She nodded then shook her head. "No. Everyday cases—with normal, everyday husbands and wives—just seemed a little too...real," she said.

His blue eyes burned into her and his grip tightened on her hand. "So, guys like me aren't real?"

She swallowed hard. He felt real...He felt more than real—he felt amazing. His arm wrapped around her felt deceivingly safe and his hand holding hers felt warm and secure. God, she could see herself giving in to these painfully real feelings..."You're probably one of the more real ones," she said, hoping he didn't detect the slight quiver in her voice.

He nodded slowly as though unsure whether her words were a compliment. "Have you ever been married?" he asked, rotating them in time to the music.

"That's crossing a line into personal."

"Kids?"

"That's less personal?" She raised an eyebrow.

He smiled. "Guarded much?"

The effect of his smile from a safe distance was knee-weakening. This close, it was downright dangerous. She quickly averted her gaze to the other couples on the floor. "How long is this song anyway?" She felt trapped the way she had in tenth grade when Robbie Gropes-a-Lot Harris had tricked her into dancing with him at the winter formal to "November Rain"—the full eleven-minute extended version. Except Ben's breath smelled minty fresh and not like tacos, and his arm draped across her lower back made every fiber in her being spring to life, making her want to flee for a completely different reason than the one Robbie had evoked.

"Do I make you uncomfortable?"

Damn right. And it should be *her* making *him* uncomfortable. There needed to be a power shift between them and fast. "Of course not."

He pulled her closer. "You make me uncomfortable," he murmured, his expression suddenly serious. Every inch of her body was pressed to his and she could barely catch a breath. Dancing was a really bad idea—a torturously bad idea. Being in his arms reminded her of all of the things she'd sacrificed for her career, of all the things she'd told herself she didn't need…

"G-good," she said, her voice cracking. "As I said, my client…"

"I don't mean the divorce case. I mean you." He touched

her cheek and her skin burned. Thank God he was holding her so tightly because she couldn't trust her legs.

Their stare locked and held for what could have been a lifetime, as everything seemed still and quiet around them.

Still and quiet.

The song had ended.

She yanked her hand free of his and stumbled away from him, inhaling a gulp of air into her deprived lungs. "Well, dance is over. I'll…uh…see you."

He nodded, the charming polite smile back on his face and for a second she wondered if she'd imagined the intensity in his gaze seconds before. "Goodnight, Olivia."

Olivia.

Her own name sounded foreign coming from him. She longed to hear the sound again, and she was an idiot for wanting something so dangerous. The NHL's biggest playboy had just worked his charm on her, and she'd lost all common sense.

She turned and headed straight for the table, leaving him on the dance floor.

She had to pull it together, but she also had to admit the unfortunate truth. Never before had she been tempted to kiss the enemy.

Damn hormone injections.

CHAPTER 7

❧

Seven pairs of eyes stared at him expectantly around the dining room table. Ben ignored each and every one as he reached for the mashed potatoes. He scooped three big spoonfuls onto his plate and set the bowl back. Reaching next for the carrots and peas, he helped himself to a generous portion, despite having zero appetite.

He could sense they were all perched on the edge of their seats, waiting to pounce, and he refused to acknowledge the tension around the table.

Finally it was his eleven-year-old niece, Taylor, who summoned the courage to speak first. Or maybe her mother—his sister Becky's—kick from under the table prompted her to ask, "So, Uncle Ben, when do I get to meet my new aunt?"

He shot his sister a look. He used to like his niece, until recently, when she started demonstrating far too much of her mother's annoyingness.

Becky shrugged and leaned forward, looking eager to

hear his response. Her baby girl, Lily, was in her arms, sucking obliviously on a bottle.

Lily was his new favorite family member, her inability to speak placing her on top of the list.

He scooped a lump of potatoes onto his fork and dipped it into the gravy boat in front of him. "Don't believe everything you read in the tabloids," he said.

"So, you didn't get married in Vegas on New Year's Eve?" his brother Jackson asked, holding a tray of their mother's honey-glazed ham—the primary reason he'd come for dinner—ransom until he responded.

"It's all a misunderstanding. I'm taking care of it."

"So, we won't get to meet her?"

He snatched the tray of ham and stole the end pieces with the crispy glaze, hoping his family would shut up about all of this long enough for him to enjoy the only home-cooked meal he would get until the fourth of July—if his team made it to the playoff finals.

When. Not if.

"Of course not."

"Actually, Becky and Jackson, you two would have probably met her already," his mother said.

He dropped his fork. "Really, Mom?"

"What?" She frowned at him. "I'm not the one who got married and doesn't remember." She turned her attention to Becky, the oldest, and the one who might have the best recollection of their time in elementary school. "Do you remember Kristina Sullivan from school in Denver?"

Becky tapped her fingernails against the table as she thought.

Jackson shook his head. "I don't remember much about Denver."

Good. They'd all been too young. He reached for his fork,

the smell of the slightly burnt honey glaze overpowering the nauseating family discussion.

But then across from him, Becky's eyes lit up. "I do remember. Wasn't she that little girl everyone teased?"

His stomach turned and he continued to chew the piece of meat, not trusting himself to speak.

"Her parents were terrible, and they lived in that trailer park outside of town. Is that her?"

His mother nodded. "That's her."

Becky looked sad. "I heard she was taken away from her parents a year after we left Denver. She grew up in foster homes."

He forced himself to swallow and avoided Becky's gaze.

"That's so sad," Abigail, Jackson's fiancée, said.

"The team's lawyer is handling it?" Jackson asked.

"Yes."

"Does Kristina have representation?" Jackson asked.

His mother nodded. "Yes. And she's absolutely lovely."

Ben shot his mother a look. "Really?"

Beverly waved a fork full of potato. "As if you haven't noticed. I saw the way you looked at her at the charity event the other night."

Becky kicked him under the table.

"Ow…what the hell?"

"Language!" his mother said.

"You're hot for the opposing lawyer?" His sister looked disapproving, but not entirely surprised.

"I'm not hot for her…I was trying to charm her into leaving my balls alone."

"Ben, not at the table," his mother said.

"You started it," he said, pointing his fork at her.

"What's her name?" his niece asked, taking out her iPhone.

"None of your business," he said. "And no phones at the table."

His niece shrugged. "I'm sure the tabloids will announce it all soon enough, and I'll Google her then."

He sighed. "Her name is Olivia Davis."

Across from him Abigail's expression confirmed his worst fears. He was screwed.

"She's that good, isn't she? She's going to destroy Sanders in court." Appetite officially killed, he dropped his fork and sat back in his chair.

Going to the charity to see her had been a bad enough idea, but he hadn't been able to resist. He'd wanted to see if the connection in her office had been real. Flirting with her and holding her close while they danced had only confirmed it…This insanity needed to stop. Now. For years, he'd kept women from getting too close, and Olivia was the last person he should break his own rules for. She was too beautiful, too smart, too tempting, and she was making him feel too much.

Seeing her laugh and joke with his mother last night had warmed him in a way he'd never experienced before. He'd only ever introduced one woman he was dating to his family, and Janelle had never gotten along so well with his mom. Olivia and Beverly had chatted all night like old friends, and he hadn't even minded his mother sharing stories about him.

"I won't lie to you Ben. She is pretty fantastic," Abby said, shooting him a sympathetic look. "I didn't know she'd changed firms or moved to Denver…she was in L.A. before."

Part of him wished she'd stayed there. Another part remembered how it felt to have her in his arms.

Jackson shook his head. "Look, man. You messed up. After only a couple of months, what's the most damage this

Kristina Sullivan could actually do to your bank account and reputation? She can't be entitled to much of a settlement, and well, your status with the ladies was starting to take a dive anyway." His brother's attempt to ease his stress failed. "Hang in there—you'll be divorced in no time and back to playing the field."

Not if Olivia Davis was a good as he suspected she was.

* * *

The Grumpy Stump was loud, busy, and exactly what Ben needed that evening.

"Another round?" Gigi asked as she passed their table.

Jackson nodded. "Keep 'em coming," he said, his speech slightly slurred.

"You know what, I think we're good," Ben said with a smile.

Gigi checked her notepad. "James Dessner from the hardware store and Kiffer Patrick from the fire hall are still waiting to buy you guys a round, and I'll lose my job faster than Ben filed for divorce if Wilson hears me turning down paying customers," she said.

"Nice, Gigi." Someone just had to say something.

She touched his arm with a warm smile. "You know I couldn't resist, honey. What do I do about the drinks?"

It was the same every time he and Asher were in town for a few days. He appreciated the locals' appreciation, but with him and Asher not drinking much during the season, poor Jackson reaped the benefits of the free booze with a nasty hangover. "We'll take them in rounds of soda," he said, tossing a large tip on her tray.

She beamed. "You got it." The wink she threw his way and the extra sway in her thin hips as she sauntered back toward the bar for their next nonalcoholic round was wasted. He didn't get involved with women from his hometown. He wasn't a complete idiot. Breaking hearts and keeping things fun and casual on the road was one thing, but the moment he messed around with a local, he was doomed. He was a hero in town, and he wanted to keep it that way. Besides, he'd grown up with all of these women; they all seemed like extended family. It would be like dating his sis…He shook his head. Jesus. Gross.   ·

He prayed Kevin Sanders could get him out of this marriage mess quickly. So far, no one in town appeared to have lost respect for him, but he knew he was walking a thin line with this quickie wedding and divorce. And everyone was already watching him, waiting for any sign of "the choke." Since making it to the NHL, the pressure to be the best, to not let down his fans, had only increased the better he played.

"So, tell us about this woman," Jackson said, leaning closer.

"I really don't want to talk about Kristina Sullivan," he mumbled.

"Not her—the lawyer—Ms. Davis," Jackson said. "Mom hasn't stopped talking about how fantastic she is."

So much for family loyalty. "I don't want to talk about *her*, either." It was bad enough he couldn't stop thinking about her. An image of her curves in the white dress had plagued him all night. The more time he spent with her, the more his attraction for her grew. Despite her reputation for getting her clients everything they wanted in court, she was kind and easygoing. Strong and determined, but not the ballbusting, man-hating attorney he'd thought she'd be.

And he knew she was fighting a similar attraction to him. He could sense it in the way she looked at him when she thought he wasn't looking, the way she'd stiffened in his arms and ran away as soon as the song ended.

"Abby says she's beautiful."

He nodded and shrugged at the same time. "So are a lot of women."

"Exactly. Ben's not about to let some woman get in his head and affect his game, right?" Asher said, looking to him for confirmation.

Too late for that. He drained the contents of his glass and looked around. "Where's Gigi?"

Asher's expression changed to a panicked one. "Ben…"

Man, was the cup the only thing anyone cared about? "Look, don't sweat it, okay? She's not in my head. She's just…aggravating." And hot and tempting as hell.

"Aggravating," Asher repeated, shaking his head. "Shit, here we go again."

"You don't know what you're talking about." This thing with Olivia was nothing like the thing with Janelle. He'd been head over heels for his ex…He ran a hand over his hair and checked his watch. He had to get back to Denver. But he stayed in the booth, noticing Dr. Chelsey approach.

"Hey, boys, how are you?"

The older man was once the head gynecologist at the local hospital, and he'd opened a fertility clinic several years ago. His reputation and the clinic's success rate had couples flocking to the small-town clinic. His question may have been directed at the three of them, but he was studying Ben.

"Don't worry, Doc. That cup is as good as ours," he said wryly.

"Oh, I wasn't worried."

Sure.

"I came over because I need something from you boys," the man said, sliding into the booth next to Asher and setting another round on the table.

"No can do. My swimmers belong to one woman only,"

Jackson said, picking up his empty beer glass and tipping it back to catch the last few drops.

Ben grinned at the doctor's expression. "He's cut off." He moved the new pints of beer out of Jackson's reach. "What can we do for you?" He wasn't willing to donate sperm, either, but he didn't think the man went around soliciting it.

Ben doubted a family and kids were in his future, but he could appreciate how important they were to couples who longed for a family. Watching his nieces grow up was enough for him, but he saw the love and special bond his sister and husband had with their girls. And even the way Jackson had stepped into the role of stepdad for Abby's daughter, Dani…But after things ended with Janelle, he'd pushed away the thought of children.

An image of Olivia flashed in his mind; the look on her face when he'd asked her about kids—and a husband—had been telling. She obviously did have hopes for a family, so why she didn't have one, he was interested in finding out.

Which was just stupid. Getting to know her any more on a personal level was only asking for trouble. If he had a hard time forgetting about her after the brief glimpses she'd allowed him, he wasn't sure he could walk away unscathed if he found out more.

"That's not what I meant," Dr. Chelsey was saying. "Karen and I are hosting a dinner party with a silent auction next month at the country club, and I'd love to have autographed jerseys, sticks…anything you boys can provide."

Asher opened his coat and retrieved a puck.

Ben grinned. "You carry a puck around?" Ben loved the sport, but his little brother took the obsession to a whole new level.

"You don't?" Asher countered. He pulled the cap off of

a white marker and scribbled his name on the puck. "There you are."

Dr. Chelsey smiled. "Great. Thanks, Asher." He studied the puck. "Actually, if I can get another one of these, I'll keep this one for myself. Ben, could you sign it, too?"

Asher frowned, but reluctantly handed over the white marker as Ben took the puck from the doctor. Then he made sure to sign his name bigger.

"Thanks, boys. Now I've got the autograph of this year's Stanley Cup winner and a player on the US World Hockey Championship team."

"That's if he gets an invitation," Ben said.

His brother's hand gesture was less than polite, and Ben laughed. The delay in the invite was causing his brother to sweat.

"*I* didn't get an invite," Jackson mumbled.

"I think it's time to get you home to Abby," Ben said, sliding out of the booth.

The doctor stood as well. "Great seeing you boys again. I'll pick up the donated items from your mom's place next week?" he asked.

"I'll drop everything off at the clinic in the next few days—save you the trouble," Ben offered. He hoped to avoid his mom for a while. She was a little too determined to make him admit his feelings for Olivia, and he was still determined to move past them as quickly as possible.

The doctor shook his hand. "Thank you...and good luck with the semifinals."

Translation: *try not to screw up.* He nodded and waved to his brothers. "Ash, I have to get back to Denver. You're on Jackson duty."

Leaving the bar, he headed toward his Hummer. His cell phone rang as he reached it. Sanders. This late at night?

His heart raced. Late-night calls were hardly ever a good sign.

"Hello?" he said, climbing into the vehicle and starting it. He set the cell phone on the holder on the dash as the Bluetooth connected.

Sanders got straight to the point. "We have Kristina Sullivan's statement. I wanted to give you the highlights, and I'm hoping it might jog your memory of that night. The more you can remember to refute, the better."

Unless he remembered getting roofied, he wasn't sure much would help. "Go ahead."

"She says you ran into one another in the lobby of the Bellagio Hotel and started drinking there."

He thought for a moment. "I'm pretty sure I'd started drinking before I met her, otherwise I wouldn't have gotten into this mess, but we were staying at the Bellagio, so it's possible that part is correct." He turned the vehicle onto a side street and pulled to the curb.

"She says when she approached you, you were offensive, believing she was a fangirl whom you'd already had relations with…" Kevin sighed. "Women," he muttered. "You'd think that would have been enough to send her on her way."

"You'd think," he said slowly, a fuzzy image of that night appearing like a vague dream.

"Anyway, she says you two went for several drinks in the hotel's sports bar…You both got wasted. She says she told you about her son, Brandon, and his aspirations to make it to the NHL someday. You were supportive, yada, yada, yada…"

He could hear the man flipping a page as parts of that night returned. So far, everything she said was true…and it confirmed his suspicions that she wanted him to help her son.

"Then she says Janelle's sportscast aired, and her co-worker…"

"Yeah, yeah, I know this part," he said quickly. Janelle's surprised expression and tears of joy as she accepted her co-anchor's marriage proposal was etched in his memory. The only thing from that night that was hauntingly crystal clear.

"Then you suggested the wedding."

"I suggested it?"

"That's what she says."

Ben rested his head against the seat. "Fine. Maybe I did." Shit, this sucked. "So, what does she want?"

"Only for you to live up to your word."

He tensed. "Of happily ever after?" She couldn't really keep him married, could she?

"No. She says you promised to try to help her son," Sanders said.

"How?"

"I don't know, man. But if you want out of this marriage quick, you better figure it out."

CHAPTER 8

The little cluster of cells in the center of the petri dish
could potentially be her new baby.

The thought both excited and terrified her.

"Olivia, you okay?" Dr. Chelsey asked, gently touching
her shoulder through the thin pink medical gown she wore.

His touch made her jump. She'd almost forgotten he was
in the room. She tore her eyes away from the dish and nodded. "Yes. It's all just…"

"A little overwhelming? Scary? Intense?"

"Yes," she said, the doctor's understanding putting her at
ease. She was so grateful she'd chosen this particular clinic.
Would Dr. Chelsey be interested in being honorary grand-
father to this baby? The idea that she would be completely
alone during the process was the scariest part—the pregnancy, the delivery…the raising of a non–serial killer. She
wasn't sure of her parenting ability, and a support system
would be so helpful.

Maybe she should move back to L.A.; at least she had

friends there. But a new firm in L.A. would be reluctant to hire a pregnant woman.

"Unlike the egg retrieval, implantation is noninvasive and will be no worse than a Pap smear," Dr. Chelsey was saying, cutting into her thoughts.

"That's good news." She'd already read that the procedure would only take a few minutes and then she'd be on her way.

The thought of leaving the clinic didn't appeal to her. At least here she had someone to talk to about the whole thing…someone who could reassure her that things would work out the way they were meant to.

She sighed. How had she let her life become so void of things that mattered—family and friends, support?

"So, whenever you're ready, we'll get started with the embryo transfer."

She nodded. The doctor probably had countless other patients to see that morning and no doubt she was putting him behind schedule, but this decision hadn't felt completely real until now. There would be no turning back. "Can I have a few moments?"

"Of course. I'll knock, and if you're still not ready, just tell me to come back." The doctor stood and left her alone in the room.

The door clicked shut behind him and she was alone with the petri dish. Alone with her future child. *Potential* future child. The success rate wasn't high enough for her to feel comfortable getting her hopes up yet.

She stared at the fertilized eggs. In a few minutes, her life could be changed forever. The process had been surreal, going through the motions, deciding on a sperm donor, cultivating eggs for retrieval…

What kind of mother would she make?

A memory of her own mom flashed in her mind, and she felt tears stinging the back of her eyes.

Of all the memories that could resurface in the moment, she remembered the day she'd gotten lost at the mall. She wasn't actually lost. She'd known exactly where she was—looking at a pair of sparkly blue Cinderella slippers in a toy store's window display. It was her favorite fairy tale; Prince Charming finally wising up and following his heart…At least in the version her mother told.

"Liv!" Her mother's voice had sounded frantic. "Liv! Olivia!"

"Here, Mom!" she called out, but she saw her mother walking in the opposite direction. "Mom!" she yelled, pushing her way through the crowd, until finally reaching her.

Her mother's eyes had been full of tears, and the look of relief on her ghostly white face as she'd bent to hug her had brought tears of fear to her own eyes. "I'm sorry, I was looking at Cinderella shoes," she said, crushed into her mother's chest.

Her mother had pulled away. "Don't ever wander away like that again, okay? You terrified me." Her voice and expression had softened. "I thought I'd lost you."

"I was right there, Momma," she'd said.

In the end, it had been she who'd lost her mother. And she'd known exactly how her mother must have felt that day. Only so much worse. Losing her parents in a drunk driving accident had changed her life. She'd moved to Colorado to live with her father's sister, Helen, and while her aunt had tried her best to give Olivia a good life, she'd lacked the maternal instincts her mother had had, the nurturing, caring side that a heartbroken ten-year-old girl had longed for.

Her mother had been so wonderful. Could she be that for her own child?

A loud voice in the hallway outside the examination room made her tears stop in their tracks and her heart echo in her ears. Already on edge, a new kind of anxiety threatened to undo her.

What the hell was Ben Westmore doing at the clinic on her fertilization day?

What the hell was Ben Westmore doing there *any* day?

Her eyes widened. Was he a donor?

With her heart barely contained in her chest, she struggled to recall the details of the donor she'd selected. Dark hair, blue eyes, six foot—*pound, pound, pound* against her chest cavity—pro athlete. Her hands shook at her sides. Since the charity banquet, the memory of what it felt like in his arms had played on repeat in her mind. She honestly thought she might be going crazy as every now and then she thought she could still smell his cologne on her skin. The radio station seemed to play that stupid Ed Sheeran song a million times a day.

Her mouth went dry and her tongue felt like sandpaper. Water…she needed water. They really should provide water—after all, she was paying ten grand for this procedure.

Forcing a calming breath that got stuck somewhere in her throat, she stood and paced the room as she heard him laugh.

God, she hoped the baby got his laugh.

Damn it! What the hell was wrong with her?

She heard him speaking, but the words were muffled through the door, and all she could think about was the sound of his deep voice, strangled and slightly sexy—okay, a lot sexy—telling her she made him uncomfortable.

Naked under her hospital gown, three minutes from having a potential life placed in her care, she was pretty sure he wouldn't find her as intimidating in that moment…or as desirable, if in fact she'd read his expression right every time she caught him looking at her.

She swallowed hard. Confidentiality agreement or not—she was finding out if her egg had been fertilized by Ben Westmore's donation. Because there was no way she could cross that crazy line knowingly. Right?

She hit the button on the wall to call the doctor and clenched her hands together at her chest as she continued to pace the room.

An eternity too long, he entered, a wide smile on his face. "Feeling better? Ready to get started?" he asked, reaching for a new pair of latex gloves.

She held him off as he approached. "Almost. Um…one quick thing." She paused. How on Earth was she supposed to ask the question? She was pretty sure he wasn't allowed to answer it, but maybe she'd be able to tell from his expression or the way he answered. She bit her lip.

"Olivia, you had a question?" he asked, pulling out a stool and sitting.

"Yeah, just a second. I'm working though something in here." She gestured around her head. Funny how a second ago, a million concerns had raced through her mind in these final decisive minutes, now there was just one burning thing that seemed like a deal breaker.

"Are you okay? What is it?" the doctor asked, looking concerned. "Do you want me to go over the procedure again or…"

"Am I getting Ben Westmore's sperm?" she blurted out.

Dr. Chelsey looked surprised, then he laughed gently, offering her a sympathetic look. "You wish," he said with another soft smile. "Unfortunately, we haven't had the pleasure of trying to create a new local hero, I'm afraid."

Relief flooded through her. After that panic, she was certain she could handle any other stress she might encounter going forward with this procedure, the pregnancy, and beyond.

"Then I'm all set."

* * *

In nine months—forty weeks—she could have a baby. The thought brought on so many different emotions as she walked along Main Street in Glenwood Falls an hour later. Happiness was definitely the leading one, but also nervousness and self-doubt—different than the kind she'd experienced earlier. Before, she'd been second-guessing her decision to go through with the procedure, but now that it was done, her concerns and fears about motherhood grew exponentially.

Dr. Chelsey hadn't led her astray, though—the implantation process had been almost *too* easy and pain-free, making her doubt whether he'd actually done anything. And other than the stress of the whirlwind emotions, she felt great—the vitamins and supplements she'd been taking in recent weeks had done wonders for her skin and hair. She was surprised they didn't inject folic acid into beauty supplements.

Ignoring the tempting aromas coming from the bakery, she crossed the street, noticing a sign on an overhang that said BABY CHIC. It was obviously far too early to be buying baby stuff, despite the extreme temptation to do so, but she could look. No harm in that.

A bell chimed overhead as she pushed open the door to the shop. The place was empty, and she didn't see an employee or store owner anywhere as she entered. Boxes lay on the floor between shelves painted vibrant primary colors, and the store's name was painted in block letters amid a mural of baby animals along the back wall.

Taking in the cash register and debit/credit machines still sitting in boxes on the counter, she realized it must not be open for business yet. Pieces of light hardwood flooring were still missing from the far end of the store.

"Hi there," a woman said coming from the back of the store. "Sorry for the mess. The store's not technically open."

"Sorry to wander in." She looked around. "The door was unlocked…" The designs in the window on the child-sized mannequins—the good kind with heads, not the creepy headless ones—were the only things displayed, except for tables covered in baby clothing to her right.

The woman smiled. "My brother must have left it open on his way out. He's supposed to be bringing me a latte, but he's no doubt delayed." She sighed.

"No problem. I'll leave. But, do you have a business card?" Maybe the woman had a website she could order from. If the clothing in the window was any indication of the rest of the line, she'd no doubt drop a small fortune on a baby wardrobe. Once the pregnancy was confirmed of course.

The woman nodded, but after rummaging through stacks of papers on the desk and opening several drawers, she shook her head. "Apparently not." She laughed. "Can you tell I'm new to this whole owning your own business thing?"

"That's okay…a website?" She could remember if it was something easy.

The woman looked embarrassed. "A work in progress. Like everything else," she said gesturing around the space. "I just started unpacking things—if you want to take a look, you're welcome to, but I won't be able to sell you anything today."

"Oh no, that's…" She stopped, for the first time noticing the baby in a sling against the woman's chest. Obviously a few months old, but still so tiny, she barely saw a head of dark brown hair peeking out over the top. "Wow, you can work with the baby sleeping there like that?"

The woman laughed. "This little one could sleep anywhere, and yes, trust me—if I don't work now while she sleeps, nothing will get done."

Olivia swallowed hard. "Babies are pretty time-consuming, huh?" Was she crazy to think she could have both—the career and the family? She worked long hours at the office and most nights she was up past midnight reviewing court documents and preparing legal briefs. Hiring a full-time nanny had been on her list of things to do while pregnant, but that would only help during the daytime hours when she returned to work. What about nights?

Again, the lack of support system worried her. Most people had parents, brothers or sisters, close friends they could call on for help. What if she couldn't do it all alone?

She squared her shoulders. She could.

The woman was shaking her head. "I mean, yes, they are, but I may spend too much time staring at her." She laughed again, gently touching the top of the sleeping child's head.

"I can see why." Olivia moved closer to peek over the sling. So small. So precious. The little girl was sleeping with her tiny hands tucked beneath her chest, her tiny body falling and rising in a deep comforting sleep on her mom's chest. "She's beautiful."

"Thank you. Anyway, please feel free to look at the items on those tables. There's no real organization yet—boys and girls clothing mixed together—but they are labeled for size and price. I can hold anything you might want until we officially open."

She nodded, tearing her gaze away from the baby. Would she ever look that comfortable and natural holding one? "Okay, thank you." She really should leave to let the woman

set up. She could come back. After all, she was getting a little ahead of herself.

Instead, she made her way toward the clothing on the table.

Sorting through the items, she could tell they were all hand-
made. Unique designs and gender-neutral color patterns were
a welcome relief to the mass-manufactured Disney-logoed
clothing she'd seen in every kids' clothing store she'd ever
walked past. Each piece was beautiful, and she couldn't decide
which she liked more—the boys' items or the girls'. The jeans
and hoodie sets with dinosaurs and puppies on the front were
the coolest little boy clothing she'd ever seen, and the sun-
dresses for little girls made her chest ache. It would be
impossible to decide which were nicer. Not that it mattered;
she didn't care of it was a boy or a girl, as long as…

She paused.

Nope—she definitely wanted a girl. She picked up a pale
yellow dress, the fabric covered in sunflowers, white piping
around the collar and base. So soft, so tiny. The tag read
NEWBORN, and the price was more reasonable than she
would have expected for an independently owned boutique
in a small town.

Just put it back.

She didn't even know if she was pregnant yet. And she
could have a boy.

She set it down and continued to look through the pile,
but her gaze kept returning to it.

Damn.

"Could you hold this one, please?" she asked, carrying it
toward the counter. She hated to leave it in the store even
temporarily. The one-of-a-kind design would sell as soon as
the doors officially opened, and with the less-than-organized
chaos inside the store, she worried it might find its way back
onto a sales rack by mistake.

The woman smiled. "I love this one, too. I made it for Lily, but she grew too fast on me. So it was made with a little extra love." She grabbed a piece of paper, pen, and safety pin to attach her info to the dress. "Your name and phone number?"

"Olivia Davis. My cell number is three one zero…" She paused when the woman stopped writing and stared at her. "Something wrong?" Did she doubt she'd return? "I can pay for it in advance, too." That would be better. In fact, maybe she could pay for it, take it now, and the woman could ring it in as a sale later. She didn't require a receipt or anything. She opened her purse to retrieve her wallet, but the store owner shook her head.

"Oh no, no. Sorry," she said, her cheeks reddening. "I'm…You're just…My brother is Ben Westmore. I'm his sister—Becky."

Right. Leave it to her bad luck to stumble back onto enemy turf. And here she was buying baby clothing.

Well, nothing said she was buying the dress for her own child. Maybe she was buying it as a gift, for all this woman knew. "Um…this dress is…"

Becky waved a hand, cutting her lie short. "None of my business. And here at Baby Chic, we have a strict customer confidentiality policy."

Olivia smiled. "Thank you."

Becky nodded, writing her name on the paper. "So that number was three one zero?"

Olivia gave her the rest of the number.

"Great," Becky said, safety-pinning the paper to the dress. "All set. We should be open in a week…Or I could have it shipped?"

"I'll be around," she said. She'd need to stop by the clinic to confirm her pregnancy and for her first three months of prenatal appointments, before Dr. Chelsey would refer her to an ob-gyn in Denver. "Thank you."

"Sorry if my brother is giving you a hard time," Becky said as Olivia turned to leave.

She smiled. "Don't worry. I'm used to dealing with stubborn, strong-willed athletes."

"Yeah? How about cocky, annoying ones that still haven't made it back here with my latte?" she asked with a smirk.

She laughed. "Them, too." She could see the resemblance in the siblings—they had the same crystal clear blue eyes. In fact, Becky looked like a younger version of Beverly, obviously with the same sense of easygoing humor Olivia had enjoyed in the other woman. Ben Westmore's sister was a woman she could like. So far, she liked the entire family—too much. It caused her heart to ache even more not having one of her own. "Thanks again," she said as she headed toward the door. She paused and turned back. "So, that coffee place…"

Becky pointed down the street to the left. "Two blocks that way. You'll smell the baked goods before you see the sign for Kelli's Delicatessen."

She nodded. "Thanks, Becky." She'd already smelled the bakery goods, seen the sign shaped like a steaming coffee cup, and obviously had walked right past the temptation of the pastries *and* Ben Westmore without even knowing it.

Leaving the store, she glanced to the left, then went right.

CHAPTER 9

*H*ere you are. One latte with extra foam," Ben said, handing his sister the third latte he'd had to buy in order for it to be hot when he delivered it. She'd sent him on the caffeine run almost an hour ago.

But he couldn't help it if everyone in town stopped him to talk. He was a local superstar, and he rarely spent a lot of time in Glenwood Falls. He wouldn't even still be there if Jackson hadn't finished the renovations on Ben's lake house and he'd stuck around to see the place.

"This tastes like real cream," she said, taking a sip.

"It is."

"Ben! I'm trying to lose the baby weight."

Wow, talk about ungrateful. "Fine. Give it back." He would be buzzing on caffeine after three lattes in an hour, but his sourpuss sister didn't deserve the drink if she was going to complain about a little fat.

She moved it out of reach. "I had Doritos for breakfast anyway. Neil isn't back from a training mission for another few weeks—my diet officially starts tomorrow."

His brother-in-law was an air force pilot and was currently training pilots in Afghanistan. Ben was happy his sister had her new venture to help keep her mind from worrying so much. "What about the store? When's it going to be officially open?" he asked.

She glared at him. "You have two choices: hold your niece and shut your face, or set up my cash register."

He immediately reached for the baby girl. "Hand her over. Jackson's the handyman, not me." Besides, he needed to take advantage of the opportunity to cuddle his new niece before she got bigger and inherited her mother and older sister's mouthy gene.

"Someone say my name?" Jackson asked, entering the store.

"Finally! You were supposed to be here this morning to set this up. I already had to turn away a paying custo..." She stopped. "Never mind."

Jackson folded his arms across his chest. "You know, I could leave and you could learn how to do this stuff yourself."

Becky sighed. "No. Thank you for getting here so quickly," she said through gritted teeth.

"That's more like it." Jackson said, ignoring the box of machine parts she extended toward him. Instead, he touched Lily's cheek. "How's the only nice female in the family?" he asked the baby girl, making her giggle.

"Jerks," Becky mumbled.

Jackson laughed. "The rest of the lighting is done at the lake house," he told Ben.

Their sister scowled. "You're late because you were working on Ben's house—one he won't need until..."

Jackson silenced her rant by heading toward the door.

"No! I'm sorry, okay...come back," Becky said. "Just please get this set up today."

Jackson checked his watch. "Okay...but it can't take longer than an hour—Abby, Ben, and I are having dinner at the lake house."

Ben frowned. "What? No. I'm heading back to the city. I have a game to play tomorrow night and a practice first thing in the morning."

"Is *everyone* in this family ungrateful?" he muttered. "I just got all that shit done for you in record time in case your lame playing gets the Avalanche kicked out of the playoffs this round—again—and you need a place to sulk in your underwear."

Ben switched the baby to the other arm so she wouldn't see his less than nice hand gesture. "Fine. Dinner at the lake house. I'll barbecue steaks. Becky, you in?"

"Can't. Look at this place. I can't keep turning away customers."

"Who came by today?" Jackson asked.

Her cheeks reddened and she was uncharacteristically silent as she avoided their eyes. "No one special...Anyway, get to work." She took Lily from Ben. "And you," she added, "try not to be such a jerk."

His eyes wide, Ben shot Jackson a look as his sister disappeared into the back room. "What the hell did I do?"

"You breathe, man. With women, that's all it takes."

*   *   *

Olivia tightened her grip on the paper shopping bags she carried across Main Street. Where had she parked? She thought her car was directly across from the deli...She switched the bags in her arms, struggling under the weight. Maybe picking up the items she needed in Glenwood Falls instead of waiting until she got back to Denver hadn't been the best idea.

"A little out of the way for grocery shopping, isn't it?" a voice said behind her.

She shut her eyes and smothered a sigh. God, that voice, so rich and smooth, made her insides do stupid things. Though this time, she'd wandered onto *his* home-turf, and his sister had warned her he was around. She should have gotten out of there sooner.

Especially after Dr. Chelsey had gushed about the town hero while he'd performed the implantation. Apparently, Ben hadn't been at the clinic to donate seed but instead to sign hockey gear for a charity auction. Only a boy who never forgot where he came from would take time from his playoff schedule to do that, the doctor had said, pride in his voice.

She wondered whether or not anyone's feelings about Ben had changed or would change as more news about his current bad decision surfaced in the media, and she found herself hoping they didn't.

Damn. Why couldn't he have been just another faceless, arrogant opposition? That would have made her job so much easier. Not for the first time since meeting him did she regret getting involved with this case.

She turned around slowly and spotted her car half a block away. "Hi," she said tightly. Dressed in a pair of jeans and a black sweater that hugged his chest and biceps, he looked as amazing as he'd looked in the tuxedo. She suspected he made his hockey jersey look good, too. She averted her eyes and stepped around him.

"Are you stalking me?" His tone was suspicious as he blocked her path and bent lower to meet her gaze.

"That's ridiculous."

"Is it? So you're not trailing me to get more info for the case?"

"Tell me you're kidding."

"The only other thing I can reason is that you were desperate to see me."

Oh please. She should let him believe it was an intel mission. Unfortunately, if it were, she'd have discovered nothing but good things about him. "None of the above."

He peered inside the paper bags in her arms. "So, what then? They ran out of pickles at the supermarket in Denver?" he asked, shooting her an odd look.

She quickly moved the bag out of his view before he could also notice she'd stocked up on each and every brand of home pregnancy kits. Plus signs, two lines, the word *yes* in the window—couldn't get much clearer than that, probably the only one she needed really. But, when the time came, she knew she'd have to see it all to believe it.

And, well, the pickles were for the cravings…whenever they started.

After all, she didn't have a devoted and caring husband to run out when a craving attack struck in the middle of the night, now did she?

She'd have picked up ice cream, too, but it wouldn't have survived the drive from Glenwood Falls.

His intense gaze continued to make her uncomfortable, and when the mild, warm breeze carried the scent of his familiar cologne closer, she needed to get away. Her momentary panic when she heard his voice at the clinic had spoken volumes—she wasn't immune to Ben Westmore's charms, not even close. She just wanted to get this case settled and put all thoughts of him behind her. With any luck, her life was about to get complicated—in a good way—and she couldn't lose sight of what was important to her. "I like pickles," she mumbled with a shrug, heading toward her vehicle.

Ben followed. "Do you have friends…family out here?" he asked.

"No."

"A client?"

Reaching the car, she set the bags onto the passenger seat and slammed the door. "No."

He opened his mouth to say something else, but a woman's voice crossing the street toward them stopped him. "Oh my God—Olivia! What are you doing out here?"

Her former client Abigail Jansen. Great. A reunion. Right when she wanted to get home to put her legs over her uterus (it was supposed to help with the implantation), eat a pickle (to proactively ward off any cravings), and take a pregnancy test (just in case). She forced a smile. "Hi, Abigail, how are you?"

"Wonderful. Engaged to this troublemaker's brother," she said, nodding toward Ben.

The troublemaker's eyes were burrowing a hole in her forehead, so she didn't look at him. "Congrats, that's great."

The awkward silence that followed hung heavy on the air around her and she needed to escape. "Anyway, I have to go." She opened the driver side door. "Nice to see you again…Abby," she said to clarify that she didn't mean Ben.

"When did you move to Denver?" Abby asked, obviously not planning to let her escape.

"About ten months ago…just as we finalized your divorce."

"A little different from L.A. right?"

Ben was still staring at her.

She nodded. "A little bit…See you. Take care."

"Hey, why don't you stay for a while?" Abigail touched her shoulder to stop her from getting into the car. "We were just heading over to Ben's new lake house for dinner. You should join us."

"Uh…" She glanced at Ben quickly, but he was looking at

Abby, an are-you-out-of-your-mind expression on his face. "I can't," she said as another man joined them.

Dark hair and identical blue eyes. Another Westmore. Fantastic. The guy wrapped an arm around Abigail's waist. "Hi, I'm Jackson Westmore—the good brother."

"Oh, come on," Ben groaned.

Olivia was happy to see that he looked at least as perturbed by this reunion as she was. Obviously, he'd reached the same conclusion she had after the charity event—avoidance was best. Yet, she couldn't deny the slightest pleasure of seeing Ben again. "Anyway, I…"

"I love the effect you're having on my brother," Jackson said with a smirk directed at Ben. "Very humbling. He needs that sometimes."

"Jackson." Ben's tone was meant as a warning, but the other man smiled even wider.

"I was asking her to join us for dinner at Ben's new lake house," Abby told him.

Surely, Jackson would see the conflict of interest in that dinner invite, even if Abby were choosing to ignore it. Instead, he smiled. "That's a great idea."

"It is?"

Had *she* vocalized the thought or had Ben? They were so in sync, it was difficult to tell.

"Yeah. I mean, you may as well see firsthand the property your client is probably going to get in the divorce settlement," Jackson teased.

Next to him, Ben's face paled. They may be on his home turf, but somehow she had gained the upper hand. "Well, since you put it that way…"

CHAPTER 10

$\sim\!\!\infty\!\!\sim$

*T*he enemy was in his lake house. Worse—the woman
who had been on his mind, in a disturbingly good way,
for days was in his lake house. And she was smiling, sitting
with one leg curled under her on his new leather sofa, near
the wood-burning stove they'd lit moments before. As the sun
set and the early spring weather turned cool, Olivia Davis
was in *his* lake house looking comfortable and relaxed.

Ben was sweating bullets. Seeing her on the street had
been unexpected, and at first he'd thought he was imagining
it. She'd been on his mind so much, it wouldn't have surprised him if he'd fabricated her from his thoughts. But
she'd been real. Real and beautiful, dressed casually in a pair
of tight black leggings tucked into ankle boots and a pale
pink sweater that hung off one shoulder. The fabric looked
soft, but it was her porcelain skin that had tempted his touch.
When she'd walked away, he should have let her go.

He continued to scrape the squeaky clean barbecue grill,
staring though the window from the deck. "Don't worry

about helping clean up guys…I got it," he mumbled. "I just have a playoff game tomorrow night—no biggie."

The sound of his brother's laughter coming from inside only irritated him more.

The next time they were alone, he was going to kill Jackson. Abigail inviting Olivia to dinner was bad enough, but his brother backing the idea went against every bro code possible. And they were *actually* brothers— therefore it was like a double violation of the sacred code.

Yet, despite his annoyance, he couldn't say he hated this situation. His gaze landed on Olivia's face, illuminated by the light escaping the fireplace, her cheeks slightly flushed from the heat, and his breath caught in his chest.

There had been no shortage of women in his life—beautiful, fantastic, interesting women—but no one had him feeling this tortured, this confused…Not since Janelle.

But he still knew nothing about her. He didn't even know why she had been in Glenwood Falls that day, and he wasn't about to let his guard down and let her get close to help her case. There was no way she'd just been in the neighborhood. She was up to something. Maybe the charity event had been as much of a setup on him as he'd tried to make it on her. Maybe she really was one step ahead of him all the time. Maybe she really was that good. Well, he didn't know what kind of information she was after…but he was giving her nothing.

Though what *he* did or didn't do, didn't really matter. His brother and soon-to-be sister-in-law were babbling on endlessly, giving Olivia more information about him than she could ever need. Any minute now, Jackson would mysteriously pull a baby album out of his ass. The evening had to end before things got…complicated.

He put the scraper away and put the cover back on the barbeque before going inside. "Well, it's starting to get late…" he said from his tense position near the living room doorframe. The only place left to sit inside the room was right next to Olivia, and he'd already made the mistake of getting too close in the kitchen when they'd both reached for the fridge door at the same time. Her soft, delicious scent had nearly destroyed him as an ache of longing to see if she smelled that way everywhere had consumed him.

It had been weeks since he'd been with a woman, and his unusual dry spell was making him extra…sensitive. Maybe that's all this was. Damn, he hoped so, but the hollow, slightly nauseating sensation in his gut told him it wasn't as simple as that.

"You're right. We should go," Abby said, jumping to her feet and grabbing his brother's hand. "Come on, Jackson."

"I'm not finished with my…"

Abby grabbed his wine glass and drained the contents. "Finished. Let's go."

Ben's eyes narrowed. No wonder his brother had given up a career in hockey for this woman. Jackson had been head over hockey skates for Abby Jansen since they were kids. Ben swore he'd heard his brother's heart shatter the day Abby had married his best friend. But somehow, they'd found one another again. And now they were apparently partners in crime.

But thankfully Olivia stood as well. "Yeah, I need to get back to Denver, too," she said, checking her watch.

"It was great seeing you again," Abigail said, collecting her purse and sweater and tossing Jackson his coat. She hugged her quickly. "Don't be a stranger." Dragging Jackson by the hand, she tried to leave.

Ben blocked their escape. "It's rude to leave before guests."

"I'm right behind them," Olivia said, grabbing her own things.

"It's late, maybe you should stay..." Abby started, but even Jackson shot her a look that said *That's a little too far.*

She looked deflated, but then a wide smile appeared on her face as they all walked outside.

Ben turned to look at whatever was making her look like a cat that swallowed a canary. "Oh, you have got to be kidding me. Is that one of your guys?" he asked Jackson, pointing to the big construction truck blocking his and Olivia's vehicles in his gravel driveway.

Jackson squinted, reading the side of the truck. "Yeah, those guys are pouring a basement next door for me tomorrow. I'll call the owner of the company."

"Think they'll be able to move it tonight?" Olivia said, looking distraught to see her tiny car completely blocked by Ben's Hummer and the big truck.

Jackson nodded as he reached into his pocket for his phone.

"I think it's fate," Abby said.

"It's not," Olivia said, but her cheeks turned a shade of pink that suited her far too well.

"Just the kind of suspiciously bad luck I seem to attract around you two lately," Ben mumbled.

A moment later, Jackson put the phone away. "I left him a voicemail...Told him someone needs to get the truck moved as soon as possible."

Ben eyed him. Could he trust his own brother?

"Seriously, man, as fun as it is to torment you, I want you to bring home the cup this year more than anyone. I know you have to play tomorrow night, and I made sure Tom knows it. Someone should be here soon."

He hesitated. Maybe he should force Jackson to drive

them back to the city now. He could come back for the Hummer…

But Abby was already at the truck. "Come on, Jackson. We have to pick up Dani from your sister's house."

"I'll keep calling Tom," he yelled as he climbed in.

"Funny how *they* weren't blocked in," Olivia said, looking as annoyed to be left stranded together as he felt. Or wanted to feel.

"Well, I guess we wait."

Olivia sat on the swing on the porch.

"You can come back inside," he said. He could behave. He hoped. Of course it would be easier if she wasn't wearing that off-the-shoulder sweater, teasing him with the view of a pink bra underneath, and those leggings that clung to her beautifully tempting curves. The fact that he knew how her body felt didn't help things, the way her waist gave way to sexy hips…Maybe outside was safer.

She must have agreed as she shook her head. "Nah, that's okay. It's nice out here. I rarely get a view like this one in the city." Her gaze was on the snow-covered mountains casting a reflection on the dark lake, lit only by several street lights.

The view of the mountains was his favorite part of lakeside living. Once the season was over, he planned to spend most of his time there. He hesitated. "I'm going to grab the rest of the wine…then I'll come back and wait with you?"

"It's your house."

That wasn't what he wanted to hear. "Right. But are you okay with company? *My* company."

"Sure. But no wine for me. I will have to drive eventually, hopefully…" her voice trailed off as she stared at the blocked vehicles.

Going inside, he released a deep breath and emptied the remaining red wine into a glass. He hadn't had any with dinner, and he wasn't a big wine drinker, but he needed something to calm the anxiety that had been increasing from the moment he'd seen her on Main Street.

"Be good. She's off-limits," he said to himself as he opened the screen door and rejoined her.

Placing his glass on the end table next to the swing, he sat, leaving as much room between them as possible. "So you never did say why you were in Glenwood Falls today."

"Just felt like getting out of the city," she said noncommittally. He sensed it was a lie. Her expression held a peaceful look he hadn't seen on her before. He could certainly understand wanting to escape for a while.

"It is a great place to recharge the batteries," he said.

"That's what you're doing? Recharging before the next game?"

He laughed. "I wish. No, I had to drop off some donation items at the fertility clinic—the head physician and his wife are holding a fundraiser and I said I would. And then my sister needed help putting up some shelves in her new baby clothing store. So, no, there was no relaxing or recharging batteries for me today." Even if that had been his mission, she'd have shot that to hell by showing up, but it was hard to feel stressed in that moment with her, surrounded by a peaceful silence. For the first time all evening, he started to feel the awkward tension slip away, replaced with a different kind of sensation—a warm, unfamiliar, electrically charged feeling coursing through him. She was just an arm's reach away…but he kept his hands to himself. Touching her would only make a bigger mess of things.

"Have you lived in Glenwood Falls most of your life?" she asked, freeing her feet from her boots and tucking them under her on the swing.

He reached for the blanket on the back of the swing and

opened it, draping it over her legs. She smiled in thanks and
he swallowed hard, struggling to remember the question.
Those perfect, nude lips were so tempting. He averted his
gaze. "Since I was ten. Moving here from the city took some
getting used to, but then Jackson made friends with some
older kids who played hockey out here on the lake every day
in winter, and once I started to play with them, I learned to
appreciate the quiet, slower pace of the small town."

"That's how you started playing—on the outdoor lake?"

He nodded. "To be honest, I wasn't interested in
hockey—I actually preferred football. Jackson was the
hockey-obsessed one, but his love of the game was infec-
tious. When I started playing, I could barely keep the puck,
which for a competitive, naturally athletic kid like me was
a blow to the ego. So I learned fast, and then I was unstoppable," he said with a grin.

She rolled her eyes. "Of course you were. I bet you're
sickeningly good at everything, aren't you?"

"Not everything. But most things."

She shifted on the seat, her expression turning to one
he couldn't quite name. "And you probably get everything
you want, don't you, Ben?" Her dark eyes held no trace of
annoyance, just a curiosity that made him slightly uncomfortable. They were moving into territory about his life, a
place he preferred not to go. Couldn't go without letting her
in even more.

The smile slid from his lips ever so slightly. "Not always,
but most of the time, yeah."

"That must be nice," she said, looking away, her attention
back on the lake.

The smallest glimmer of resentment in her voice made
him move closer, lifting the edge of the blanket to slide beneath it. His thigh brushed hers and he turned slightly to face

her, letting his arm rest behind her. "Is that a bad thing? You make it sound like a bad thing."

She shook her head. "It's not a bad thing…if you're *you*." She continued to avoid his gaze.

"What about you, Olivia? You work hard. You must get what you want. I hear your court win record is something I should be terrified of." Turning the tables on her was his only defense. He refused to give too much without getting anything in return.

She nodded. "Career-wise, I definitely achieve the goals I set for myself."

The added "career-wise" part intrigued him. "And outside the courtroom?"

"Crossing the line into too personal again."

She'd started it, and all of a sudden, he refused to retreat. "Are you always this shut down, closed off? Or has someone ever gotten in there?" He nodded toward her heart.

She hesitated. "Like you, my career has been my primary focus," she said simply.

The temptation to touch her was overwhelming, so he gave in. He traced a hand along her cool cheek, and it warmed slightly under his caress. "But *I* still have fun…make time to enjoy life."

"At the expense of countless women, you mean?" she moved her face away.

He wouldn't deny it. "I like keeping things casual, yes, but the women I get involved with know not to expect any more than that. I make no promises." Another relationship was something he wouldn't even entertain…or at least he thought he would never entertain. Being with Olivia felt terrifyingly too right.

"Yet somehow you decided to marry a ghost from your past with whom you'd just reconnected hours before."

He stiffened, feeling the mood around them change. "We're back to the court case." Had they actually gone almost five full minutes without bringing it up? Though admittedly, any other conversation, any other direction in which to take the evening was probably pointless—and worse, dangerous.

"What else is there, really?" she asked, echoing his thoughts. She tossed the blanket aside and stood.

He grabbed her arm and was on his feet in a flash. "I don't know. How about this?" His mouth crushed hers and he felt her gasp in surprise, but half a second later, her arms were around his neck and she was returning his kiss with a fervor he'd never expected.

Pushing all other thoughts away, he pulled her closer, aching to feel every inch of her against him, knowing this kiss would be the one and only. Hopefully, it would be all he'd need to put this stupid yearning for the woman to rest.

His hands moved from her waist, up her back, then tangling in the hair at the base of her neck. His tongue parted her lips and she moaned, which nearly drove him completely mad. Her lips were as soft as he'd imagined, and when her fingers slid into his hair, his pulse raced.

The feel of her breasts against his chest made it impossible to think straight. He was sure she could feel his increasing hardness pressed against her, but she didn't move away. Her hands slid lower to grip his sweater as she held him even closer. The fact that she wanted this as much as he did had his body and mind in a heated battle. He wanted nothing more than to scoop her up, bring her inside the lake house, and really make a mess of things, but the beating in his chest made him fear this attraction was more than just physical. What the hell was he doing? He was supposed to be keeping his distance, but she felt too good in his arms. He never wanted to release her, which was exactly why he had to.

Fighting to catch a breath, he broke away, moving a fraction of an inch from her lips. "Olivia," he murmured.

As if the sound of her name broke the spell she'd obviously gotten lost in, she stumbled away from him, her hand going to her mouth. "Shit."

"Yep."

"No, like really, shit," she said, almost frantically, running a hand through her tangled hair. "I have to go." She bent to collect her boots, bumping her knee against the swing.

"You okay?"

"Fine. Just have to go."

She'd said that already. "Car's still blocked."

"I'll walk."

"Relax. Breathe. It was just a kiss." *Liar.* It wasn't just a kiss. It was a mind-blowing tease of what couldn't be. How *he* wasn't the one losing his shit right now, he didn't know.

Lights from a vehicle turning into the driveway cast a bright glow over them.

"Oh thank God," she said, trying to flee once more.

Against all common sense, he blocked her escape. "Wait. Tell me you didn't feel something just now." Damn. What did it matter? The kiss wasn't supposed to mean anything—wasn't that his thing? Meaningless kisses, casual hookups, no feelings, no strings…He was an idiot to be looking for answers he didn't want.

Her eyes widened and her cheeks flushed, telling him exactly what he wanted to know. She'd felt the spark between them grow stronger, too. Instead of the kiss extinguishing whatever heat and tension was between them, it had only added fuel to the fire…one he desperately needed to contain.

But she shook her head. "Of course I didn't feel anything." She was lying. The chemistry between them was real for both of them. And she was just as terrified by it as he was. "Besides," she continued, "you're still a married man." She sidestepped him and practically ran down the front steps, as the construction truck moved, freeing her car.

"And whose fault is that?" Ben muttered under his breath as he watched her drive away.

CHAPTER 11

❦

*H*ockey was a mental sport. Success required more than size, strength, and speed. What happened off the ice in a player's personal life could impact their game, something Ben knew well enough. But muscle memory had to take over at some point, didn't it?

It could start anytime now. He skated toward the loose puck in the last period of the first semifinal game the following evening, but the round, black disc disappeared inches before he could reach it.

He looked up to see his opposition was a rookie player. He almost sighed with relief as he charged ahead. Other than the goal he'd scored at the beginning of the first period, Ben could do nothing right. His feet felt clumsy on his skates and he'd yet to achieve great speed during the game. Whenever he had the puck, it was stolen. His frustration mounted, resulting in poor decisions and even worse performance.

And it seemed his line was always up against the opposing team's star players. This was the first time this new kid had shared ice time with him, and he was about to find out what happened when the puck was taken away from Ben Westmore.

He lowered his shoulder as he neared the kid, skating close to the boards, and held nothing back as he went to check him.

A second later he blinked, finding himself the only recipient of a run-in with the unforgiving advertisement for the local bank, whose words blurred for a brief count before he could shake off his own hit.

The buzzer sounded as he got to his feet. The new kid had scored, bringing the game to three to two. The clock read three minutes left in the game.

Shaking off his disappointing performance, he mentally prepared for the last three minutes of the game. He could tie this up and push the game to overtime. The coach always left him on in the final minutes, changing out the other players on the line every thirty seconds. Ben had brought their team back from a losing scoreboard countless times. He skated toward the blue line, but another player got there first. He frowned as he glanced toward the box. Must be a mistake…

But the coach was waving him in.

That shook him more than the hit.

He skated to the bench. "I'm good. Stupid bad timing on that check, that's all."

Coach Bencik gave him a concerned look. Which was the worst look of all. An angry look meant a player was pissing him off—usually for taking too many penalties. An annoyed look meant a player wasn't passing enough or venturing out of their zone too much. But a concerned look meant a player—*him*—was playing like shit, and it could only mean a life-threatening illness was taking over.

"It's one bad game, one bad night—sit out," the coach said.

There was no point in arguing. Besides, he wasn't at all confident he could bring the game back that evening, and his team deserved to have the best chance possible. Winning the first game in a playoff round gave a team confidence. It was better to be leading the series than playing catch-up with each victory. Fans hated to see their team lose on home ice. The next two games would be played away, so they needed a win while they had an advantage.

He wasn't sure he was the man for the job. "Okay," he nodded, climbing over the boards.

His coach shot him a different look—one he reserved for new players who complained too much or trash-talked in the locker room, never to back it up on ice. One that made even the most confident player question why they'd ever gotten drafted in the first place.

Ben's disappointment in himself reached an all-time high.

"That's it—no fight?" his coach said.

He removed his helmet, knowing the fight his coach had expected out of him was too late now. "I'm sorry, Coach, but I didn't think it would work."

Coach Bencik folded his arms as he turned away from him. "I want my star player back by Sunday night," he said, and it wasn't a request.

Back home after the 4–3 loss in overtime, Ben showered again, hoping the hot water would help ease some of the tension in his shoulders and neck. Then he mixed a protein drink, guzzled it, and despite it being after midnight, he opened his laptop to Skype Asher.

As predicted, his brother was awake. Asher was always awake—an insomniac since they were kids. Yet, he still functioned better than most people. "Hey, man, rough game," he said as he appeared on the screen.

Ben ran a hand through his still wet hair. "That's an understatement. See that embarrassing failed hit?"

Asher nodded. "I won't lie, I enjoyed it a little."

"Did you see me get pulled from the last three minutes?" If anyone knew how discouraging that was, Asher would. Playing a bad game was one thing; it shook a player's confidence and added a weight to his shoulders that he wouldn't be able to drop until he performed better. But losing a coach's confidence—that was devastating.

Ash nodded again. "Saw. Sorry, man. I'm surprised you didn't fight Coach on that—what's going on?"

The concern in his brother's voice and the truth of the sentiment expressed by his coach made Ben's blood pressure rise. "I was bringing the team down, man. Would you have stayed on?"

Asher shook his head slowly. "But I'm not you. *You* would have stayed on, pulled it together, and brought the team back like you've done in the past. The first game in the semifinals isn't exactly the place to get soft, Ben."

Exactly the speech he would have delivered to any of his teammates or his brother in this situation, but not one he wanted to hear himself. He gave a quick "I'm out" wave and shut down the connection.

Tossing his protein cup into the sink with a loud clang, he headed into his bedroom and lay on the bed. His brother was right. His coach was right. He had to get his shit together and clear his mind before the next game two nights from now. All day, he'd been off. At practice, at warm-up…and as much as he'd like to have blamed lack of sleep, not having made it back to Denver until after midnight, he knew that wasn't it. His mind wasn't where it needed to be. He was allowing everything happening off of the ice to reflect in his playing.

It had to stop. He couldn't let this court case or the media attention make him a different player. He couldn't let this insane attraction to the last woman on Earth he should want destroy his concentration and put him off his game. On the ice, he knew who he was—a winner.

And while that may not be the case in this personal life, he had to focus on the game. The one thing he *could* control.

* * *

"Madison, what is this on my desk?" Olivia picked up the box of raspberry tea leaves and opened the lid. It smelled nothing like raspberries and looked like grass.

Her assistant hurried over with a smile and leaned around the doorframe. "It's red raspberry leaf tea. It helps strengthen your uterus," she whispered.

"Get in here, please." She removed her suit jacket and draped it over the chair.

"Did you want me to make you a cup?" Madison asked, entering.

"No, thank you, and try not to mention my uterus." She ran a hand down her pencil skirt as she sat. Thoughts of her uterus had competed with thoughts of Ben all night until she'd finally fallen asleep from mental exhaustion. The same day she'd gone ahead with her plans to have a baby, she'd given into a mind-blowing kiss from a man who couldn't possibly be farther from father material. She had to be losing her mind. A month ago, she'd been certain this was what she wanted. Letting Ben Westmore's delicious kiss cloud her certainty was stupid.

Now that the implantation was complete, she wanted to

follow the doctor's orders of relaxing and trying not to stress about it too much until she knew one way or the other. Stress was not good for her or a baby.

Which was why she'd decided to remove herself from this divorce case. She shouldn't have taken it on in the first place, but she'd never have predicted she'd be desperately attracted to the man she was trying to keep married to another woman.

Coffee. Where the hell was her coffee?

Madison stood in the office looking determined as she showed her the box. "Read the label. It has all-natural ingredients."

It could be fairy dust and unicorn wings for all Olivia cared. Caffeine wasn't on the list, therefore she had zero interest. She was exhausted and she needed to get through the day. On top of her to-do list was scheduling a meeting with Kristina Sullivan, and she wasn't looking forward to it. Even if she could in all good consciousness remain on the case despite her attraction to Ben, she was starting to side with the opposition. Kristina's reason to prolong the divorce, hoping Ben could help her son's hockey career, wasn't exactly something Olivia felt comfortable fighting for. She couldn't argue in court that the couple should stay married when they weren't—and had never been—in love. She wasn't the best lawyer for Kristina…God, she was justifying.

Picking up her mug, she handed it to Madison, hoping it was enough of a hint.

Nope. "So many women in my family swear by this tea," her assistant pushed on. "They all drank it while they were trying to conceive and *poof*—without hardly trying."

She sighed. There'd been a lot more than a *poof* involved for her already. "My uterus is fine, and I'm not a tea drinker." She nodded wide-eyed toward her still empty mug. By now the coffee would have been the perfect temperature to start drinking.

"Yes. Your coffee—I know." Madison hesitated. "Caffeine is bad for the baby, so I thought you might want to get used to skipping your usual eight cups now so it will be easier once you know…"

Olivia thought about it. She had given up everything else in advance preparation, but coffee would be the hardest to let go of. She wasn't ready to say goodbye to the one thing that got her through her days just yet. "I need my coffee…for now…and please take that tea. Hide it somewhere so no one sees it."

Madison looked ready to argue, but she tucked the box inside her sweater and shrugged. "Fine. I'll keep it in case I ever get pregnant. I'm terrified of labor, and this stuff is supposed to make it as close to painless as you can get." She turned to leave.

"Wait." Labor was something Olivia refused to think about yet—one thing at a time—but now that the girl brought it up…"What does this tea do?"

Madison needed little encouragement. "It's a miracle tea. It helps strengthen the uterus walls, which makes the muscles stronger for delivery. You drink it every day until you get pregnant, then you stop until you're in the third trimester, then you drink it like water every day—like six cups. Then as soon as you feel the first labor pain, you drink as much as hot as possible and before you know, baby is here."

"Just like that, huh?" Nothing could be that simple.

"Do you want a cup instead of your coffee?" Madison asked, hopeful.

"No, I want my coffee." If and when she was pregnant, she would begrudgingly give up one of her life's only true pleasures, but for now, she was going to enjoy it. Could she also enjoy more of Ben Westmore's kisses? She cleared her throat. "I'll check this with the doctor first," she said awkwardly, tucking the box into her drawer, out of sight.

Her assistant smiled as she stood. "Fair enough. I'll get your coffee."

"Thank you."

When Madison left the office, she typed "red raspberry leaf tea" into Google search. Just how did this "miracle" tea work?

Her cell phone rang and she reached for it absently, her eyes scanning the amazing claims of this tea. This herbal medicine site was confirming everything Madison claimed…it also had her computer's antivirus claiming her computer might now be infected. Great. "Hello—Olivia Davis speaking," she said into the phone, shutting down the site as Madison set her coffee in front of her. "Thank you," she whispered, taking a sip.

"This is Emelia Michelin from the Colorado Center for Children's fundraising committee. How are you?"

"Great. Is something wrong?" Had she forgotten to sign her check? With Ben's unsettling gaze on her that evening, it was quite possible. When he'd held her on the dance floor, she been thinking of nothing else except how wonderful it felt to be in his arms.

"No, nothing's wrong…just wanted to remind you of your payment for your silent auction item."

Silent auction? She hadn't bid on…Her mouth dropped. He didn't.

She swallowed hard, setting her cup on her desk, afraid she might snap the handle with her death grip hold. "Can you remind me again what I bid on?" She forced a light laugh.

"Sure. You bid six thousand dollars for a skating lesson with Ben Westmore."

She closed her eyes. "That's right, I'd totally forgotten."

"Well, we thank you for your generosity. Before your bid, the highest was five thousand. People usually don't jump that much from bid to bid."

Of course not. A thousand-dollar increase was crazy. "Well, it's for a good cause," she said, mentally calculating the funds in her savings account. She didn't want to write a check she couldn't cash.

"Thank you again. The check can be made out to the hospital, and we hope you enjoy your skating lesson."

She clenched her teeth, fighting the memory of Ben's kiss.

She must have been insane to agree to have dinner with them at the lake house. She blamed her confused, exhilarated emotions that day for everything. There was no other explanation for why she'd readily spend time with a man she was going up against in court, why she'd let him engage her in unsafe conversation, or why she'd returned his untimely kiss as though he were a source of oxygen.

She sighed. Enjoy the skating lesson? Probably a little too much. Disconnecting the call, she reached for her checkbook and wrote a check for an auction prize she had no intention of redeeming. Then she sent Ben Westmore an invoice.

* * *

Ben felt better. The wake-up call warning from his coach and a good night's sleep had been what he'd needed. His mind was back in the game, and for over an hour now, the memory of kissing Olivia Davis had not crossed his mind.

And, the clock resets.

If only the kiss had sucked. If only the kiss had been enough to satisfy the urge to do it again. It hadn't.

Rotating his shoulders, he stretched, warming up for the game. He'd managed to relax a little after practice that morning, and he felt ready. As long as he could push everything else aside and focus on sixty minutes of ice time, he would be okay.

Winning the first away game would shatter the other team's confidence and tie up the series. Being down by two games and playing catch-up was not something he wanted to deal with. That was the team's downfall the last several times they'd made it to the semifinals. Not this year.

His teammates all looked ready for the game, but he knew they were watching him to see if *he* could pull it together. He was ready to prove he deserved to wear that *C* on his jersey tonight.

He took a breath. Good. Another solid five minutes of not thinking about Olivia.

In his locker, his phone chimed with a new email message.

Leave it. Anything important would be a call or text…

Reaching into his bag, he retrieved the phone. Opening the inbox, his mouth went dry. The message from the woman driving his thoughts wild for the last few weeks had a two-word subject line: *Not funny.*

He knew what this was about.

He read the short message.

You owe me $6,000. Invoice attached.

He sat on the bench. She was right. The auction bid was meant to be a funny, jerk-face move. He'd had every intention of paying the six grand and providing the lesson to watch her squirm a little more…but not now. Not after that kiss. He'd pay her back immediately, but there would be no lesson.

Safer to deal with things through his lawyer and stay

away from her. The more distance he could put there, the better, and soon enough she'd just be some woman who tried—and failed—to ruin his life...with the most tempting body and irresistible lips...

Hitting Reply, he typed, *That's one expensive kiss* and grinned despite himself.

Her reply was instant. *Don't try to be cute. You can keep the lesson, I just want the money.*

He hesitated, then typed, *I understand if you don't trust yourself around me.* He hit Send and put the phone away, immediately regretting it. Damn—he was stupid. Flirtation seemed to be an autopilot reaction for him. Continuing this dangerous cat-and-mouse game with this woman was the worst thing he could do. The power she held over him since the day they met was a foreign feeling to him, and it had nothing to do with the court case. No other woman had ever occupied his mind this long. She needed to get out. And spending more time with her certainly wasn't the answer.

Luckily, he knew she'd never take him up on the skating lesson. She was immune to his juvenile tactics.

A second later, her reply was back.

Anytime, anywhere, Westmore.

Shit. She'd called his bluff.

CHAPTER 12

❧

"I can't believe you don't know how to skate."

She couldn't believe she'd fallen for his bullying technique, but she hadn't shied away from a challenge since she was three years old, and his taunt had resulted in her not thinking clearly before she'd inadvertently agreed to the lesson. In the days in between, she'd composed a dozen emails canceling, but had been unable to send any of them.

And it was taking all of her strength not to question why.

She certainly wished she had now, shivering in the cold, crisp air. Outside it was sixty degrees; inside it had to be thirty degrees colder. "This is the first time I've ever worn a pair of skates." Growing up in California with her parents, winter sports weren't really her thing, and the move to Colorado with her aunt hadn't changed that. Aunt Helen hadn't encouraged her to participate in sports, instead focusing heavily on academics.

Ben knelt in front of her to lace up the bulky, awkward men's skates she'd rented from the arena, and she tried desperately not to think about the countless pairs of sweaty feet that had been in them. Thank God for the extra layer of thick, warm socks she'd worn.

"Well, you're in for a treat." Ben yanked on the laces and she winced. Watching his hands expertly tie the skates, wrapping the tattered extra-long laces around the back of the skates several times, then knotting them, she experienced an odd sense of vulnerability. She wasn't used to anyone doing anything for her. Even a gesture as small as this one felt far too intimate, as if she were being taken care of. She didn't want or need to be taken care of. She'd always been independent, and her plan to have a family alone was her most recent solitary venture, proving she didn't need a man for anything. So why was her stomach fluttering? It was just her nerves about this lesson, that was all. "Are you sure they need to be that tight?"

"Unless you want to break an ankle."

"I actually don't want to do this at all." Why had she entered into this stupid battle of wills with him?

He finished tying the first skate and switched to the other one. "You know, I can list a hundred women who would be dying for the opportunity for a private skating lesson with me on an empty ice rink," he said, placing her foot between his legs to steady it as he started the yanking all over again.

She scoffed. "Right. As if a skating lesson is what they want."

"Are you saying I'm sexy?"

"Wow—way to blow my simple statement way out of proportion," she said and winced again as he pulled the laces, practically cutting off her circulation. "All I'm saying is some women are attracted to men like you—good-looking, powerful, wealthy…"

"But not you?"

She shook her head, knowing the outright lie might choke her to death if she vocalized it.

"So that kiss at the lake house—there was no passion there? No sexual tension? No spark?" He yanked the laces tighter, daring her to deny it.

"Nope. None. Like kissing a brother."

He raised an eyebrow. "You'd kiss a brother like that?"

She sighed and pushed him away, finishing the laces herself. She wanted to get this over with, then get to the office. This wasn't exactly the way she'd ever thought she'd be spending a morning before work—getting an unwanted skating lesson from the opposition's client. Soon to be ex-opposition client...She quieted the annoying reminder. Her meeting with Kristina that afternoon was the second ordeal she wasn't looking forward to.

Standing, she made her way to the ice, hesitating at the door. The moment she placed a foot out onto the ice, her leg would jut forward and she would fall on her butt—she knew it.

"Grab the side," Ben said behind her.

The smell of his cologne—strong and manly, yet smooth and warm—and the heat radiating from his close proximity did nothing to soothe her nerves. *Better get this over with.* She sighed and did as he instructed. The ice felt smooth as glass beneath her skates and she clung to the two-inch side board as she slowly moved her feet.

Ben stood beside her and extended a hand. "Let go."

No fucking way. "You know, I think I'll just hang on to the boards and go around." The ice was dangerous. His touch was lethal.

He shrugged, then disappeared.

She watched as he expertly glided across the ice, his legs *swish-swishing* back and forth in opposition to his swinging arms as he made his way across the surface. He made it look so easy, graceful…He was confident, self-assured…sexy as hell in his ripped jeans and black sweater that hugged his sculpted, muscular chest. Without a doubt the hottest man she'd ever needed to avoid, and yet here she was. Why couldn't she stay away from him? What was it about him that she failed miserably to resist? No other man had this effect on her.

He winked at her from directly across the ice and she lost her balance. He had to stop doing that. And she had to get it together. She stared at her feet on the ice as he disappeared out of her line of sight.

Slowly letting go of the boards with one hand, and steadying herself with a death grip with the other, she started to slide her feet. One foot, then the next one…okay, so it wasn't as hard as she thought.

She pushed her right foot forward a little faster and further, and as she was about to do the same with her left foot, a pair of hands seized her around the waist and pulled her away from the safety of the boards. She gripped his wrists, her eyes widening as they picked up speed. "Ben, stop. This is not fun."

"For who?" he asked, whispering in her ear as he picked up even more speed.

She swallowed hard, her spine stiff as a board as they approached the first corner. Oh God…his plan was to kill her. A skating accident. Innocent enough. "Ben—corner…Ben…" Her voice had adopted a slightly shrieking panicked nuance. One she was certain she'd never heard come from her own mouth before. Her grip tightened and her nails bit into the flesh at the back of his hands.

"I've got you. Relax, bend your knees a little, and lean forward," he instructed.

She tried to do it, but her feet slipped backward, and he

caught her just before her nose hit the ice. His arms around her waist as he lifted her back to her feet made her pulse soar. Too much adrenaline. Too much tension and nerves. This couldn't be good. "I'm done," she said, attempting to free herself from his hold.

"Do you really want me to let you go?" he asked.

Yes. She surveyed the distance back to the safety of the boards. "No," she mumbled. "But please return me to the boards."

He moved to stand in front of her and took her hands in his instead.

Better. But not much. Now he could see the look of terror on her face, and she could see how annoyingly gorgeous he was. His hair in a spiked, gelled mess, the thin covering of stubble on his face, and those damn blue eyes that she couldn't escape from had her at a complete disadvantage. And yet his hands wrapped around hers—big, strong, supportive hands—made her feel safe.

"One lap around. If you hate it, I'll bring you back inside, we'll take off the skates, and you're free to go, and I won't think you're a wimp."

She sighed. She desperately wanted to prove she wasn't a wimp, but already her feet were aching and every muscle in her body felt tense. Did it really matter what he thought of her?

Obviously it did. Otherwise she'd have dropped to her knees and crawled back to safety by now.

"Come on. Trust me and let go. We'll go slow this time, I promise," he said, the teasing glint in his eye making her wonder if they were still talking about skating. He slowly released one of her hands and she reached for his hand back.

"No! Wait. Don't let me go yet."

He smiled as he steadied her. "Okay. Relax, bend your knees a little, and lean forward."

She did her best, but the relaxing part was impossible. His touch sent a tingly sensation up her arms and into her chest. How were his hands so warm in the freezing arena?

"I'm going to let go of this hand now and skate beside you," he said.

"Okay."

When he was next to her, he pushed forward, dragging her with him. "Try moving your feet. Right…left…right…"

She was moving. It was slow, but she was moving. She must also be cutting off circulation in his hand, she realized, releasing her grip ever so slightly.

"Want to try on your own?" he asked as they moved a little faster, approaching the first turn.

"No." Holding his hand was dangerous, but compared to being on her own on the ice, it was the lesser of two evils.

He picked up speed and she tensed. "Ben…"

"Trust me, you're doing great," he said, moving a little faster.

She shut one eye as her skates rounded the first turn and released a sigh of relief when they were once again on a straight stretch. "I survived."

"We weren't exactly going at a breakneck speed, but yes, you survived."

Finding courage from some foolhardy place, she wiggled her hand free. "I think I'm okay now."

He smiled. "Great. Race you to the other end?"

The words were meant as a joke, she knew, but her new-found confidence had her nodding. "Sure," she said, taking advantage of the element of surprise and dashing off…as fast as she could stumble.

A second later, he was matching her pace. He could easily win this race, but he skated alongside her. "One lesson and you're taking on a pro hockey player in a speed race—that's a little ambitious, don't you think?"

"Without a doubt. I guess I'm hoping you'll trip over your overinflated ego," she said with a smirk. Feeling herself lose balance, she turned her focus straight ahead again and slowed a little. *Do not flirt. Just skate.*

He took the lead, skating backward to look at her. "That's what you think I have? An overinflated ego?"

She nodded. His intense gaze on her was making her own confidence wane, but still she picked up speed as they approached the boards—a long-repressed competitive nature rearing its unexpected head. If she got close enough, she might even push him...and maybe win the race by cheating.

"You're probably right," he said, "but you're not exactly lacking in the ego department."

"Excuse me?" She stumbled and waved her arms to regain her balance.

"Your reputation in court precedes you," he said.

He wouldn't have to worry about it after that afternoon, but she wasn't about to tell him that. "You scared?" she asked, teasing, but his expression turned serious.

"Terrified," he said, slowing his pace to stand in front of her.

She swallowed hard as the moment simmered between them. His expression was full of desire, and she hadn't realized how alone they were in the big arena until now, when the sound of her heart seemed to echo off of the concrete walls. How was the ice not melting beneath their feet? "Good. You should be," she said, but her voice was an unrecognizable creak. She toyed with telling him that she was removing herself from the case, but at that moment it might be the only thing keeping his lips off of hers. And that's what she wanted. Right?

"Maybe you could go easy on me…" He moved even closer, and they were almost standing still. His eyes fell to her mouth and then back to hers. "Like I'm going easy on you."

Was that what this was about? Befriend the enemy? At first, she'd thought he'd been trying to kill her with this escapade. This was worse. She straightened her shoulders and, seeing her opportunity, shoved him off-balance.

The look of surprise on his face as his butt hit the ice almost made her laugh, but she kept her game face on. "I don't go easy on anyone." With that she dashed toward the boards, picking up her pace as her fake confidence grew…Until she was only feet away and going at a breakneck speed—breakneck according to her standards anyway.

Oh shit. How did she stop? She'd seen skaters and hockey players doing this sideways full stop thing that sent snow flying up into the air. It didn't look that hard…She bit her lip as the boards drew closer and her window to make a decision closed.

"Olivia—brace yourself," she heard Ben call as he scrambled to his feet behind her.

Shit. She was going for it. Twisting her body to the left at the last minute, she turned her skates sideways as she closed her eyes and hoped not to end up facedown on the ice.

"Holy shit. Did you just do a hockey stop?" Ben's disbelief made her open her eyes.

She was still on her feet. Her heart leaped with joy. Forcing a cocky grin, she turned to face him as he approached. "If hockey stop is what that expert display of talent is called, then yea…"

Her words were cut short by a light push that had her off-balance and onto her butt on the cold ice. Mouth open, she blinked away her surprised expression. "What the hell?"

"That was for hustling me."

CHAPTER 13

❦

"Wow, I think this woman is going for everything but the poor guy's kidneys…and maybe one of those just in case," her colleague Kendall Schiller whispered in the back of the courtroom later that morning. They each had a case on the docket.

"No kidding." Usually sitting in the room and hearing other cases while she waited for her own to be called didn't bother her, but today she was starting to feel bad for the couple. Three kids and twenty-six years together down the drain—why? Because he worked too much to support her and the kids? Hardly an offense. The worst of it was the poor man seemed like a decent guy, who was about to lose everything…

Oh God—she was getting soft. Was that a side effect of the hormone injections, too? "I'm going to get some coffee." Water actually. She hadn't had coffee in days, not being able to stand the look of disapproval on Madison's face every time she saw her with a coffee cup. Lack of caffeine had to be why she was losing her edge. She'd blame it on that at least.

But when she stood, every muscle in her body ached and she grimaced.

"What's wrong with you?" Kendall asked.

"Nothing…just a tough workout this morning."

"You don't work out."

"Hence the hurting."

"Hey, get me one, too," she said, rummaging around in her oversized purse for change.

"I got it," Olivia said, hobbling painfully toward the door, her annoyance with Ben Westmore growing with each painful step. Not only did her body feel like it had been ripped apart, but she'd also noticed a big purple bruise on her left butt cheek when she'd gotten out of her second shower that day. If she ached this much already, she'd be immobile tomorrow.

Pulling her phone from her purse, she scrolled through her contacts looking for his number, which *he* put in her phone, not her. And which she just hadn't had a chance to delete yet.

You could delete it now, a nagging voice taunted.

Instead, she texted, *My body hurts everywhere.*

She tucked the phone into her suit jacket pocket as she reached the coffee kiosk at the back of the courthouse.

The blond guy behind the counter smiled in recognition. "Double Americano?"

Oh God, it was tempting.

"Not today. Just a black coffee and a bottle of water please," she said, as the phone chimed.

He nodded and left to pour the coffee as she read, *Do you need me to fix that?*

What an arrogant jerk.

Though he had a point. What *had* been the purpose of her text?

Just letting you know that you were a terrible date. As soon as she hit Send, she gasped. Damn it! *Date?* Seriously? And though she was annoyed, she was pretty certain her tone would come across more flirty in his no-woman-can-resist-me mind.

She was right.

Date? Sweetheart, that was hardly a date. But since you thought it was and I disappointed—do over?

Her heart raced. No. Of course she didn't want a do-over. She hadn't wanted the first one. God, it was easier to manipulate the truth all day for other people than it was to lie to herself. She started this mess—again. She had to end it now.

No. Plain, simple, short.

"Here's your coffee and water. That'll be six dollars," the guy behind the counter said.

Olivia handed him the cash and took the drinks. Her phone chimed…once, twice, three times. Holy crap, was he writing a novel?

Setting the drinks down on the ledge near the window outside the courtroom, she read,

Dinner and drinks with the lakeside view of the mountains…

Tempting.

Followed by a full body massage to work those kinks out…

Even more tempting…

Finished off with a late night soak in my hot tub.

She deserved a freaking medal for willpower.

No.

Oh, but damn, how she wished she could say yes.

* * *

Man, he was losing his game. Ben frowned at the two-letter response from Olivia, before tucking the phone into his locker. No. Just no after *she'd* started the exchange. After the kiss and then the insane chemistry between them on the ice, he'd promised himself he wouldn't contact her. There was complicated and then there was stupid, and he had enough stupid to make up for at the moment.

But when he saw her message on his phone, he wasn't going to ignore it.

"Westmore, what the fuck are you waiting for? Let's go," the team's assistant coach said, pushing open the locker room door.

"Coming," he said, slightly annoyed with himself that he'd actually waited for her reply. His phone was a constant stream of text messages from women, though less so since he'd changed his number after Vegas, so why was the one from the woman he couldn't have so important?

Maybe because he hadn't been able to shake the image of her falling on her sexy ass on the ice all morning. The look of shocked innocence as she realized he'd pushed her had made him laugh to himself more than once, earning him odd looks from his teammates. Then seeing her unexpected text on his phone had surprised the shit out of him.

And now, after initiating the flirty back and forth, she'd shot him down with a simple *no*. He put on his helmet as he walked out to the rink.

Not that he needed an explanation. Obviously, their situation was the reason she was putting the brakes on this crazy attraction between them. Because it sure as hell wasn't because she wasn't into him. The kiss at his lake house had told him everything he needed to know, and the sexually charged tension between them had almost melted the ice. He'd wanted to kiss her again. He'd intended to kiss her again, before she'd pushed him.

He knew she'd felt it. She was trying to resist the connection between them. And that had been okay, smart even...until she'd reopened the can of explosive worms with her text.

There was no point in trying to fight his attraction any longer. He didn't want to. This situation might be complicated and messy, but he no longer cared. He would do what he had to to get out of this marriage as fast as possible, and then he was going after the woman he wanted. The time in between would be torture, but he couldn't continue something with her until he was a free man.

But the minute he was...

*   *   *

"Ms. Davis, Ms. Sullivan is here," Madison said, buzzing her office later that morning.

Like pulling off a Band-Aid, do it quick and get it over with. Olivia forced a steadying breath. "Okay, send her in."

Through the glass window, she watched Kristina walk down the hall and open the door. Her stomach did a flip. This sucked. Never in her twelve years practicing law had she walked away from a case. Especially not for a reason like this. But that morning with Ben confirmed she couldn't continue working on this one. Despite the fact that she wouldn't let anything more happen between them, staying on with such a huge conflict of interest was wrong. Being off the case also ensured she wouldn't have to deal with Ben anymore.

Disappointment crept into her chest and she sat straighter, shaking it off. It was for the best. Ben was not the right man for her.

Kristina smiled as she entered, and Olivia forced her own

lips to curl into the best version of one she could muster. "Hi, come on in," she said, gesturing to the seat across from her.

"I was surprised to get your meeting request. Is everything okay?"

The temptation to say yes was strong, but she had to grow a set and tell the woman the truth.

That she'd kissed her husband? Her stomach turned again and she thought she might throw up. Okay, she couldn't exactly be that truthful, but, "Kristina, a situation has come up, and I'm sorry to say that I can no longer represent your case." There.

The woman gave her a blank stare. "What do you mean you can no longer represent me?"

Her annoyance was to be expected, and Olivia had prepared for it. Kendall was on standby a few offices down, waiting to step in and take over as soon as Olivia explained this situation—or rather, lied to her. Of course, she hadn't exactly revealed the real reason to Kendall, either. She simply stated that her caseload had gotten heavier and she wanted to make sure Ms. Sullivan's case got the attention it deserved.

She was going to hell.

"I apologize, but when I took the case my workload wasn't as heavy, and I feel as though you would stand a better chance in court with a different—equally competent and aggressive—lawyer by your side. Kendall is an experienced divorce attorney." The truth of it was bittersweet.

"Oh, I get it. You're in love with Ben."

Blink. Blink. Blink.

Where on earth had that accusation come from? And why wasn't a defense coming quickly and naturally to mind? This was what she did for a living.

Was the question/statement true?

She shook her head. No. She wasn't in love with Ben.

The kiss had been the best one she'd had in years, but it was just a kiss. While she knew she was attracted to him...she couldn't be falling for him, could she?

The man was a self-proclaimed player. And that was fine with her because she wasn't even considering a relationship with him. Right?

"Well, I guess that answers the question," Kristina said.

Shit. All that rambling in her mind, and she'd forgotten to say the "no" part out loud. "It's...no...I'm not." She paused, but knowing a better, more believable statement was needed she tried to explain. "I represented his soon-to-be sister-in-law last year, and I hadn't thought that would pose a problem, but it has. A conflict of interest has arisen." There. That sounded professional. And technically it was true. Had she known Ben was Abby's future brother-in-law, she never would have offered to represent Kristina.

"So, this conflict of interest is about a former client and has nothing to do with you dating Ben?" she asked, calling up that day's *People* magazine on her cell phone.

Her chest tightened. Damn. The two of them together hadn't made the big news, but the small pictures of them in the parking lot of the stadium were telling enough.

How did these publications move so freaking fast anyway? The shot had been taken less than eight hours ago. No other industry moved at such a lightning pace. Apparently, gossip didn't sleep in.

"There's no point trying to deny it," Kristina said.

Obviously. "We were together this morning, it's true... but not in the way it appears."

"I'm not stupid, Olivia. I saw it here in your office—that connection, that sexually charged tension between the two of you. At first, I tried to tell myself I'd imagined it or that it was something between you and Mr. Sanders."

She shuddered involuntarily at that thought. "I swear there was nothing happening that day. There's still nothing happening." It was partly true. Her feelings for Ben had been primarily superficial that first day in her office...things had really started to change at the charity event when they'd danced, when his arms around her and his gaze locked with hers had a knee-weakening effect she'd never experienced before.

"Maybe not for you. But he certainly was interested."

Olivia sighed. Whether it was true then or not, didn't matter. He was attracted to her now. "I'm sorry about all of this. I never meant for this...complication to occur."

"Complication." She seemed to consider the word. Then she stood. "Unfortunately I don't agree to you abandoning my case."

"Well, it is your right to insist that I stay on, even if I'm advising you that it is against your best interest."

"So, you'll stay on?" she asked.

"No. It means I'll have to file a motion to withdraw with the courts. Which could also cause a delay in your case."

"We wouldn't want that, would we?" Kristina said snidely. "The longer he's married to me, the longer you have to wait to have your turn with him."

Olivia bit back a defense of Ben. The guy she was getting to know wasn't the same heartless, love-'em-and-leave-'em player the media made him out to be. He wasn't interested in a relationship, and admittedly that was a problem for most women...but not her. After all, she didn't want one with him, either.

Kendall tapped on the door with a smile, having waited the designated time to introduce herself to Kristina, but Olivia shook her head. Her coworker rolled her eyes to signify she sympathized then continued down the hall.

Kristina gathered her things. "So, I guess I wait to hear from you?"

"The office will call you with the court date." She stood as well. "I am sorry, Kristina."

The other woman offered a small, humorless smile. "Guess not even the toughest hearts can resist Ben West-more's charm."

CHAPTER 14

❧

Olivia let out a deep breath as she waited at the front of the courtroom a few days later. Kristina hadn't arrived yet, and the judge was giving her five minutes to appear. Olivia hoped she'd realized that her stepping down was in Kristina's best interest—if also self-serving—and not appear that morning to oppose her decision.

She just wanted off this case.

The courtroom doors opened and Kristina rushed in, destroying Olivia's hope for an easy, quick decision. She was exhausted, not having slept the night before, and emotionally drained. She'd canceled all of her appointments for that day, and after this, she was going home.

For three days, all she'd thought about was Ben. She'd resisted the urge to contact him to let him know she was dropping Kristina's case, because what would be the point? She wasn't in a position to start a relationship right now, especially not with a man like Ben. The fact that she hadn't heard from him either should be making this easy;

maybe he was realizing what she had: things couldn't go any further.

The thought depressed her more than she was willing to acknowledge.

She had to pull it together long enough to get through this.

She turned in her chair as Kristina took a seat opposite her and the judge called the case to order.

After they were sworn in, the judge turned his attention to her. "You're filing a motion to withdraw on the divorce case Westmore versus Sullivan, on the basis of conflict of interest. Is that correct, Ms. Davis?"

She nodded. "Yes, Your Honor."

"And you, Ms. Sullivan, would like the court to deny that request?"

"Yes, Your Honor."

"Okay. Well, first, I'd like to advise the defendant that anything Ms. Davis says to argue her side—whether it be flattering to yourself or not—may be used by Mr. Sanders, whom I see in the courtroom today, for your future hearing on your divorce case."

Olivia shot a glance over her shoulder. Sure enough, Kevin was sitting in the back. So much for this being private and quiet. Ben would be finding out in less than an hour. Her heart raced. Would he reach out to her then? When part of the problem preventing them from seeing one another was eliminated?

She shook it off. She was hopefully having a baby. No matter how this case went, that was enough reason not to pursue things further.

"I understand," Kristina said.

"And you wish to proceed?" the judge asked.

"Yes, Your Honor."

Of course she did. She knew Olivia had little that could tarnish her case. Before everything had gotten complicated with Ben, she'd seen their defense, and it was weak. Ben had admitted that Kristina's statement was accurate. He'd even confessed to being the one who'd suggested the wedding in Vegas and had actually convinced Kristina to go through with it. He hadn't been tricked or forced. And while Kristina's unwillingness to sign divorce papers until Ben delivered on his drunken promise to help her son wasn't exactly admirable, it wasn't completely unreasonable, given the circumstances.

The judge turned back to her. "We'll start with you, Ms. Davis. Why do you make this motion to withdraw today?"

She took a deep breath, willing her voice to remain steady and strong. "Your Honor, since accepting Ms. Sullivan's case, a conflict of interest has arisen, and I feel that I am not suitable representation for her going forward."

The judge made a note. "This conflict of interest is between the two of you?"

"No, Your Honor. It's between myself and Mr. Sanders's client, Ben Westmore."

The judge flipped several pages in the file on his desk. "You state in the file that you represented Mr. Westmore's brother's fiancée last year, is that correct?"

"Yes, sir."

"So you have existing ties with that family?"

She did. Strong ones. Ones that were slowly wrapping around her heart. An image of his mother, followed by one of Becky and then Abby and Jackson played in her mind. They were all such wonderful people. Such a supportive family…Ben was lucky to have them. *She* longed to have them. Damn it, there was no more denying she also longed for Ben. "Yes, sir."

"What about your contact with Mr. Westmore?"

She swallowed hard. "We had been communicating outside of the case." *Had* being the key word. Not hearing from him was killing her, even though she knew it was for the best. She missed their teasing flirty banter and the sound of his laugh, the way his touch felt, and God, she couldn't even think about his kiss without warming from head to toe.

The judge nodded. "Communicating..." He turned his attention to Kristina. "Given the fact that Ms. Davis is unable to be an impartial representative for you, why are you interested in keeping her counsel?"

"She believed in this case before, and I trust her."

Still? After all this?

"Even though she now has a vested interest in your losing?" the judge asked.

Olivia swallowed hard. Did she? Could she actually reach out to Ben once all of this was over? Her hand went to her stomach and she knew the answer. Starting a relationship with him while she was trying to start a family wouldn't be fair to either of them...or her potential future child.

Kristina must have answered the judge's question, as he was staring at her again.

"Sorry, Your Honor, I missed your question."

"I asked if you have found suitable representation to replace you on the case?"

"I have, Your Honor."

"Who is it?"

"Mrs. Kendall Schiller."

He nodded, made a note, then turned to Kristina. "With your best interest and the interest of your case against Mr. Westmore, I am ruling in favor of Ms. Davis. She will be granted approval of her motion to withdraw, and Mrs. Kendall Schiller will be your newly appointed attorney, unless you prefer to arrange alternative counsel on your own."

Olivia released a deep breath. She hadn't doubted this would go her way, but now it was official. She felt like a jerk. She felt embarrassed. She felt like the worst lawyer on the planet...but she also felt relieved.

Kristina looked disappointed as the judge continued. "Do you understand, Ms. Sullivan?"

"Yes, Your Honor."

"Case file number four twenty-eight—motion to withdraw —Davis versus Sullivan dismissed." He banged the gravel and shot Olivia a look that said, *From now on, keep it professional.*

* * *

Olivia was off the case.

The text from his lawyer had him conflicted as hell. She'd gotten the motion to withdraw based on a conflict of interest by knowing Abby, but he knew there was more to it.

And thoughts about what that meant were driving him insane. He'd wanted to contact her since their skating lesson, but he couldn't reach out. Not yet. He was feeling things he hadn't in a long time, but he was still technically married, and he couldn't afford the distraction of more complications right now. The Avalanche had taken the lead in the semifinals, three games to two, and he needed to stay focused.

But Olivia had dropped the case.

Leaving the locker room after practice, a sign announcing the Major Junior tryouts caught his eye. Tryouts were held in early May while players were still warm from their season and would be able to train with the new team over the summer to prepare for their first real season in the fall. An invite to tryout by talent scouts was next in line behind getting drafted as far as important and exciting moments in a young player's career went, and it reminded Ben of his tryout day.

He'd been so nervous, he'd thrown up in the parking lot behind the garbage cans. In front of the Major Junior coach. His nerves had turned to embarrassment until the coach had pointed out several other puke piles behind the cans and said, "Looks like we have some star performers trying out today. Rookies are too cocky to be nervous enough to puke. Professional players know what's at stake."

The words were meant to reassure, but they'd only made him even more nervous. He did know what was at stake. Everything he'd worked hard to achieve had come down to that moment in his life.

He scanned the badly handwritten names on the sign-in sheet for Brandon's. There it was, third from the last. Obviously he'd gotten an invitation. On his own. Without any help from Ben. He experienced an odd sense of rebellious pride for the kid.

He saw several other names he recognized, kids who'd attended the Avalanche's hockey program last summer. He'd love to see how they did at the tryouts. He was a game away from entering the Stanley Cup finals, but it inspired him to watch other motivated kids fighting for their own dreams. And inspiration in any form right now was more than welcome.

No contact from Olivia was killing him. Ignoring the feelings he had for her when she was still on the opposition had been tough, but now it was nearly impossible. Could he break his own rules? Could he take a chance?

Heading back to the rink, he climbed the side bleachers to the far back. Most of the kids' parents were sitting along the glass, and he didn't want to steal the players' thunder by making his presence obvious. He scanned the row of nervous-looking adults and was relieved to not see Kristina. Their court date was set for the following week, and he wasn't interested in seeing her before then.

Then disappointment for Brandon sank in. His mom wasn't there. Though it was the middle of the day on a Tuesday, and she might have had to work. Being a single mom and raising the boy alone had to be tough.

The tryouts started, and he watched the young players skate out onto the ice, wearing home and away colors for the games they'd play after warm-up. Some were fast. Some took a steadier, more calculated approach as they selected a puck from the blue line and took shots toward the net. He recognized himself in the fast ones. He knew one speed. It worked for him. But he could see the speed was affecting a lot of the boys' accuracy on their shots.

Except one kid. The one with SULLIVAN spelled out on the back of his uniform.

He had no idea why Kristina would want his help for her son. The kid was a natural on skates. Ben leaned forward as he watched. He had great precision in handling the puck. As a defensive player, he knew his position and played within it, but he wasn't afraid to advance the puck when he saw an opening. He protected his goalie without getting in the way, and he looked comfortable, confident, and relaxed on the ice.

Unfortunately, once the game started, his obvious skills made him an instant target for the slightly bigger, slightly less talented players. The first time his body was crushed against the boards, the kid's gloves were off and he was swinging.

Now he understood Kristina's need to help her son.

He sat back. A temper like that would never get the boy

to the NHL. Not these days. Years ago, big brawly players were something coaches appreciated having on their team, and a good defensive player without a fear of fighting was still secretly on every coach's wish list, but a smaller player who was simply a hothead? No.

The ref broke up the fight, and the boy was sent to the bleachers for a five-minute time-out, limiting his opportunity to demonstrate his fantastic puck-handling and scoring abilities. Watching Brandon from the bleachers, he saw him hit his stick against the seat and sit with his head in his hands.

Damn.

Against his better judgment, Ben waited for him outside the locker rooms an hour later. When the door swung open and the kid nearly collided with him, he said, "Hey, Brandon?"

The kid's expression was one of mixed disbelief and awe—the same one each of the boys leaving the room had worn when they saw him—but Brandon's quickly faded to annoyance. "Wow. Mom has zero pride."

Ben wanted to think if he ever had kids, he'd do whatever he could to make them happy and help them reach their goals, too. "Your mom didn't send me," he said. It was technically true. He'd refused to give in just to have her sign the papers, putting his trust in Sanders in court the following week. "I was watching the tryouts. I like to see who might be kicking my senior citizen butt out there in a few years." The joke was meant to lighten the tension that was so thick between them.

But the boy didn't even crack a smile. "I'd like the chance, seeing as how you married my mom and now you're trying to ditch her."

If the roles were reversed…"I bet you would. Look man,

I'm sorry about everything that's going on. The last few months have been crazy." He hadn't even thought about the boy and how all of this must be affecting him. Guilt washed over him. "I know it must be hard."

"Try awkward as fuck."

"Hey! Language." A coach wouldn't put up with a mouth like that.

Brandon smirked, but it was colder than the air in the arena. "Okay, *Dad*."

Shit, this had gone sideways fast. Ben clenched his teeth and fought the urge to say *Oh well, I tried.* "Let's start over. I'm not here to talk about what's happening between your mom and me. Quite honestly, I can't even wrap my head around that, so let's talk about what I saw out there today—as one professional player to a soon-to-be pro."

The kid's face softened just a fraction. "You think I can play?"

"I think you've got what it takes to make it as far as your dedication and determination and hard work will take you, but you need to check that temper, man."

"Seriously?" He pushed past him, heading toward the exit.

Damn. Were all kids this stubborn and hardheaded? "You're a really good player," Ben called after him. "It's too bad you're going to blow your shot at this opportunity, because believe me, there's no better path to the NHL."

Brandon stopped. "It's too late. Coach already said that my chances are slim after that time-out. I lost too much time on the ice, and that fight…" His voice trailed as he turned around.

"He said slim. Not completely gone." Ben walked toward him. "Do you want this opportunity or not?"

The boy stared at him for a long moment. Most people

would have assumed his hesitancy was because he lacked the drive to do what was necessary to achieve the success he sought. Ben knew it was the kid deciding whether or not to trust him, so he waited.

"Yes," he said finally.

"Okay. Here's what you're going to do. Write a letter to Coach Sample apologizing for your behavior…"

The kid nodded.

"And one to that Grayson kid you nearly knocked out."

"No way. You should have heard what that asshole said out there." Anger was back.

Ben laid a hand on his shoulder. "It doesn't matter. You can't let someone else's words or actions determine how you act. He only taunted you because you were playing better than him. Better than anyone else out there. Being skilled makes you a target. Being able to brush aside insults makes you a professional. Some fighting can't be avoided, but try. Now, two letters of apology as soon as possible, before team selection is made."

The kid looked as though he'd rather clean the locker rooms all season, but he nodded. "Okay."

Now the hard part. "And contact the Colorado Anger Management Center. They have a program for teens with anger issues."

"I don't have anger issues. The guy was just an asshole," Brandon argued.

"Fine. Call it an asshole management course if that makes you feel better, but enroll and tell the coach you've done that in your letter."

"You think that will work?"

"No guarantees, but it will show that you're doing everything you can to curb your…to succeed," he said. "It will go a long way."

Brandon sighed. "I don't know, man. My mom's already riding my ass about school and shit."

Ben shrugged. "It's your future, Brandon. The choice is yours. It's always yours, remember that." He tapped the kid on the shoulder as he passed. He'd tried. Brandon's fate came down to how badly he wanted this for himself. He could only offer advice and hope that something he'd said would stick.

"Hey, Westmore," Brandon said behind him.

He stopped and turned. "Yeah?"

"Could you give me a ride to that center?"

*   *   *

"Well, good news for your boyfriend," Kendall said, poking her head around Olivia's office door the next morning.

Olivia glanced up from her computer monitor, her eyes tired from lack of sleep. After dropping the Sullivan case, she was putting in extra time on the other files she had on her plate. Staying busy helped keep her mind off of Ben and her possible pregnancy and the mixed emotions strangling her over both. "I'm sorry—what?"

"Westmore. Kristina Sullivan dropped the case. She's coming in to sign the divorce papers later this afternoon."

Olivia blinked. Had she fallen asleep at her desk? She sat straighter and shook off the exhaustion. "Why? Did you try to talk her out of it?"

Kendall shot her a look. "Trouble in paradise?"

She sighed. She knew her coworker had seen the picture of them at the skating rink, but luckily she hadn't mentioned it to anyone else in the office. "There never was any paradise, just a complicated mess." One that she hoped she could put behind her quickly, but so far, her chest still contracted at the mention of Ben…or any reminder of him. "Are you sure she wants to do this?" Given the circumstances, Kristina had a great chance of getting what she wanted in court the following week—an extension on her marriage and forced counseling with Ben.

A thought that shouldn't have such a heart-wrenching effect on her.

But Kendall nodded. "She said she didn't want to be with someone who doesn't love her, and keeping Ben married is unfair."

Olivia wouldn't argue against that. "What's Kristina asking for in a settlement?" she asked. She'd reviewed Ben's financials herself—the man had a lot to lose if Kristina was still looking for some kind of retribution. For the first time, Olivia was seeing the other side of the proceedings, and it was definitely hindering her abilities on her other cases. She was constantly reminding herself that they were different. These other men were not Ben.

"Just enough to cover our legal fees. And I had to plead with her to do that." Kendall shook her head. "Why do I keep getting these cases?"

"Sorry. I thought this one was in the bag." She really had. With Ben's statement and the shared history between the two, the case had seemed like a no-brainer with a win for Kristina. Of course, Ben would have had the right to reapply for a divorce, but who knew what might have happened in that time.

But he was free. Or would be soon.

"Well, now the path is clear for you two," Kendall said.

Olivia shook her head. While there may no longer be a divorce case, there was still a potential pregnancy and baby to consider, and she didn't suspect Ben was the type of man who dated pregnant women. Not to mention the fear of being hurt beyond repair when he moved on. Which he always did. She wouldn't for a second allow herself to think she could be the one to change him. Make him want to commit. "No, that was a momentary lapse in judgment, that's all."

"You sure you're not having another one by letting him go?"

CHAPTER 15

❧

*H*e didn't have time for this shit right now.

Hitting Ignore on the call from his lawyer, Ben resumed tying his skates. This was the last practice before what could be the final game of the semifinals, and he had to focus. His team depended on him to perform the same way tonight as he'd been performing so far in this series and advance them to the finals. Finally. Text messages from his mother, his brothers, and just about everyone else who had his personal cell number wishing him luck had him on edge already.

He couldn't choke this time. He had to push past the personal.

Focus on the game. Live only in this moment. Don't mess this up.

He stood and pulled his jersey over his head.

"Hey man, how you feeling?" Owen asked, coming into the locker room, the mascot's head under his arm.

"Good. Solid."

His friend studied him, then, seeming convinced, he grinned. "Just wait until you see the routine I've got planned as soon as that winning goal sails straight into…"

Ben's cell rang again. "Damn it!" Picking it up, he tossed it to Owen. "It's Sanders. Tell him whatever it is can wait until after the game." He turned away to get his gloves and helmet as Owen answered.

"This is Ben's personal assistant, Owen, speaking."

Ben placed his hands on his hips.

"No, he said to tell you that if you haven't noticed, he's going to win game six of the semifinals tonight, so if you could fuck off until then…"

Ben swung around. "Not quite what I said." He reached for the phone.

Owen pulled away slightly, his eyes wide as he listened.

Ben could hear Sanders on the other end. No doubt telling Owen where to shove the mascot head. "Give me the phone."

He slowly handed it over.

"Hey, Sanders, sorry…"

The line was dead.

Damn. "What did he say?" he asked Owen. Whatever it was he could handle it. Or rather push it aside along with everything else.

His buddy smiled. "Seems as though you already had one win today."

"What?"

"The chick—your wife—dropped the case. Sanders filed the divorce papers this afternoon."

Ben's legs felt slightly unsteady as he processed the good news. A weight he hadn't fully realized he was carrying lifted from his shoulders, and he hugged the big furry in front of him.

He was a free man.

* * *

A week and five unopened, unread, unanswered...yet *undeleted* text messages from Ben later, Olivia marveled at the man's persistence. As soon as the divorce papers were filed, he'd started trying to contact her. Which made her believe that he'd been resisting their connection while he was still technically married.

Only making him that much more appealing.

She suspected he'd never had to work hard for a woman's attention, and this lack of acknowledgment from her must be driving him insane. It was really the only explanation for his attempts at contact.

She was certainly losing *her* mind. The temptation to read the messages was overwhelming, distracting her from their weekly office meeting with the firm's partners, and she knew she should delete them, but instead, she scrolled over them. *Not* reading them.

She knew the Avalanche had won the semifinals and advanced to the finals. Lyle had shown up to work the day after wearing a snow-covered mountain peak foam hat in celebration and hadn't shut up about it. Olivia would have thought the upcoming finals would be Ben's only focus.

Apparently not, as another text from him arrived.

"Olivia, what do you think?"

Damn.

"Um...I think..." Quick. What had they been discussing? She glanced at the meeting agenda, feeling Lyle's gaze on her. The partners, too, waited for her to say something.

Madison scribbled something on her pad and discreetly nudged it toward Olivia. *Mediation agreement changes,* it read.

Right. "I think we should implement the requirement. It

would certainly cut down on the time we spend in court, and the firm makes more money from those sessions anyway. They usually take about six hours, which we can bill the client directly for, and the government funding for mediations will offset any drop in billing."

He was nodding. "Good point. All in favor of approving the changes."

Olivia smiled at Madison. So far her assistant was keeping her secret, and she was even respecting Olivia's privacy by not asking about it.

Back in her office a few minutes later, she removed her suit jacket as she sat, and Madison followed her inside. "Thank you—you saved my life in there. I'd completely zoned out."

Madison closed the office door. "Yeah, you seemed a little preoccupied." Going to the office windows, she closed the blinds as well, blocking the view to the hallway.

Olivia shot her a look. "What's happening?"

Peeking through the blinds, Madison looked up and down the hall before rushing to the file cabinet on the other side of the office.

Olivia marveled at the height of the heels the girl was wearing—five inches at least. Three was her limit, and even then she was terrified. She may have grown out of her braces, but clumsy never seemed to go away.

"While you were in there, these came for you," she said, pulling a vase of lilies from the side of the cabinet that was hidden from view.

Olivia's jaw dropped. "Oh no…"

"Don't worry. I told the women waiting in the reception area that they were sympathy flowers."

She nodded. She hadn't even been thinking about that, but Madison was right. The last thing the bitter soon-to-be-divorced women in the waiting room would appreciate was a sign of love and affection in their face. "Does the card say who they're from?" she asked, trying to sound nonchalant, but she was certain Madison must be able to hear her heart pounding.

She handed her the card.

Stop ignoring me, or this will become a daily habit.

Damn. He'd signed his name—his *full* name. There'd be no lying to her assistant about these now. Feeling heat rush to her cheeks, she struggled to find the right words. "Listen, Madison, this is…"

"Exciting," she said, quickly taking a seat, folding one hot pink pant leg over the other and swinging the white stiletto–clad foot.

Exciting? Hell no. More like career-hindering. The partners had heard about her motion to withdraw from the Sullivan case, and they'd accepted her reasoning of having represented Abigail as a valid one, but they wouldn't be impressed if they knew the whole truth. She'd been lucky that none of them were subscribers to *People* magazine. She shook her head. "No. It's not what you think."

She frowned. "So, you're not having a thing with Ben Westmore?"

Olivia winced. That would depend on one's definition of *a thing*. Did it include having dinner with him at his lake house? Kissing him? Agreeing to a skating lesson? Being tortured by constant thoughts of him? Then yes, in that case, yes she was having a thing. Oh God. She swallowed hard. She may be trusting Madison with a lot already, but there was no way she was adding this to the pile. Forcing her voice to remain steady, she said, "No. Definitely not. He's been trying to contact me, and I've been avoiding him." That was true at least.

Madison frowned. "Isn't his case resolved?"

"Yes." She eyed the lilies on the desk, then reread the card. Daily flowers were the last thing she needed. Though they were beautiful…and the only ones she'd ever received from a man. She shook her head. "Can you take these away?" She'd buy her own damn flowers. She'd never needed a man to do anything for her before, and she didn't need one now.

But what if she wanted one? God, Ben was making her crazy. Even if she did want a relationship, he wasn't a relationship guy. Going any further with him would only lead to disappointment and heartache. And if he wasn't interested in marriage, he certainly wouldn't be willing to step into the role of father, if she was pregnant.

"What should I do with them?"

"I don't know. Just don't tell anyone where they came from." Helping Madison to her feet, she handed her the flowers and shoved her gently toward the door.

"Are you sure you don't want to keep them?"

"One hundred percent." And she'd have to make sure Ben didn't deliver on the promise of sending more…which meant contacting him.

Damn, he was sneaky, and the worst of it was she knew it wasn't an empty threat. Sitting in her chair, she squared her shoulders, took a deep breath, and picked up her cell phone, hesitating for an eternity before texting,

Are you insane? No more flo

"I hope that's a 'Thank you, the flowers were beautiful' text." Ben's voice in her office doorway made her jump and hit the Send button before she was ready.

Shit. "What are you doing here?" she hissed, looking past him to the reception area. Madison wasn't at her desk. Where did she go?

"If you're looking for your assistant, she's locked out of the building."

Her eyes widened. "What?"

"I buzzed in, said I was delivering something, and then I slipped past her into the building."

She sighed. "You're impossible."

His cell chimed and he read her text. "And insane apparently. What does *No more flo* mean?" he asked with a grin.

"Okay—out! This ends now, Ben," she said, grabbing her office keys to let Madison back in before someone else did.

"Not until you agree to have dinner with me." He crossed the room and sat in the chair opposite her desk. No intention of leaving, obviously.

"That can't happen. Please leave before someone sees you in here." God, she'd have so much explaining to do if one of the partners saw him. And if Lyle did, he'd keep Ben there all afternoon, signing every Avalanche logoed item in his office. And she needed him gone—out of sight—immediately. In a pair of gray dress pants that hugged his thighs in droolworthy fashion and a light blue dress shirt—which was the exact color of his eyes—opened at the top to give her a glimpse of the muscular chest her hands had explored at his lake house, he was the hottest man she'd ever had to turn down.

Ignoring her, he picked up a magazine from her desk. "I'm not playing tonight, so I've got nowhere to be."

Why was he making this so hard? He had women falling all over themselves just to be near him, and yet he wanted to have dinner with her? She'd be flattered if her own common sense wasn't cautioning her to stand her ground. Ben saw her as a challenge. As soon as she gave in, he'd lose interest, and she'd be the one looking like an idiot.

Hearing the door buzzer, she checked the hallway

quickly. "Stay right there while I let Madison back into the building."

"Seriously not going anywhere," he said, flipping the pages of the magazine.

Rushing out into the lobby, she went behind the desk and hit the outside intercom button. "Madison, come in," she hissed.

"Sorry he…"

She released the button and ran back to the office, closing the door. "What do you think you're doing? Flowers? Showing up? Even though your case is resolved, this is all such a huge conflict of interest. If the partners find out you're here…" She fanned herself with a hand. The office suddenly felt too small with him in it, and had someone turned off the air-conditioning? Breathing became a challenge, and she unbuttoned the top button on her blouse.

His eyes left hers and fell to the opening she'd created in the fabric.

The desire in his expression was undeniable, and she felt a rush of heat flow to her cheeks. A memory of the same look right before he'd kissed her had her mouth going dry. When he stood and walked toward her, she willed herself to retreat away from him, but her feet were glued to the carpet.

"Yeah, and if they knew we kissed and spent time together…" He let out a low whistle and shook his head, stopping just inches from her. "We'd really be in trouble." His eyes dropped once more to the opening in her blouse. "Is that pink lace?"

She quickly redid the button, her cheeks on fire. "You think this is a joke?" This was career-jeopardizing for her. Dating him so soon after dropping the case would raise eyebrows and could lead to an investigation into her conduct. "Ben, please leave," she said, her voice barely above a whisper as she stared at anything other than him. If he didn't go soon, she was afraid her resolve would weaken. Ben Westmore was a man who normally got what he wanted, and now she could understand why.

He touched her chin, forcing her to look at him. "Leave? Or leave you alone?"

Damn, those eyes! She could get lost in them if she allowed herself. Which she couldn't. Wouldn't. He had heartbreaker written on every bone in his body. "Both."

"Wrong answer."

She released a desperate-sounding sigh as she took a step back. "Look, I realize this might be fun for you. I'm sure you rarely get to experience the thrill of a chase, but I'm not interested."

He laughed.

"Wow. You take arrogance to a whole new level."

He moved toward her again, and one more step back took her to the office wall. Nowhere else to go. "It's not arrogance. It's the way you kissed me with as much passion and desperation as I kissed you that has me believing you may be just the tiniest bit interested."

Understatement. And he knew it. And he knew she knew it. She released a deep breath. She couldn't believe she was going to do this. "I'm having a baby."

Target hit.

He blinked, looking genuinely confused. "You're pregnant?" His eyes went to her stomach, and she wrapped her arms around her waist.

"Not yet."

"Clarification needed."

"I'm doing in vitro. Artificial insemination with a sperm donor."

He looked dubious. "I'm not sure I believe you."

"That's why I was in Glenwood Falls that day you saw me outside of the market."

"I like to refer to it as the day we kissed."

"Please don't, and shhhh…" The walls of her office were paper-thin. "I was at the Glenwood Falls Fertility Treatment Center to see Dr. Chelsey—a man who thinks you're a freaking saint, by the way," she said, rolling her eyes. "I'd just gotten…inseminated." Having this conversation with Ben was sucking the life out of her. No one else knew—except Madison—and Ben was the last person she'd ever expected to be telling. But surely now he'd back off.

Which was a good thing, so why was her chest hurting?

He studied her, taking several steps away from her.

Did he think pregnancy was contagious?

"You're serious?"

"Yes." Any second now, he would hightail it toward the door. Her gut twisted at the thought, and a deep disappointment she knew was stupid to feel overwhelmed her. It was for the best, but the idea of not seeing him again made a lump rise in her throat.

Crazy hormones.

Instead, he continued to stand there. He was silent for so long, she picked up a piece of paper, balled it, and tossed it at his forehead. "Wake up!"

He watched the paper land at his feet, then slowly picked it up, took aim, and tossed it expertly into the wastebasket near the door. "I don't care," he said with a shrug.

"What?"

"I still want a dinner date."

Was the guy out of his mind? The temptation to give in was strong. "No."

"Unless you're married—which you're not—or a lesbian—which again, you're not—there's no reason you can give me that I'll accept. My case is settled and we are both free to do whatever we want. *Whatever* we want," he repeated, his blue eyes blazing heat as they fell to her lips.

Oh God. "I could have you arrested for harassment," she said, but the argument was weak. They both knew she wouldn't. His persistence was starting to break her.

"Do it." He folded his arms across his chest, the fabric of his collared shirt tight on his biceps the sleeves rolled up in an impossibly sexy casualness that had her mouth watering and palms sweating. *Whatever they wanted.*

She was screwed.

"Fine." She must be out of her mind. Not a good idea. Definitely not a good idea. "One dinner, then you promise to leave me alone?"

"I didn't say that."

"Ben!"

"Text me your address. I'll pick you up at seven." He headed toward the door.

"No!" There was no way she was telling him where she lived. "I'll meet you somewhere." Maybe.

He cocked one eyebrow. "You must want company this afternoon," he said, moving back toward the chair he'd vacated.

He was dead serious about this date. Even though she'd just given him the best reason possible to walk away. He was killing her. "Fine, fine, fine! Just get out." She could feel sweat beading on her spine.

He looked as cool and unfazed as always. Smiling, he headed toward the door. "Text me the address."

She picked up the phone angrily and did. "Done."

"Thank you. You won't regret this decision."

"I already am," she muttered. "And fair warning—if your cell phone rings tonight with a call from Rebecca, Isabelle, or any other woman—date's over."

He grinned, and she immediately wished she could pull the jealous-sounding words back. "Phone on silent all evening, I promise."

She noticed he couldn't promise there wouldn't be any calls.

"Oh, and I rescued the lilies before Madison could toss them. I'll bring them to your place tonight," he said with a wink.

CHAPTER 16

❧

$\mathscr{I}$t was too early to test. Implantation was only three weeks ago. Technically, she hadn't even missed a period yet. But she felt…different. Pregnant women had a sense about this, didn't they? Maybe not the ones on that show where the participants didn't know they were pregnant, but most women. She applied a pale pink gloss to her lips, her gaze locked on the home pregnancy test box sitting on the sink. She'd surrounded herself with positive images to help the positive thinking…yet having this out in plain view with Ben on his way to pick her up—probably not the best idea.

Oh, sure—because that was the bad idea. Once again, her chest tightened at the thought of what she'd agreed to do. A date? With a man who most certainly, without a doubt, she'd never see again after this dinner? After she was no longer a challenge? Every ounce of her common sense screamed the reasons why she was crazy to be doing this, but her stomach fluttered at the thought of him, and common sense took a flying leap.

She bit her lip and leaned against the sink in her bra and underwear, staring at the test box. What if she wasn't pregnant? What if one more reason not to be with Ben was removed from the equation?

But then she wouldn't be pregnant. The in vitro would have failed. And she'd be devastated.

Screw it. She had enough tests to test every week for six months. She reached for the box, tore it open, and removed the stick. She didn't need to read to instructions—she had a masters' degree in law. Just pee and wait. How hard could it be?

Of course she didn't have to pee, so she had to mentally will a few drops out of her bladder. Then replacing the cap, she sat clutching it and waited. One pink line appeared immediately, but the box said that would happen to let her know the test was working. It said the other pink line—should it come—could take...

Oh my God! There it was. Faint. But there. Definitely there. She squinted and blinked. Still there. She waited for it to darken, but it never did.

But it was there. She was pregnant?

Thankfully her past self knew her future self pretty darn well. She reached for another box from the drawer—the yes/no kind. She couldn't leave the biggest moment of her life up to a faint, barely there pink line.

And of course, she still didn't have to pee.

Sheer will and determination produced just enough, and she waited again.

This one took longer, and as she sat with the two pink lines in one hand and the taunting I'm-going-to-take-my-designated-three-minutes test in the other hand, her heart raced.

She'd been nervous about her date with Ben. Now that

anxiety paled in comparison. If she was pregnant, how was she supposed to go through with this date?

This wasn't exactly the way most women celebrated this news. No, most women trying to get pregnant had a loving, supporting partner to share the anxiety, the waiting, the squinting at two indefinite pink lines. She swallowed hard. It was her decision to do it this way.

Finally, the display lit up and the word *yes* on the screen left no more room for doubt. She was pregnant. The treatment had worked. Tears threatened to destroy her freshly applied mascara, and she took several deep breaths as she stood and tossed the sticks into the trash can—she wasn't that sentimental to keep sticks she'd peed on.

Was she?

She retrieved them and tucked them into the bathroom drawer.

She smiled as she glanced at her reflection in the mirror. She was pregnant. In thirty-seven weeks she would have a baby, the family she wanted. Emotions spiraled through her as her doorbell buzzer rang.

And in thirty-seven seconds, her date would be on his way to her apartment.

* * *

Being unable to read Olivia's expression wasn't new. The woman had mastered confusing, noncommittal looks. When she opened the door that evening, Ben studied her, dissecting the layers, as though evaluating a fine wine. Apprehension was definitely there—understandably so. But also an excitement…with a tinge of pre-date regret?

I'm getting better at this. He smiled, his confidence choosing to cling to the excitement part, as he handed her the lilies as promised. "You ready to go?" She looked ready and more beautiful than his imagination had done justice. Her dark hair was loose around her shoulders in light waves, and the black v-neck cashmere sweater she wore looked soft and warm.

The strength of the desire to take her into his arms surprised him. He resisted. Barely. He wanted this date, he'd worked harder to get it than any other in his life, and he knew she'd never go through with it if he pushed too far, too fast.

"Just about…Come in for a sec," she said, moving aside to let him in.

He stepped over the threshold into her apartment and nodded appreciatively. "Great place." The dark hardwood flooring contrasting with the cream-colored furniture gave the space a modern classic look. The matching mocha-colored marble countertops and backsplash in the open-concept kitchen and dining room were similar to the color scheme in his home. In fact, their choice in décor was even similar; they both preferred basic, uncluttered, expensive pieces placed strategically for design and comfort.

"Make yourself comfortable. I'll go put these away," she said, but instead of going into her kitchen, she disappeared down a short hallway and into a bedroom.

He ignored the temptation to follow and rearrange the proper order of the typical date. He'd be lying if he said he wasn't interested in eventually seeing her naked, but he was looking forward to taking her out, showing her there was more to him than what the tabloids proclaimed. He was interested in getting to know her.

It was a foreign concept to him. Something he hadn't felt in a long time. A red flag that should be sending him packing. Instead, he studied the pictures in a decorative dressing screen dividing the space. The first set of collage photos were obviously her as a little girl with her parents. He leaned closer to look. She was a cute kid—dark, uncontrollable ringlets and chubby cheeks. The woman she was now looked a lot like her mother, but she obviously got her coloring from her father.

In the next set she was older and the other woman in the picture wasn't her mother. A grandmother, perhaps? Though she didn't look much older than Olivia's parents. But whoever she was, she remained the constant in the pics as he continued through Olivia's timeline up to her high school graduation.

Had she lost her parents at a young age?

"That's my aunt Helen," she said, reappearing behind him.

"She raised you?" he asked, turning to face her.

She nodded. "My parents were in an accident…a drunk driver."

Her tone was tight. Obviously time hadn't made it easier to talk about. A loss so young was heartbreaking. "I'm sorry. And no brothers or sisters?" As much as they drove each other crazy growing up, Ben couldn't imagine not having his siblings.

"Nope, just me." Once again, her expression was unreadable, but one thing was clear: she didn't want to talk about it. "Ready?" she asked.

"Yes." She could change her mind at any minute, and he knew he had to seize the moment. He'd made dinner reservations at the best seafood restaurant downtown, and he had a public art walking tour planned for them in Denver's Golden Triangle cultural district. "Do you have a jacket?"

She reached for a light denim jacket from the hook near the door. He took it and held it open while she slid her arms in. He lifted her hair gently over the fabric and allowed the smell of jasmine-scented shampoo to fill his senses as he rested his hands on her shoulders almost too long to be safe.

He'd missed that smell.

Luckily, she stepped away and opened the door; otherwise, he would have probably stood there, touching her, for who knew how long. He followed her outside and waited as she locked up, then he led the way to his Hummer.

"That's right I forgot—you drive a tank," she said.

He opened the passenger side door for her. "But, you'll notice, I only took up one parking space this time."

"How thoughtful," she said, accepting his help into the tall vehicle.

Her soft hand in his sent an electric current through his arm. If a simple touch had that affect, he wondered what kind of damage she might inflict on his emotions if she were to touch him everywhere. Releasing her hand, he closed the door and got in behind the wheel a second later. "What kind of music do you like?" he asked, starting the car and immediately reaching for the radio dial to switch channels. He listened to old-school classic rock, and more than one date had wrinkled her nose at his taste.

"This is good," she said as an old Bruce Springsteen song played.

"Really? Classic rock?" He nodded his appreciation, turning it up a little louder as he backed out of the space.

She laughed. "I'm probably the first woman you've had in here who's old enough to recognize these songs, right?"

Damn. Come to think of it, she *was* probably right. She was far from old, but being in her thirties put her about ten years older than most of the girls he went out with. Young girls weren't looking for commitment—they were out to have fun, which suited him and his own intentions—but explaining that would no doubt make him sound worse, not better, so he just grinned and shrugged. "My mom can sing along."

She punched his arm and he grabbed her hand, bringing it

to his lips. He turned the palm up and kissed it gently before letting it go, aware of her surprised stare.

He cleared his throat. "So I thought we'd have dinner at Kleine's—I hope you like seafood."

"Ben, I'm pregnant," she said, the words coming out in a rush.

He'd always been terrified of hearing a woman say that, but in this case, he couldn't possibly be at fault. Still, his stomach knotted as he glanced at her. Hadn't it just been three weeks since she'd done the egg thing? She'd said it was the day she'd been in Glenwood Falls…The day they'd kissed. And she was pregnant already? Wow. Had he known, would that have stopped him from kissing her? Probably not, seeing as how it hadn't stopped him from wanting this date. "When did you find out?" Earlier in her office, she'd been unsure.

"About ten minutes ago."

He laughed. "Couldn't wait until after the date, huh?"

"I should have canceled, but…"

He wanted to reassure her she shouldn't have canceled, that strangely enough her revelation didn't change the fact that he wanted this time with her more than any other date in too long. But he waited to see what her "but" was.

"I don't know. I guess I wanted to see if the connection between us was real. Even though I have no idea what to do if it is. And I'm hoping like crazy that it isn't," she said.

Honesty. Just one of the many things he liked about her. "Well, I'm glad you decided to go through with this evening." And he was happy to hear his suspicions were correct—that she felt this strong pull between them as well. "I'm happy for you." Reaching across the distance between their seats, he squeezed her hand. "That is great news. In fact, change of plans," he said, an idea forming in his mind as he switched lanes.

Her eyes widened. "Surprises are not really my thing Ben…"

He grinned. "Yeah, well, dating pregnant women is not really *my* thing. Guess we both need to adjust a little for this to work, huh?" And the thought that he wanted this to work, despite the fact she was going to be a mother in nine months, only scared him a little a lot.

* * *

"How the hell am I supposed to learn all of this in nine months?" Olivia stood open-mouthed and overwhelmed in front of the parenting section in the bookstore on Sixteenth Street ten minutes later.

Ben reached for one on pregnancy. "You don't. You just find the ones relevant to you and only read what you have to. For example, in this book, the first three chapters deal with conceiving—you've nailed that part already." He flipped through the book. "The rest is just"—his face tuned a shade greenish—"disgusting and a little scary." He tucked that book in the back of the shelf. "Forget that one."

She shot him a look. "This is your idea of an epic date?" she asked, though, inside, her ovaries were overjoyed at the thought he wasn't freaked out by the situation. In fact, he'd completely surprised her with his thoughtfulness to change their plans. He'd claimed that this was an important moment in her life, and she should enjoy it the way most women would.

The gesture made her wish they were back in her apartment. The man was sex on a stick most of the time, but that evening—blame it on hormones or the fact he was embracing her life-changing news with impressive maturity—he was all kinds of tempting. The tight hip-hugging jeans and black dress shirt rolled at the sleeves, revealing muscular forearms, weren't helping her keep a clear head, either. She hadn't even known forearms could be so sexy. The men she'd dated in the past had all been good-looking guys, but Ben took handsome to an unhealthy level.

Her body was betraying her every instinct to keep her distance. She longed to be as close to him as possible, breathing in the tantalizing scent of his cologne, feeling the muscular body beneath his shirt. As much as she'd fought against this date, now that she was on it, she wanted it to feel like a date. A real one. With touching and kissing…

As he reached for another book, he said, "Okay, so maybe *epic* was a bit of a stretch, but I can honestly say it's a first for me—so I should at least get points for unique, right?"

She laughed. "Okay. I'll give you unique."

And anything else he wanted. Right now.

She felt her cheeks grow hot and turned to scan the row of books. Astrology guidance in planning your pregnancy…that was different. She took it and opened it.

Ben put his book back with a shudder. "Not that one, either." He joined her, leaning over her shoulder as she did the math in her head, making the calculation of her due date a million times harder than it should be. His breath against her neck, and the feel of his body against hers, had her thoughts going fuzzy and her body awakening to sensations she hadn't felt in a long time.

There was no denying it. She wanted Ben Westmore—broken heart waiting to happen and all.

"April conception would be a January baby," he said, flipping to Capricorn.

Thank God, he'd figured it out. She'd forgotten what she was even trying to do. She forced a breath, reading the sign's description. "Practical, cautious…Always thinks things through." She nodded. Like her—an earth sign—feet firmly planted in the dirt. She could raise a child like that. Without even planning it, she was in for a personality that matched her own. She wasn't one to place a whole lot of stock in astrology forecasting, but when the predictions made her feel better…"That sounds promising."

"However, January could also be Aquarius," Ben said, taking the book and flipping the pages. "Like me," he added with a smirk.

Her smile faded. He didn't even need to read the description of the sign for her to get a sinking feeling in the pit of her stomach. Like him. In other words—a charismatic charmer, outgoing, fast talker? Nope. That was not something she could feel comfortable with. But maybe Ben was nothing like his typical sign. She held on tight to that hope as he read.

"A born rebel, forward thinking, risk taker."

She snatched the book away. "He…or *she* will be a Capricorn." She'd induce labor if she had to.

* * *

"You know that men who buy large vehicles are usually trying to compensate for shortcomings in other…um…areas," she said as they walked back toward his Hummer, which was taking up nearly three parking spots at the back of the lot half an hour later.

"Trust me, that's not the case this time," he said with a wink.

The simple little gesture had her wanting to rip his clothes off. Damn. These pregnancy hormones were going to be the death of her common sense.

Flatlined. Do not resuscitate.

If she was this way now, she couldn't even begin to think

about how she would deal with the sexual drive increase as her pregnancy progressed. She'd read about women being insatiable, and she was wondering if Ben would be up to the challenge of being at her beck and call for booty calls.

He stopped next to the vehicle and tossed her the keys. "Why don't you drive?"

She caught them awkwardly and shook her head, extending them to him. "No way. You've seen my car."

"Exactly. I want to show you what you're missing," he said with more than a hint of flirtation in his voice.

"No. Forget it. I think we're both safer with me not knowing." Definitely safer.

He stepped closer. "Safer is boring." His warm breath on her cool cheek made her shiver. She longed to rip her suddenly too warm sweater from her body—followed by the rest of her clothing. The thought didn't help to cool her. "Live a little," he said, tucking several strands of hair behind her ear as the wind blew them across her face.

She couldn't breathe. He was too close, too attractive, too dangerous to her heart…and he smelled too damn good, like the crisp, chilly mountain air mixed with a cozy warmth. She stepped away from him. "That's the thing—if I drive, we could both die," she said, breaking his gaze to size up the vehicle. The tires practically came to her waist. She wasn't the best driver under normal circumstances, in a normal-sized vehicle. Combine the size of the Hummer with her lack of clarity around him, and no one would be safe on the road.

"You're being overdramatic. A car is a car—there's really only one way to drive. Come on, give it a try. Just around the parking lot—it's practically empty. You can't do much damage." He shoved his hands into his pockets as he led the way to the driver's side.

"Famous last words," she muttered as she followed him.

He unlocked the door and helped her climb in behind the wheel. His hand holding hers sent shivers dancing down her spine, and the other placed gently on her back made her body tingle. What would it feel like to have his hands running all over her body?

"Hit that button to start her up," he said, pointing to the keyless ignition.

She did and the beast roared to life. Huh, kinda sexy. She gripped the massive steering wheel; she'd never driven anything so powerful with such a big engine.

"There's the button to adjust the seat," he said, pointing to the electronic dash, which looked more like a computer monitor.

She hit it and the seat slid forward until she could reach the pedals.

"And this one adjusts the side mirrors," he said, leaning past her to reach the button. His arm brushing against her thighs made her clench them together as she tried to focus on what he was saying and not the dampness of her underwear.

The mirrors swiveled back and forth until she nodded. "There. That's good." She wasn't sure she'd even need to use mirrors. She was seated so high, she could see everything.

"Wait for me," he said with a smile as he shut her door.

Watching him walk around the front of the vehicle, she forced her emotions in check. She was behind the wheel of a tank. She needed to think clearly.

A second later he climbed into the passenger seat. "I've never sat on this side before."

Her head swung toward him. "No one's driven your truck before?" She'd assumed this was one of his regular dating protocols. Allow his date a false sense of power and control.

"Nope." He reached for his seatbelt and fastened it. "Okay, whenever you're ready," he said.

She hesitated, glancing around. "Are you sure?" She slid her hands nervously up and down the steering wheel. She could do quite some damage with this thing.

"Yes. Let's go." His eyes fell to her hands and the up-and-down motion on the wheel, and his expression changed. "But please stop doing that."

So, she wasn't the only one fighting sexual urges.

She put the vehicle in drive, slowly easing out of the parking spaces. The good news was the visibility was great—being up so high with so many big windows—and he was right—the lot was practically empty.

"You can go a little faster," he said, pointing toward the exit. "Let's take it out onto the road."

"You said parking lot," she said, though admittedly it was kind of fun to drive the monster vehicle.

"Don't wuss out."

She shot him a look, then pressed the gas harder, picking up speed as they turned onto the street.

He gripped the oh-shit handle over his head, and she saw him wince as she bit the curb, but the big tires ate it with ease, and she felt little more than a small thump. In her car, driving over a curb would have impaled it. She relaxed a little. "Okay, I'm starting to see why you like this…just a little."

He smiled. "Welcome to the dark side. Should we head to a used-car dealership next?"

Her smile faded slightly. "Actually I will need something else when the ba…something with a backseat, safer to drive in crappy weather." Her vehicle had let her down on one too many snowy, icy Colorado roads that winter. Alone was one thing. She wouldn't take that chance with a child in the car. Her child. Her grip tightened. "Just a small SUV or something."

"Are you excited?" he asked.

She nodded without hesitation. She wanted to tell him she

was also terrified, riddled with self-doubt over the decision, and worried sick something would go wrong, but she wasn't capable of being that vulnerable with him. She was already starting to fall for him—in lust, at least—and that left her in a bad enough predicament. No sense handing him all of the ammunition he needed to destroy her. Which he no doubt would. "It wasn't a decision I made lightly."

"That wouldn't be your style."

His tone wasn't judging. It was soft, caring, respectful. Full of things that could make her lust-filled attraction teeter slightly over the edge into love. "You're right—I'm cautious. I weigh the pros and cons in most situations—it's true. In this case, there were almost enough concerns not to go through with it, but in the end I was ready to deal with any of the challenges that arose. I want a family."

"Without the husband?"

She focused her attention on the road ahead. "It just didn't work out that way. I spent my life building my career, and relationships weren't a priority." After her parents died, she'd gotten used to being alone. Her aunt Helen had been on her own so long, she hadn't known how to fill the role of parent that Olivia needed.

She hoped she wasn't too closed off to be what her baby would need.

She was relieved when Ben didn't press for more, but she needed to turn the tables on him. She wasn't ready to reveal too much more yet she knew if he asked, she would.

She cleared her throat. "So, that night in Vegas…"

He shifted in his seat. "Do we need to talk about this? The case is over."

The tightness in his voice was almost enough for her to say no, but she was still curious about what could possibly have made him want to get married—however alcohol-induced.

"It's just you are so anti-commitment, I can't even fathom what would have possessed you to…"

"My ex got engaged on national television." He sighed, sitting back against the seat.

She frowned, searching her repertoire of what she knew about him—whether directly or from hours of cyberstalking. He was never tied to anyone for long. The countless photos of him snapped by paparazzi at different events, he'd had a different woman in almost all of them, except when his mom served as his date, which was often enough to be endearing. She thought hard…"Do you mean the sports broadcaster—Janelle Adagio?"

He shot her a surprised look. "Someone's done their homework," he said, his tone light, but she sensed an underlying anxiety about the subject.

"I'm thorough." She shrugged, turning the big vehicle onto a quieter side street. "So, she got engaged. Continue." There had to be more to it than that.

"She got engaged on New Year's Eve. On television. The guy's an anchor—it was their top story of the evening." His voice was devoid of emotion.

"Cheesy," she muttered.

"Right?" Ben looked relieved that she agreed on that front.

"Absolutely." Public engagements were so over the top. It was like the couple was more interested in declaring their love for the world to see than caring about the connection they had and the promise they were about to make to one another. She heard stories that started with them all the time—pro athletes were kings of the public engagements: scoreboards, on home plate, in center field, or halftime at the Super Bowl…gag, gag, gag. They usually ended up divorced quickly.

"Anyway, I saw it, I started to drink, I ran into Kristina in the lobby of the Bellagio, and yeah, pretty much everything happened the way she claimed." He ran a hand through his hair.

He was avoiding the point. "Right, but *why* did it happen? Why a wedding?" She wasn't seeing how his ex getting engaged could spark such a drastic move on his anti-marriage heart. If it was a race to the altar thing, that was pretty lame, and nothing about Ben—even his mistakes—could ever be lame.

He blew out a deep breath, his gaze settling on something in the distance or nothing at all. It was hard to tell. "When we were together Janelle claimed that I was never going to settle down. She wanted more, and she said I couldn't give it to her."

Sounded about right. Ben said as much himself. Wasn't that his morning-after exit speech? So why had his expression darkened?

"So, I bought my house in Denver and asked her to move in with me. She'd lost a job opportunity that she'd been hoping for, and she jumped on the chance to start building a life with me."

Obviously. Look at him—who wouldn't?

"Things were going great. It was New Year's Eve six years ago, and like a fool, I had been waiting for the right time…When I finally asked, she said no. She'd been offered her dream job as a broadcaster in Vegas. She left the next day."

Olivia blinked. "Wait. Go back. *You* proposed?"

He nodded.

"So she was…"

"The love of my life." His gaze met hers and for the first time since meeting him, gone was his flirty demeanor. In its place was the raw vulnerability of a man who'd had his heart broken.

And there went the tipping scale of her emotions from lust to something a little more terrifying.

Oh. Shit.

Then the sound of crunching metal and a high-pitched squeal made her jump. Tearing her eyes from Ben, she slammed on the brakes.

Both heads turned toward the windshield.

What had she hit? She leaned forward, but could see nothing. So much for visibility. Whatever it was must be lodged underneath the vehicle. Oh God, please don't let it be a Smart car.

"Stay here. I'll go look," Ben said, but his face had paled.

Olivia shook her head. "I did this. I'm coming." Her voice and hands shaking, she opened the door and climbed down. She saw the source of the high-pitched squeal at the same time she saw the bike crushed beneath the tire of the Hummer. Her chest filled with relief. "Thank God—just a bike." No kid. No other vehicle. No one hurt.

The kid standing on the sidewalk didn't appreciate her relief. "Just a bike?" he said. "Lady, that bike was my birthday present. It's only hours old."

Guilt washed over her. She'd always wanted a bike, but had never had one. Like everything else fun, her aunt had thought it too dangerous. Now she'd ruined this kid's birthday. "I'm sorry…"

Ben put up a hand to stop her, turning his attention to the kid. "If it was so important to you, why did you leave it on the street?"

The kid's eyes darkened. "I didn't. I jumped off of it when I saw that tank coming toward me." He readjusted his bike helmet on his head.

Oh no. She'd almost hit a kid? Her confidence in her parenting abilities plummeted. "I'm so sorry. I didn't see you…"

"Olivia, relax. He didn't bail from the bike," Ben said, re-assuring her and calling the kid's bluff. He moved closer and studied him. "There's not a mark on him. I've jumped off of a moving bike before—a ripped knee or scratched up hands would be guaranteed at least." He gave the kid a stare-down, which the preteen countered for all of four seconds.

"Fine. I left the bike in the street." He glanced toward his house behind him. "My parents are going to kill me." Now he looked genuinely devastated.

"I'll replace the bike," Olivia offered. "I can go buy a new one right now and have it back to you before they realize this one's trashed." It was her fault. Partially at least, as she'd been lost in Ben Westmore's gaze and not paying attention.

The kid's eyes lit up. "Really?"

She nodded. "Of course." At that moment, she'd offer to send the kid and his family to Disneyland for punitive damages, she was so relieved that the kid hadn't been hurt.

The boy turned toward Ben. "Will you sign the frame for me?"

Ben laughed. "Sure, kid. But no more lying, and take better care of your stuff." He playfully punched the boy's shoulder and something in the pit of her stomach turned. In that moment all of her preconceived notions about Ben vanished, leaving her with only a terrifying thought.

Ben Westmore might possibly make a fantastic father, and combined with the knowledge that at one time he'd been ready to settle down and commit to one woman, she knew her heart was in trouble.

CHAPTER 17

❧

Two hours later—bike replaced, too much Chinese food consumed, and Ben back behind the wheel—he turned into a visitor parking spot in front of her building. "There. I promised you an epic date. Did I deliver?" he asked, putting the vehicle—which had suffered zero damage in the incident—in park.

She laughed. "I can honestly say I've never been on a date even somewhat close to this one. I'd say take it as a win."

Removing his seatbelt, he turned to face her. "I had a great time tonight." Never in a million years would picking out baby books and replacing a kid's bike be on his list of things he'd find enjoyable, but with Olivia, every moment was fun. A concept he'd forgotten existed. Usually fun with a woman meant trying to set a new record in getting her naked, but while he wouldn't be opposed to getting Olivia naked, it wasn't his only priority. Being around her made him happy.

He hadn't even felt weird talking about Janelle. Sharing that part of himself—a part he usually kept hidden—had felt right. For some reason, he'd wanted her to know that there was more to him than what the media saw. He wanted her to trust him, to trust that he wasn't just wasting her time or playing her. Though where they went from here—when she was pregnant—he honestly didn't know.

"Well, if you thought that was fun, maybe next time we can go nursery furniture shopping or something," she said.

It was meant as a joke, one that normally would have sent him tearing out of her driveway before she'd shut the passenger side door, but the idea of being there for her in those important moments of her pregnancy, of being someone she could rely on, didn't freak him out. Which, in itself, should have freaked him out. "Deal," he said instead.

Her expression was one he'd seen many times before he was about to get laid.

His dick, which had been on standby all evening, woke up, but his mind for once screamed *Proceed with caution!* This wasn't just a normal date with a normal woman. She wasn't someone he'd hooked up with for an evening. She was someone he respected, someone who, despite the circumstances, he liked…a lot. Hurting Olivia was the last thing he wanted to do. "Well, let me know whenever you need someone to carry the heavy boxes," he said. This had to be an all-time first—he wasn't actively trying to get her into bed. Not that he didn't want to.

All evening, whenever their bodies touched, there was a spark of electricity that threatened to set him on fire. Every time she'd looked at him with those big dark eyes, he'd found himself losing his train of thought. He certainly hadn't been on his game that evening, and yet it was probably the most satisfying date he'd ever been on. Even if his dick wasn't getting satisfied.

Across from him, Olivia seemed to be having her own internal struggle. "Do you want to come in?" she asked finally, nervously.

There was the invite. Shit.

He ran the play over in his mind. If he gave in to the begging in the lower half of his body and followed her inside, in less than three minutes they would be naked. And not too long after, they'd both be fighting with their conscience, things would be awkward as hell between them, and then everything would be a whole lot more complicated.

He had to do the right thing this time. Even if it wasn't what he wanted to do.

He sighed. "I should go. I have a game tomorrow night and practice early tomorrow morning."

The disappointment in her eyes almost made him change his mind. "Right. Of course."

Damn. "Believe me, it's not that I don't want to," he said.

She nodded quickly. "No, you're right. It was a bad idea anyway."

God, did she have to be so beautiful, so smart, so sexy? Maybe now wasn't the time to be turning over a new leaf. After all, she wasn't looking for something more from him. Hell, twelve hours ago, she'd wanted nothing to do with him, and after that evening…who knew what would happen? Assuming that taking advantage of something they clearly both wanted would be hurting her was actually pretty egotistical.

Or was he rationalizing?

He reached over the center console and pulled her into the space next to him, wrapping his arms around her waist. "Yes, it would be a bad idea, but that doesn't mean we shouldn't do it." His gaze burned into hers, and any shred of resolve disappeared seeing the same look of desire in her eyes that he knew was reflected in his.

"No, Ben. You were right…"

He placed a finger to her lips. "No. You're right—things are already messed up, what's one more complication?"

"I didn't say that," she said, but he noticed she remained in his arms.

"Okay, I did," he said, hitting the button to drop his seat backward, as he scooped her up and brought her down on top of him.

Her eyes widened when her legs landed on either side of him. "What are you doing?"

"Exactly what you want me to do," he whispered at the base of her neck, watching as goose bumps rippled the smooth skin there.

"So, this is for me?" she asked, pushing her body closer and sliding her hands beneath his shirt. Her breasts pressed against his chest had him swallowing hard as he gripped her waist. Her top position gave her control—control he wasn't ready to give up. Yet.

"It might be a little bit for me," he said feeling himself grow thick in his jeans. His erection was betraying his false sense of bravado, and the knowing look in her beautiful eyes told him she was seeing right through it. "Okay, a lot for me…mostly for me," he said, sitting up and flipping them so he was on top.

He lifted her sweater and pulled it over her head, revealing a fitted red tank. All evening, brief glimpses of the lacy part peeking over the top of the v-neck at her chest had nearly driven him mad. This up-close look had been worth the wait. The thin, silky fabric clung to her shape and rose a little to reveal her stomach. He traced a finger along her soft skin. "You have the sexiest body…"

She wiggled beneath him, reaching for the shirt to pull it down, but he stopped her hands. "No. Don't cover up." In fact, he wanted to see more. He wanted to see everything.

He tossed her sweater into the back of the Hummer, then lifted the tank top higher.

She sighed, reluctantly lifting her arms to allow him to remove the shirt. "As much as I hate my stomach now, it's only going to get worse," she said.

"It's perfect."

She scoffed. "I'm allergic to exercise. Believe me, it's far from perfect."

He lowered his head to her collarbone, breathing in the jasmine-scented skin. The smell had teased him all night, and he couldn't wait to find out if she smelled this sweet everywhere. He kissed the base of her neck, leaving a trail of kisses over her shoulder, across her chest. He watched it rise and fall beneath his lips as her breathing became more and more labored.

He loved that a few kisses were having this effect on her. He wanted to make her feel like the only woman to ever steal his concentration, because that was the truth. "So delicious," he muttered before sliding his tongue along the edge of her bra, then moving down the line between her abs to her belly button, feeling tiny goose bumps form on her flesh below his lips. "You taste perfect," he said, raising his hands to cover her breasts, massaging gently through the lacy bra. She filled his hands easily and he hardened even more with the anticipation of what was beneath the fabric.

Her breathing grew heavy as she ran her hands through his hair. "Ben, that feels incredible."

He was just getting started. He reached for the button on her jeans, but she stopped him again.

"Not fair. I'm half undressed already. Take something off," she said.

Fair enough. He reached for the hem of his sweater and, grabbing the sweater and his undershirt, removed both, exposing a body he was proud of. "Better?"

She wrinkled her nose. "It's okay, I guess."

He grinned. "*Okay* you guess?" He flexed his biceps and tightened his stomach muscles.

"Fine. You're sickeningly perfect," she said, sliding her hands along his oblique muscles. A tingle chased down his spine as she found his one and only ticklish spot below his belly button. Her touch drove him mad, and his thighs gripped her hips tighter as she reached for the button on his jeans.

She hesitated, but if she was waiting for him to stop her, she'd be waiting a long time. He'd wanted her since the moment those mesmerizing dark eyes had shot daggers at him in her office parking lot. And his attraction had only increased. "Don't stop now," he said, making sure to infuse a note of challenge into his voice, knowing she would never back down from one.

She popped the button free and searched for a zipper, then shot him a look when she didn't find one. "A button fly? Seriously? You couldn't make this more difficult?" she asked, yanking open the first two in one quick pull.

He laughed. "I wasn't really expecting you to put out on the first date." He took over when she struggled with the bottom ones, made tighter by his ever-increasing hard-on.

· She narrowed her eyes at him.

Shit. Good one, Westmore. Do you want to go home with blue balls?

But then she shrugged. "I figure I'm pregnant anyway. What's the worst that can happen?"

Just the word *pregnant* should have killed his erection, but it didn't. It didn't matter that this situation was complicated as hell because he knew this wasn't just about sex. Not this time. This time was different. He was attracted to her body, her mind, her heart…every part of her that she'd let him see so far. And he wanted to continue pulling back the layers, discovering more…even though it terrified him that he might just discover all of the things he wouldn't be able to walk away from.

For the first time, walking away wasn't his intention.

The sound of tapping on the window followed by an insanely bright beam of light made them both jump.

"Shit. Police," he said, reaching for their clothes.

Her eyes widened. "Oh my God. Quick, put your thing away," she said.

Glancing down, he saw that he was poking through the folds of his underwear. He tucked himself inside and clasped the top button on the jeans.

"Police. Roll down the window please," a voice called from outside.

"Shit, shit, shit," Olivia said trying to cover herself with one arm as she struggled to right her inside-out tank top. "Can he see us?" she hissed.

"Don't worry. Tinted windows—as dark as factory possible." Which no doubt would earn him at least one ticket from the cops right now.

She stopped shielding herself and his dick twitched again at the sight of her beautiful full breasts spilling over the top of her red lace bra. He hoped the police wouldn't ask him to get out of the car, because they'd probably think he had a concealed weapon in his pants.

Yanking his shirt over his head, he climbed off of her, allowing her to scramble back over to the passenger seat as another tap, tap, tap came on the window. "Open up please."

He glanced at her quickly, saw she was wearing an inside-out tank top, but at least she was decent, and he rolled down the windows. "Hi. Problem, officer?"

The beam of light shone directly at his face, making him squint.

"You're double parked," the officer said.

He glanced outside. It was almost midnight and there were no other vehicles parked in the visitor spaces outside her building. "Sorry, sir. I'll move right away."

The officer looked past him to Olivia. "You okay, miss?"

"Fine," she croaked, sounding anything but. The look on her face could easily be construed as *Help, I'm being held against my will.*

Ben shot her a look that said *Pull it together before I get arrested* before turning his attention back to the cop. "I was dropping her home after a date," he said quickly.

"Is that right, miss?" the cop asked, shining the light in his face again.

She nodded. "Yes."

At least that sounded a little more convincing.

"Well, why don't I wait to see that you get in safely?" the guy said.

"Really?" Ben frowned. They were kind of in the middle of something. The date hadn't quite ended yet. He waited for Olivia to tell the cop to take a hike, but she gathered her things quickly.

"Yeah, okay…thanks, officer," she said, stretching to reach her sweater in the back, giving both men a great view down her top.

Ben glared at the officer, and the man averted his eyes. "Are you sure you're ready to call it a night?" he asked Olivia. Maybe she'd invite him in again. In hindsight, accepting her invitation to go inside, instead of this spontaneous hookup, might have been the better plan.

She looked past him at the officer, then nodded. "Yeah. Um…thank you for the date."

All that lead up, then *wham!* Shot down. His disappointment had to show on his face, but the untimely interruption had only slightly deflated his enthusiasm. It would take a simple touch from her, a silent look to get him rock hard again. He nodded. "Okay. I'll walk you to the door." He really didn't want to see her go. The night had gone too fast, and he was already looking forward to the next time he could see her, which with the finals starting would be longer than he liked.

"Not necessary, sir. I'll see that the lady gets inside," the officer said, and it sounded more like a warning to stay in the vehicle.

He turned to Olivia. "Are you sure you're okay with that?" He wasn't about to piss off a cop, but neither was he going to let the guy make her uncomfortable.

"It's fine," she said.

"Okay. Well, I'll also wait to see that you get in safely."

"Bye," she said awkwardly, the look in her eyes letting him know that she was just as disappointed to let the night end…but also maybe a little relieved.

The relief made his heart plummet.

"Bye," he mumbled as she climbed down from the Hummer and shut the door.

He watched as the officer walked her to the front door. Once she'd disappeared inside and the door closed behind her, he put the vehicle in reverse.

Then hit the brake as the cop flagged him down.

"Shit," he muttered under his breath as the guy approached the window, ticket book in hand. "Yes, officer?"

"These window tints are illegal. I need to ticket you."

"You ruined my date. Call it even?" he asked only half joking.

The cop continued to write the ticket. "Afraid not, Mr. Westmore. You see, I'm a Boston Bruins fan."

Right.

CHAPTER 18

∽◈∽

A two-hundred-dollar fine.

Olivia laughed as she replied. *So worth not having that creepy dude seeing me in a compromising position.*

She still couldn't believe she'd been *in* a compromising position. She hadn't been thinking straight...or at all yesterday. Agreeing to the date could be rationalized by the fact that she'd needed him out of her office. Going on the date? That was a little tougher to explain. The only thing she could come up with was the fact he'd looked better than the model on the latest issue of *GQ*, and the moment she'd answered her door and let him in, common sense had walked out. But then letting him get as far as he had...with no intention of stopping him...Her cheeks flamed at the memory, and she jumped as her phone chimed again.

There would be no fine too costly to protect your virtue, my lady.

She smiled. Her fingers hovered over the keyboard. Should she reply? Tell him that she'd had a great night?

To what end? They hadn't made plans to see one another again.

She put the phone in a drawer and closed it.

She bit her lip, wondering if he did want to see her again. She doubted Ben Westmore did second dates. She'd also doubted he'd be texting her that day, yet less than twelve hours after dropping her off he was contacting her.

Which shouldn't make her feel as happy and excited as it did.

Shaking her head, she signed into her computer and opened her email. Sixty-eight emails. Forty-two of them marked urgent. Good. That should keep her busy and her mind occupied. She opened the first one from the opposing counsel on a case file she'd started the day before. The man's client was asking for an extension to get his income tax forms submitted…

Her gaze drifted from the screen to the desk drawer. Ben said he was playing tonight anyway, didn't he? Opening a new search engine, the team's website confirmed there was a home game starting at seven.

Good. So even if she'd wanted to invite him to her place that evening, he was busy. Saved from the embarrassment of getting shut down.

The texting was obviously him being nice. Just like his going through with the date after she'd revealed she was pregnant. Now that he'd eased his own conscience about ripping her clothes off the night before, she'd probably never hear from him again.

Her gut twisted in a tight knot.

Why had she allowed herself to fall for Ben Westmore? Last night she'd opened herself up to him in a way she never had with anyone before. His support and acceptance of her pregnancy had made her feel like she wasn't completely alone in it…for a few hours at least. He hadn't actually meant it when he said she could call on him for baby furniture shopping, but in the moment, just the thought had been nice.

A knock on her office door made her jump and she straightened. "Come in," she called to Madison, visible through the open blinds.

"Hi, Ms. Davis. This just came for you," she said, handing her an envelope.

"Thanks," she said, noticing the Colorado Avalanche logo in the corner as she took it. Her hand immediately shook and she swallowed nerves rising in the back of her throat.

"Is it tickets to tonight's game?" Madison asked, eyes wide.

"I don't know. I haven't opened it yet." The excitement bubbling up in her chest made it almost impossible to hide a smile.

Madison waited.

"Phone," Olivia said, hearing it ring at her assistant's desk.

Madison sighed. "God forbid we let it go to voicemail just once," she mumbled as she left to answer it.

Alone, Olivia tore open the envelope and pulled out a ticket. A player's complimentary seat right behind the home box. Her heart echoed in her ears Ben was inviting her to tonight's game. Did that mean he wanted to see her, too? She flicked the ticket against the palm of her other hand, weighing her options. She could go and in doing so admit that she too wanted to see him, giving him the upper hand in whatever this was between them, or she could say she was busy, leading him to believe she'd never even entertained the idea of seeing him that night…or ever again.

Jeez, she had to pull it together. She shouldn't even be thinking of going.

Before her heart and mind could battle it out further, her phone chimed again. The sound echoed loudly in the drawer and she contemplated ignoring it, but knowing she'd get zero emails answered and nothing done that day anyway, she reached for it.

So will you come?

She grinned at his word choice and without thinking replied, *I guess that depends on how skilled you are.* She bit her lip. Sending flirty, slightly sexy messages at 8:09 a.m. would make for a long freaking day of anticipation if he continued to make her wait.

Another long moment of silence followed, then:

I promise you won't be disappointed in my performance this evening—on and off the ice.

She believed him, and all of a sudden, there was no doubt that she'd be attending the first game in the Stanley Cup finals. She didn't care that she had no idea where things could go between them; she just wanted to see him. But she wasn't about to let him know that just yet.

I'm not a fan of hockey, remember?

I bet I can change that.

She suspected he could. In fact, given a chance, she suspected Ben Westmore could change a lot of things.

* * *

Olivia climbed into the passenger side of Ben's Hummer after three exhilarating hours of hockey. Her voice was hoarse from cheering on the home team in the nail-biting game. Colorado was off to a strong start, but the next game was two days away in Boston. From what she'd learned from the hockey wives, girlfriends, and family members sitting around her in the reserved seats, the Bruins would now be more determined than ever to try to catch up on their home ice.

She'd also learned that she was the first woman Ben had ever invited to watch him play. That tidbit of information had warmed her in the chilly stadium.

Watching him play was a lot hotter than she could have imagined. The way she'd admired his grace and skill during her private lesson had been nothing to the way he'd impressed her that evening. It didn't surprise her that the team and the fans put so much pressure on him to bring home the cup.

As she reached for her seatbelt, her nose wrinkled and her eyes nearly watered. "Oh my God—what died in the back-seat?"

Ben hit the button to lower all four windows. "Sorry. I always take my hockey gear home during home games and it doesn't smell pretty after ninety minutes on ice sweating in it."

"That smell is your *gear*?" How the hell could he stand it? She stuck her head through the window, not caring that it had started to rain. She needed to escape the rancid scent killing her sense of smell.

"Yeah. Guess after twenty years, I kinda got used to it. But it actually explains a lot about why I had trouble picking up girls after games in high school."

She shot him a look, her hand covering her nose and mouth. "You had trouble picking up girls? I'm not buying it." The guy could have SERIAL KILLER on his license plate and women would still get in his car. She knew how danger-ous it was to be sitting in it, and yet, there she was.

He laughed. "You're right. I never had any trouble. I used to send my gear home with my baby brother, Ash."

"That's mean."

"Why? He wasn't interested in picking up girls." He

started the Hummer and peeled out of the stadium's now empty parking lot. "He's almost thirty, and I'm not sure if he is even now. Hockey is his life."

Kicking her feet free of her heels, she tucked her legs beneath her on the seat, pulling her skirt around her knees. She'd felt slightly out of place in her work clothes among the jerseys and jeans, but Ben's once-over and look of appreciation when he'd met her in the stadium entrance after the game made her glad she hadn't gone home to change. "I thought hockey was your life, too."

"It is, but I enjoy the perks that come along with it as well." He glanced at her with a grin.

Talking about his sex life wasn't a conversation she was anxious to have. She knew his reputation, and she was already struggling to figure out how she fit his profile. A woman he shouldn't want? The thrill of the taboo, maybe? She banished the thoughts, not wanting to turn the evening into a session of analyzing what was happening between them. "What's the deal with your other brother—Jackson?" she asked.

He shot her a look. "Your girl Abby—that's the deal."

"He gave up hockey for her?"

Ben nodded.

"I take it you think that was a bad choice?"

"My brother tried for years to play in the NHL. He gets his shot, and he turns it down." He shrugged. "His life, I guess."

"But it bothers you." That much was obvious.

"More than it bothers him."

"Doesn't he coach?"

"Junior league in Glenwood Falls."

"Did you just shudder? What's wrong? Not a fan of children?" She felt a tug at her ovaries…or at least she imagined she did. Ben Westmore would make beautiful children and the way he was with the kid the night before, signing his bike, his trading cards, and his jersey, had made her heart swell. But just because he was good with kids didn't mean he enjoyed them. Just because he was dating her, knowing she was pregnant, didn't mean he planned on stepping into any father figure role.

Not that she was expecting. Or asking. Or hoping.

But he surprised her. "I love kids."

Her mouth fell.

"Other people's children," he clarified.

Right.

"My nieces are awesome, and Abby's kid, Dani, is one of the best Junior league players I've ever seen on the ice—her father plays for the L.A. Kings."

And slept with every NHL cheerleader of legal age. "Yes, I know all about him." Too much, in fact. She was happy Abby and Dani were starting over with a new life and seemed to be doing well. "So, you don't want kids of your own?" She wished she could shut up and let the subject drop.

Ben shook his head. "Some people are not meant to be parents. My career would make it challenging to be a father, leaving my wi…" He nearly choked on the word.

"Wife?" she assisted.

"Yeah…that. I just think it's unfair to the other person left holding down the fort."

She eyed him.

"Fine. The entire concept of marriage and kids makes me gag."

She rolled her window down even further. "The *smell* in here is making me gag." She needed to change the subject. The man had practically just said he wasn't the marriage and father type—confirming what she already knew. Yet, she wasn't asking him to pull over and let her out. She must be insane. Or more far gone than she realized. "How much longer to your place?" Funny. She hadn't asked where they were heading when they left the stadium and he hadn't said, but somehow she'd sensed he wasn't in any rush to let the night end. And neither was she, despite the previous conversation.

"We're here," he said, turning into a cul-de-sac in a high-end neighborhood. The homes in that area cost over a million dollars, and his was the biggest on the block. She tried to conceal her look of surprise as he pulled into the circular stonework driveway and turned off the Hummer, but the house was beyond impressive. She should have known to expect extravagant based on his NHL-star salary and the type of vehicle he drove. Ben was a go-big-or-go-home sort of guy, and his home was certainly big.

"Home sweet home," he said.

"It's a little small, don't you think?"

He laughed, looking slightly embarrassed. "I may have gone a little crazy with the place. I'm actually thinking of selling it and moving into the lake house in Glenwood Falls."

"Another shack," she teased, opening the door and climbing down as he met her on her side.

"I know that's where I'll be spending most of my time once I retire, so there's not much point keeping both properties."

"When will that be—your retirement?" She knew it was a sensitive topic for most athletes. They often longed to play well beyond the point that their bodies could deliver the performances needed to keep them on top. She wondered if Ben would be one of those athletes who kept playing beyond his prime. He was in his thirties already; getting out while he was still one of the best probably meant he was looking at retiring in less than ten years.

"Six years...maybe five, if I re-sign next year with Colorado for the deal my agent is trying to negotiate."

She knew from reviewing his financial statements that his last contract had been thirty-eight million for five years. He could retire tomorrow and be fine, if money was his only motivator.

He unlocked the front door and she followed him into the house. The lights came on automatically, obviously operating on sensors, and her mouth dropped. Outside was magnificent. Inside was overwhelming.

Her entire two-thousand-foot condo could probably fit in the expansive foyer. The spiral staircase leading to the second floor had large, oversized stairs in a dark mahogany wood and embellished railing with wooden pillars. Overhead was the most unique chandelier she'd ever seen—large, teardrop shaped, with frosted glass hangings, each at a different height and getting smaller the closer they were to the ceiling. A waterfall cascaded down a brick and stonework wall, trickling into a bed of large beach pebbles in a dark marble base.

She'd taken two steps inside the house and already it was an architect's dream.

His cell phone rang, revealing a call from Asher. "My brother—he calls after every game."

"Go ahead," she said, feeling slightly out of place all of a sudden. This was a glimpse into a completely different world—a level of fame and fortune she'd only glimpsed as the pieces fell apart in court.

"I'll tell him I'm busy. Feel free to take a tour," he said.

"I'm afraid they'd find my body three months from now in a sixteenth and forgotten bedroom," she said.

He laughed. "Oh come on, there're only nine bedrooms. Kitchen is straight ahead. I'll be right there."

"I see a fridge," she said as he disappeared into a space that looked like a den.

She'd barely had time to drool over the white marble finish of the countertops and the stainless steel double oven when he rejoined her, his hockey bag in hand.

"How's your brother?" she asked, noticing a frown on his face.

"Injured. He thinks he might have torn his ACL."

"Shit—that sucks. I thought he was done playing for the season?"

"He was, but he was invited to play in this year's World Championships once the Devils were eliminated from the playoffs." He shook his head. "I'm sure he'll be fine by next season," he said, but the concern she detected in his voice was endearing. "Drink?" Going to the fridge, he took out a bottle of wine and grabbed two wine glasses from where they hung over the island in the center of the kitchen.

"Oh, none for me," she said as she climbed onto a breakfast nook stool.

Turning the bottle, he presented the label. "Alcohol-free."

She smiled at his thoughtfulness. "In that case, sure." She held the glasses as he poured. Then he held his in a toast, the teasing gleam back in his breathtakingly blue eyes. "To…gaining a new fan?"

He was definitely gaining a fan. On and off the ice. "Getting there," she said, taking a sip.

His blue eyes peered straight into her soul, and she knew there was no hiding her growing feelings. "I'll take it." He sipped his own and winced. "Wow, that's awful. You don't have to drink that."

"I like it." What she liked was that he'd once again thought of her and had the foresight to do something like this.

"Okay...Just give me a second to get this stuff into the washing machine before the smell brings down the property value in the neighborhood."

Her mouth gaped. "You do your own laundry?"

He grinned. "You met my mother. Do you think she comes over to do it?"

Olivia laughed. She suspected Ben and his siblings had learned to do their own laundry a long time ago. It just surprised her that he didn't pay someone to do it. "Don't you have a housekeeper?" The house was at least six thousand square feet. She'd hire someone to clean her two thousand square feet if she was ever in it long enough for it to get messy. Once the baby came along...

He was shaking his head. "I'm too particular. And I'm not a fan of having a stranger in my house. My sister was doing it for a while, but she gave it up once the baby arrived, and now she has her own business."

Right. The clothing store holding the baby girl dress. She wondered if Becky had kept her secret. Ben didn't mention it, so she just sipped her wine.

"So, you do all the cleaning?" The place was spotless. She was certain she could eat off of the heated marble-tiled flooring.

"Yes. Impressed?"

"More so by *this* information than anything else you've tried." What woman didn't appreciate a man who could clean and who took care of himself?

"Good to know. Maybe I'll create a custom bumper sticker for the back of the Hummer that says 'Cooks, cleans, and not too bad on the eyes.'" He winked. "Be back in a sec. Make yourself at home."

Carrying her glass into the living room, she scanned the cozy, inviting space. The décor was admittedly the last thing she would have expected for a bachelor athlete. Leather furniture and glass-top tables seemed to be the trend in the men she'd dated. But instead Ben had cream and tan plush sofas, dark wood end tables and lamps. The fireplace mantel was dark marble, and the hardwood floor was stained a red cherry oak color. Warm and welcoming. And perhaps the first room in the house that felt truly homey and comfortable.

She approached the fireplace and surveyed the family photos. She recognized his mother and sister and Jackson. The older man must be his father, and the younger duplicate version of Ben must be his brother Asher. Fantastic-looking family. The photo of them, all wearing jeans and black sweaters under a large maple tree, could be an ad for *Beautiful Family* Magazine.

The last family photo she had with her parents had been taken on the beach in Maui, the year before they died. The vow renewal ceremony for their tenth anniversary was like something out of her fairy tale books. Her mother had worn a simple yet elegant ivory satin dress, her hair swept up in a loose bun, tendrils of hair escaping and dancing around her shoulders in the island breeze as the sun started to set over the ocean. Her father had dressed in a pair of tan shorts and a white short-sleeved dress shirt open at the neck, revealing his lobster-colored skin from too much sun that week, and she'd felt like a princess in a pale pink sundress and sandals with the tiniest heel, her hair done in loose curls down her back.

She'd sat on the sand, watching her parents reaffirm their love and commitment for one another as the sun disappeared beneath the water, the beach lit up with countless tiki torches, and the sounds of the island vibe filled the air.

They'd been so in love.

The same glow of happiness existed on the faces of Ben's

parents in every photo of them. The look of admiration and respect in the shared glances, the pride in their family so evident even through time and these still images.

She took a sip of her wine and sighed. Would she ever be able to give her own child such a loving family?

* * *

Leaving the laundry room, Ben stopped in the kitchen to grab his glass of the nonalcoholic wine. What he really wanted was a beer to celebrate the team's first win, but he'd show support in solidarity. He'd turned down an evening out with his teammates faster than his final slapshot had sent the puck sailing into the Bruins net. He'd been relieved that she'd come to the game that evening, and she was the only person he wanted to celebrate with.

Entering the living room, Olivia's back was turned and she was looking at the photos on his mantel. Just as it had seeing her look so relaxed and comfortable in his lake house, his chest tightened now, too. She looked good in his home.

Then he noticed the photo she held.

Shit. He thought he'd gotten rid of those. Being on the road so much with the team and spending a lot of his free time with his family or going out, he was rarely at home and hardly ever in the living room. While it was one of the warmer, cozier rooms, it only reminded him of how alone he was in the big house by himself...and he didn't like when those unwanted, foreign feelings of longing overwhelmed him.

Clearing his voice, he strode across the room. "I'll take that one," he said, taking the photo from her. "That shouldn't be there." Maybe he should comb the rest of the place for any lingering signs of his ex as well, just in case Olivia decided to take that house tour after all.

She studied him. "Janelle?"

No sense in denying it. He nodded, glancing quickly at the image and immediately regretting it. It was taken the night they'd moved into the house. She was sitting in the sunroom off of the back overlooking the big backyard, a family quilt draped across her legs, staring off toward the unobscured view of the mountains. Her expression was pensive, thoughtful, peaceful—a rare moment for a woman with such a driven, firecracker spirit. He couldn't help but snap the photo unbeknownst to her. She'd looked so beautiful.

At the time he'd been fool enough—or maybe just hopeful enough—to think she was sitting there contemplating their future together. Thinking about the life she'd been talking about nonstop the last few days. That was the moment he'd decided she was the one for him. He'd known he was in love with her, and he'd been on board with everything she'd been planning for their future, but up until that moment the idea of proposing hadn't occurred to him. It had hit him then like a hockey puck to the heart, and planning a proposal worthy of her became his only focus those few weeks leading up to Christmas.

Now, he knew the truth. She hadn't been thinking about them. She'd been thinking about her—the future she'd wanted slipping away and whether or not she could be truly happy with the new one she was moving forward with.

"She's beautiful," Olivia said, cutting into his thoughts.

"Yes," he agreed, turning the photo facedown onto the end table and taking a step toward her. "Unfortunately, that beauty hid a lot of potential to do damage." He hadn't known real disappointment or the level of hurt he could experience until she'd walked away. And knowing how his pain could consume him was his armor against it. "Maybe that's why I didn't see who she really was. Didn't see how forced her enthusiasm for a future with me was or how strong her ambitions were. I didn't want to see any of that." He wrapped his arms around Olivia and pulled her closer.

She stepped into his embrace willingly, wrapping her arms around his waist.

For the first time, talking about Janelle, about the disappointment of the failed relationship, didn't leave him feeling empty or torn apart. Maybe he'd moved on. Maybe time really did heal. Or maybe the woman in his arms was evoking such feelings of passion and comfort that there was no room for any darkness or sorrow.

Olivia looked up at him. "She must have been crazy," she whispered.

"Maybe the idea of cleaning this house scared her away," he said, trying to make light of the moment. Or maybe trying to check his emotions.

She gave him a look that told him he didn't need to pretend around her, that he could be vulnerable without the consequences of another heartache as she touched his cheek. "She left quite a scar, huh?"

His breath caught in his chest at the gentleness in her touch, the understanding in her eyes, and the connection vibrating between them. "It's starting to fade," he said slowly lowering his lips toward hers. He needed to kiss her. He needed to feel her mouth against his—this insane pull toward her making him unaware of anything else.

A fraction of an inch away, he paused and she stood on tiptoes to close the gap. Her mouth eagerly accepting his as her body leaned against him. He tightened his hold on her and deepened the kiss ever so slightly before breaking away. "Fading a little more," he whispered against her lips, opening his eyes to take in her beautiful longing expression. He kissed her again, and she fisted her hands in the front of his shirt, pulling him closer, preventing another teasing break between them.

He backed her toward the wall, then placed both hands on either side of her head, his mouth never breaking contact with hers. Her hands wrapped around his neck as her tongue teased his bottom lip, demanding entry. He felt himself grow thick in his jeans, and anticipation flowed through him, making his entire body sweat and his heart thunder in his chest. The taste of coconut lip balm mixed with the familiar scent of jasmine was an intoxicating combination. Since the night before in his Hummer, he'd been craving another chance to kiss her, hold her, touch her.

This time there wouldn't be any interruptions preventing them from exploring one another. No bright lights illuminating the bad decision they were on the verge of making. This time they were in his home. He was kissing her, and she was kissing him right back. He wanted her, and there was no denying that she wanted him. This time there was nothing but their own insecurities and fears to stop them.

He knew one thing—he wasn't stopping unless she told him to. In fact, he might never stop unless she asked him to. The thought only made him harder as his hands fell away from the wall and landed on her hips. He pushed himself against her as his fingers dug deep, holding her in place as his mouth continued its frantic exploration of hers. She wasn't pushing him away; instead, she clung to his shoulders, drawing him even closer. Her breasts pressed against his chest, her pelvis pushed against his growing hardness, and her thighs tangled with his.

A long, breathless moment later, she pulled away. Her gaze flittered from his lips to his eyes and back again.

The moment of truth. Did they cross yet another line? Or would her common sense tell her to run from this, from him?

"Is there a bedroom somewhere close?" she whispered, her lust-filled, flushed expression making it impossible to look anywhere else. She was so fucking beautiful, he could barely focus on her question.

"There're four bedrooms close...you can have your pick."

"The closest one," she said, ducking under his arm and leading the way down the hall.

Catching up to her, he wrapped his arms around her waist and buried his face in her neck, leaving a trail of kisses as they hurried toward the rooms. "First door on the left," he murmured against her soft, delicious skin.

They reached the room and he shoved the door open, then scooped her up to carry her inside.

She laughed when he tossed her onto the bed and jumped down next to her. "This bed has to be bigger than a king size. I have a king size, and it looks like a single compared to this."

"It's an extra wide and long," he said, a teasing smirk playing on his lips as he brushed his thumb over her bottom lip, which was pink and slightly swollen from their kisses.

"I didn't know those existed," she said, before capturing his finger between her lips and sucking gently.

Fuck, she was the sexiest woman he'd ever been with. The playful, teasing look in her eyes was killing him. He wanted her more than he'd ever wanted anyone, and it terrified him. "You're about to find out just how real they are," he said gruffly, lying back and pulling her on top of him. Placing his hands on her face, he moved her dark hair away, tangling his fingers in its softness. "You are so beautiful."

She tried to lower her gaze, but he wouldn't allow her to look away. He needed her to see he meant it, that it wasn't just words he said before sex, that he found her so fucking beautiful it was enough to make him hesitate.

"I'm sure you've had women far more beautiful than me in here," she said, with a hint of jealousy and the first sign of insecurity he'd ever heard from her. Somehow it made him feel better knowing his wasn't the only vulnerable heart in the room.

"You're the first woman to be in here...but even if you weren't, you'd still be far more beautiful than even my best dreams."

Her forehead wrinkled. "You've never had anyone else in here?"

"No." He and Janelle had shared one of the other bedrooms in the house, but not this one, not this bed. This was his bedroom, the one he'd moved into after Janelle left. And he'd never brought another woman back to his place before. It was too personal, too committal.

Yet, he hadn't thought twice about bringing Olivia there.

She stared at him for a fraction of a second longer, before crushing his mouth with her own.

His hands left her hair, allowing the dark waves to fall forward. The smell of jasmine filled his senses once more as the thick, soft strands tickled his neck. He dragged his hands over her shoulders, down the length of her ribs, around the side of her body and down her back, searching for the zipper on her skirt. Finding it, he stopped, despite the throbbing in his cock that demanded he rip the skirt off and submerge himself inside her soft warmth. "It's not too late," he said, his desire not to hurt her, to protect her heart from him, overshadowing his own need for her.

Her breath was labored and her voice hoarse. "We both know it's definitely too late."

The hint of hesitation in her voice sounded like premature remorse, and he didn't want to do anything she would later regret. He knew he wouldn't. "Do you want me to make love to you, Olivia? Be sure." If she regretted this in the morning, it would crush him.

"Make love to me, Ben," she said, hesitation gone.

He wasted no time pulling the zipper roughly and pushing the fabric over her hips.

She wiggled her legs free, kicking the skirt onto the floor, then she reached for the base of his T-shirt.

He sat up and raised his arms to allow her to lift it over his head.

Her eyes skimmed his torso. "Disgusting," she said with a grin, as her nails raked along his chest and stomach, tickling him.

"That's not nice," he murmured, unbuttoning her blouse and tossing it aside. Reaching around, he unclasped the white lace bra and slowly slid the straps down over her shoulders and away from her body. He let the fabric fall onto his stomach and his breath caught at the sight of her exposed chest and stomach, the perfectly shaped, full breasts better than he could have imagined. "Beautiful," he said again. He'd say it a million times a day, if that was what she needed to believe it. He buried his face against her, enjoying the feel of her nipples hardening beneath his touch. His hands cupping and massaging until she moaned in delight. The mere sound almost finished him off.

"That feels incredible," she whispered, tossing her head back, her breathing coming in quick, short pants.

Damn. The sounds she was making and the look of tormented satisfaction on her face made him so hard, he reached down and unbuttoned his jeans.

Taking her rough and hard was tempting, but he forced air into his lungs and made himself slow down. He kissed her flesh along her cleavage, leaving a trail all the way to her nipple. He sucked gently, swirling his tongue around the hardened bud, then flicked his tongue across it before grazing it with his teeth. She tasted so good…Sliding his tongue along her skin, he moved to the other nipple and now she was almost whimpering above him. "You're driving me crazy with those sounds," he murmured against her skin.

"You're causing them," she said, her voice pure seduction, running her hands through his hair.

"I'm so fucking hard right now." His cock spasmed as a rush of blood left his every other extremity weak with desire. Switching position, he laid her back onto the bed, and kneeling in front of her, he quickly removed his jeans and underwear, freeing himself from the restricting confines of the fabric.

Her eyes took him appreciatively. "Extra-long and wide, huh?"

He shot her a look. "Go easy now…a man's ego can only take so much," he said, lowering his head to press his lips to her stomach, kissing a circle around her belly button, as his hands slid up the length of her legs. He reached for the band on her underwear and moved the thong down to her thighs. His eyes slowly drifted over her body and he let out a low whistle.

Below him, Olivia reached forward to stroke his cock, gently wrapping her hand around the shaft. He closed his eyes as pleasure soared through him. It had been far too long since he'd had a woman's hands on him. She applied more pressure as she stroked up and down and he had to stop her.

"Hey!" she said.

"If you don't stop, this will be over really fast," he said. Placing his hands on the inside of her muscular thighs, he eased them open and brought his lips back down to her stomach. "You're so wet," he whispered against her skin as he pressed two fingers inside her.

"Oh my God, Ben..." she said, his fingers sliding the length of her swollen, wet pussy. She arched her back, pressing her body against his touch, as though she couldn't get close enough.

He slowed the pace slightly, moving his fingers in and out, applying pressure then easing off. Knowing they were both so close to the edge, he longed to make this moment last as long as possible. Which wouldn't be that long, judging by the way his cock was demanding to be touched. With his other hand, he stroked his straining and throbbing length.

Olivia watched, her eyes barely open as her own pleasure grew more intense. She raised her hands to her breasts and massaged them gently, her gaze teasing him with seduction.

Moving away from her, he climbed off of the bed. "Don't move. Don't stop. Stay right there," he said, disappearing into the adjoining bathroom.

Opening the medicine cabinet, he grabbed a condom and seconds later he was back in the room.

She hadn't moved. She hadn't stopped. She'd stayed right there.

Oh God, he'd be a lucky man if she'd stay right there forever.

The thought nearly knocked him on his ass, but he pushed it away. He ripped open the package and slid the protection firmly in place before raising her body and positioning her over him. "No regrets," he said, swallowing hard.

She shook her head, her eyes filled with only longing and desire. "No regrets," she whispered.

A second later, a shocked cry escaped her lips as he slid her body down over him, his cock burying itself deep in the wet warmness of her. Her nails bit into the flesh of his shoulders as he pushed himself even further. "Too deep?" he asked.

She closed her eyes and moaned, "No…it's perfect…so fucking perfect."

"Olivia," he groaned as her hips moved up and down in a slow rhythm, teasing, killing him. Her hands in his hair, she kissed his neck.

It was too much. He was going to come, and he never came before he pleasured. He eased himself out of her body.

"No…come back, please," she begged, pushing herself against his erect shaft.

He was throbbing so hard he was afraid he might come anyway. He forced a calming breath as he slid the tip in again gently, then plunged deeper, harder. He repeated the torturous motion several times, his fingers squeezing between them to flick her clit and explore the folds of her pussy.

"I need you inside me," she said, and he pushed deeper, a moan escaping as she tightened around him.

"Are you close?" he whispered. He was. So dangerously close.

"Yes," she panted, riding him up and down, faster, harder, until they were both desperate for release.

His hands tangled in her hair and pulled her head backward as he kissed the base of her neck, burrowing his head into her breasts, and came undone. Losing all control, he held her firmly in place as he pulsated inside her.

She pressed her hips into him as her body rippled in pleasure, before relaxing, spent against him.

He kissed her shoulder and smoothed her hair away from her neck.

She leaned back to look at him, and he placed a gentle kiss on her lips, her nose, and her forehead.

"How's the scar now?" she asked tracing a finger along his chest above his heart.

"I would say it's almost gone."

* * *

Lying awake hours later, Olivia sleeping soundly on his chest, Ben struggled with emotions he'd never experienced before. His gut was sending out warning signals that he was heading straight back to a place he'd fought to climb out of. While he was sticking to the vow of no regrets, his mind was begging him to start thinking a little clearer around Olivia—that despite the connection and attraction between them, she had her own life plans…that may not include him. And his heart—the most ambiguous of all—was reminding him that the farther the fall, the harder the climb back up.

He'd always felt as though he'd been partially responsible for Janelle not getting the anchor position in Seattle. While he was supportive of her career, the idea that she would have to move and they'd have to somehow make a long-distance relationship work had made him uneasy. Sure, he was traveling a lot with the team, so nine months of the year they struggled to make things work anyway, but still he had been secretly relieved when she hadn't gotten the job.

With the relief, a wave of guilt had washed over him. He'd been hoping for that outcome because it made things easier—for him. Their life together was going to be challenge enough, and her not getting her dream position in Seattle was one less thing they needed to consider. It was selfish and wrong, and he felt like an asshole. His guilt was the reason he'd bought her the convertible sports car she'd wanted, against the advice of his financial manager, who warned him against extravagant purchases considering his short-term contract with the Avalanche.

But he'd never worried about his future in hockey. And at the time he was riding high. On top of the world. An NHL contract with his home team for at least two seasons and the love of his life staying in Colorado.

Heartbroken and disappointed about her career.

Seeing her so upset, her confidence waning, had nearly killed him, and he made it his mission to try to make her see the good in the situation. Everything happened for a reason, he said, along with a bunch of other crap people said when things didn't go their way. He wasn't buying into it, and he could tell she wasn't, either.

But oddly enough, she'd bounced back quicker than he'd expected, and things between them changed practically overnight.

While before she'd been reluctant to move into the house she'd picked out and decorated the month before, now she was ready to take the step. She started planning their future, claiming it was a good thing she hadn't gotten the anchor position, as she'd studied his regular season schedule and figured out when and which cities it made sense for her to fly out to see him and how to make the most of his home games.

Everything happened for a reason, she'd echoed.

And he was happy enough to believe it, without question.

He'd been too caught up in his own dream coming true he hadn't seen her pain. He'd seen only what he'd wanted to see. Heard only what he'd wanted to hear. He had everything he'd always wanted—a career on the ice, a beautiful home in the state he'd grown up in, family close enough not to miss, and a beautiful woman who loved him and wanted to spend her life living the fairy tale.

Not even his mother's words of caution when he'd shown her the three-carat engagement ring he'd bought had rung loudly enough to make him pause. He hadn't wanted to hear caution or warnings from family and friends, so he dismissed them as white noise. After all, he'd successfully silenced all of his own alarm bells.

Even the deafening ones going off the moment he'd walked through the front door after his game on New Year's Eve to find her pacing in the foyer, looking nervous and on edge.

In the years since, every time he looked back on that moment he regretted not letting her speak first.

He'd dropped to one knee the moment she'd turned to look at him, instead of waiting until they were cuddled in bed with Champagne counting away the year, the way he'd planned.

"Oh no, wait, Ben." Just those first few words should have been enough for him to realize he was about to make a mistake, but he'd stayed where he was and reached inside his coat for the ring box.

"Can I please say something first?" she'd asked, looking nervous. An expression, at the time, he'd mistaken for excitement.

"After you say yes to marrying me, you can say anything else you want," he'd said. His love for her and his sudden clarity about what he wanted in life overshadowed the odd sense that something was off. Blinding him to the fact that maybe she wasn't as ready, despite her claims.

"I can't, Ben," she'd said, taking his hands and lifting him up from his perch on one knee.

"What?"

"I can't marry you…At least not right now." Her gaze fell on the blue box, and he sensed the briefest of reconsiderations, before she continued, "I got a call this afternoon from Sports News Vegas. They offered me a job starting in January." Her excitement only made the moment worse for him.

He was proposing. Giving her what she'd claimed to

want—a life with him. And she was saying no—breaking him, while smiling? Displaying excitement over a job offer while she was crushing him?

It had taken years for him to realize his own selfishness in his lack of excitement for her. His own hurt and pain had made it impossible to feel happy for her. "So, that's it? You're accepting the position without even talking to me about it?"

Her smile had vanished, replaced immediately by a look of annoyed determination. A look he'd come to realize was far worse than anger. Anger dissolved. This look meant he was only adding fuel to her fire. "Did you ask my permission before accepting the deal from Colorado to play hockey? Did we discuss that first?" she'd asked.

"You knew that's where I was headed." She'd been there all along, watching him move through the ranks, celebrating with him when he was drafted, supporting him in his decisions…But a nagging voice reminded him she was right; he'd never actually asked her what she thought about him becoming a pro athlete, and they hadn't discussed things before he'd made his final decisions.

Unfortunately, she'd spoken again before he could say she was right. "And you'd doubted my ability to secure the future of *my* dreams, is that it?" Anger had registered on her face. "All that talk of believing in me, that was all bullshit?"

The man he was now would have stopped the fight right then and there, taken her in his arms, apologized, and congratulated her. He would have pushed aside all talk of marriage and instead celebrated her success. Made the night memorable in a different way. Maybe then they still could have had a chance. Maybe they could have figured things out. Maybe the engagement might have happened eventually.

But at the time, he'd been a selfish kid who let his own

hurt and disappointment overshadow logic and common sense. "I just thought you'd given up on that idea. I thought you wanted a different life now. You were the one who wanted all of this," he'd said, gesturing to the house he could barely afford. "You were the one talking about marriage." He shook the ring box. "Babies—how many did you say you wanted? Three? Four?" His anger rose at each aspect of the dream she was destroying.

"Ben, please…"

"Please what? Stop reminding you of the future you promised me?" How could she not understand where he was coming from? All of this—everything around them—had been for her. And now she was saying it wasn't what she wanted? That she'd changed her mind for a job that might not even work out?

She'd sighed, lowering her gaze to the floor. "I did want all of that Ben, but I guess the truth is I was really just trying to make the best of plan B."

He'd felt as though he'd been sucker-punched. Air escaped his lungs and he found it hard to focus. Plan B. That's what he'd been to her?

She'd rushed toward him. "That wasn't what I meant. It came out wrong." She'd reached for his hand, but he'd pulled away.

"No. I think it came out exactly right." He'd tossed the engagement ring onto the table next to the front door and grabbed his coat and car keys. The slamming of the front door had drowned out her pleas for him to stay and talk. There had been nothing left to say.

She'd been using him as a backup plan when her real dreams had seemed to fail. And now that she was getting another chance at the life she really wanted, she was abandoning her promises to him.

Opening the door to his car, he tossed his coat over onto the passenger side and climbed behind the wheel. The sound of fireworks in the distance told him that it was midnight. The old year was gone, the new year was here.

And in that moment, he swore he'd never be another woman's plan B.

CHAPTER 19

*B*en hit Send on a text message to Olivia and then re-luctantly turned his phone to airplane mode for the team's flight to Boston. He smiled thinking about how amazing she looked in his bed this morning. Her dark hair a tangled mess on his pillow, her discarded clothing still lit-tering the bedroom floor. He'd hated to wake her that early, but coming out of the bathroom and seeing her naked back and the top of one hip as she lay on her side sleeping, he hadn't been able to resist. He'd quickly decided that morn-ing sex was by far his favorite, and her send-off had started the day on an incredible note.

"No one smiles like that this early in the morning unless they've gotten laid," Owen said, boarding the aircraft and sitting in the seat next to him.

"Who let you in first class?" He refused to admit shit.

"Miller lost everything but his Maserati at poker last night. So, who is she?" he asked. "That sexy little reporter that was undressing you with her eyes while she interviewed you after the game last night?"

He shook his head. He barely remembered the woman in question. Damn. That hadn't happened before. He'd been in a rush to get through the mind-numbing standard questions he answered after every game, get showered, and be with Olivia. The next three nights away would suck.

That hadn't happened before either—the idea of not seeing the same woman again after an incredible night of sex bumming him out.

"Nah…it's no one you know."

Owen tucked his bag under the seat. "Well, at least you're starting to play better."

It was true. The night before he'd scored two goals and made three assists. "Yeah, I feel better. Still need to get my scoring rhythm back." The team was winning, but he couldn't claim to be the player leading them to victory so far this playoff season, and that had to change. As captain and MVP, the other players, the coaches, and the fans expected far more from him than he was delivering. He wanted to dispel the playoff choking myth that plagued him.

Luckily, Olivia hadn't seemed disappointed in his performance on the ice *or* between the sheets.

He wondered how she would feel about things with more time and distance between them. She'd been fine that morning, but he worried that without him there to remind her of his affection, she'd start to doubt him. Doubt them. His reputation could overshadow what she knew to be real.

Just the fact that it worried him made him uneasy. He'd always wanted the women he'd slept with to move on as quickly as he did, to not expect more…

Things were so different with Olivia. His attraction to her was far more than just physical.

But did she feel the same way? They hadn't discussed feelings, instead letting their bodies do the talking, but he sensed she was falling just as hard and fast for him as he was for her.

And he needed to make a decision to be either all in or out. In less than nine months, the woman he was falling in love with would be a mother, and it wasn't fair to either of them or the baby to play this game without being fully committed.

He sat back in his seat, his gaze lost out the window. The problem was he couldn't imagine going back to life without Olivia.

His heart had already made the decision to commit somewhere between meeting her and kissing her goodbye that morning.

He was all in.

No regrets.

*   *   *

Curling her legs beneath her on the sofa that evening, Olivia stared at the Skype window open on her laptop. Seeing her reflection in the screen, she ran a hand over her hair and tugged a little higher on her sweater. Online video chats always made her nervous. Skype and FaceTime were too much pressure.

Tonight's would be torture.

In thirty-six seconds, Ben would be calling. And she would be ending things between them.

She had to. She should never have let things get so far out of hand. She was starting to fall in love with him, and smart women did not fall in love with sexy professional athletes who had reputations like Ben's.

Especially not smart, *pregnant* woman who didn't have the luxury of wasting time with a man who, despite all attempts at sincerity, wasn't willing to commit. Ben had said marriage and family were not in his future...therefore neither was she.

She bit her lip as she waited. Trying to distract herself from the back-and-forth thoughts, she'd been working on case files, with the hockey game on in the background, but had only paid attention to the screen enough to see that they'd lost. The game had gone into a first round of overtime, and Boston had scored three minutes in. The series score was now tied, and the team would be playing one more game away before returning later that week to play game four on home ice.

The timing of tonight's loss wasn't ideal, and she hated giving him more bad news, but she couldn't put this off. Doing it while he was away, through a Skype connection, was lame, but even that was hard enough. If she tried to do it when they were together, when he could wrap his arms around her, kiss her, make her experience mixed feelings of comfort and passion at the same time...She'd never be able to do it. This was easier—for her.

He'd be fine. He was Ben Westmore. He'd probably be relieved that for once he wouldn't have to be the bad guy. No doubt he was probably on the verge of breaking things off himself. The moment he disconnected the Skype connection, he could have any one of—or the entire—Boston cheerleader squad in his hotel room. The thought was supposed to make her feel better, but it only made her nauseous. The idea of him with anyone else...

She jumped as the Skype connection rang. She took a deep breath and swallowed the lump in her throat. Her heart raced and her hands felt clammy on the keyboard as she accepted the call. "Hi," she said, when his face appeared on her screen.

"Hey, pretty girl. Sorry to be so late. That overtime period put us off schedule, and the bus on the way back to the hotel made several food stops." He held up a bag of Chinese food.

A memory of their first date, eating Chinese food and trying not to fall in love weakened her resolve, but she shook it off. She had to do this. She had to stay strong. She could not be swept along with something that would eventually end. "It's no problem at all. It's still early here." God, did he have to look so good? Hair wet from the shower. His short playoff beard had just the right amount of stubble on his face. And the plain black T-shirt he wore was hugging his chest and biceps so nicely. She'd be on the next plane to Boston if he asked. She missed that chest and those biceps. Waking up in them this morning had been a fantasy. *But it was just a fantasy.*

Ending things remember. "Listen, Ben…"

"Man, you are a sight for sore eyes," he said smiling as he spoke at the same time she did. The stupid Skype delay made him pause a second later. "Sorry, what were you saying?" He leaned closer to the screen.

Who knew what she was saying? She could barely remember her own name when those icy blue eyes held so much affection and sincerity she could almost fool herself into believing they had a future together. "Um…Sorry about the loss tonight." Okay, so she'd chickened out.

He nodded. "Such a close game. They needed this win, though, and they worked for it. Hopefully, we'll take back the lead in a couple of nights and then be at an advantage for the next home game. You'll be there, right?"

He looked nervous as he waited for her reply, but she refused to make any promises or commitments beyond this Skype chat. "Do you think the team will win the cup?" Why were they talking about hockey? She needed to tell him things were over. That she didn't want to see him anymore. She had to lie to him and herself and tell him that she'd had a great time, but she wasn't interested in seeing him again.

Do it. Say the words.

"I think we got this, but anything can happen." He ran a hand through his hair and his expression clouded slightly. She could sense his unease, or maybe it was her own anxiety…Either way, his vulnerability made her rethink her words.

"Where's my cocky MVP?" she asked softly, offering an encouraging smile. She couldn't do it. She couldn't tell him.

He laughed, and the sound warmed her heart. God, she was so screwed. She was defenseless against him. "Yours?" he asked, leaning closer to the screen.

Her cheeks flushed. "That's not what I meant."

"Why not? I like it," he said.

Oh shit. Even through computer screens, he had her. The way he was looking at her with those adoring eyes and soft smile—an expression she saw only on his face when he was talking to her—weakened her. "Ben, I'm not sure about this." That was a lie. She was sure. Sure it was a terrible idea. Sure it would only end in heartbreak.

He frowned. "You don't think the team can win?"

He thought they were still talking about hockey. Damn.

Just tell him! Say it. Say you can't see him anymore.

Right. Break things off with a guy in the Stanley Cup finals whose confidence already seemed shaky.

Excuses.

She'd take them. "I think the team can win. You just need your confidence back. You're the MVP for a reason, and I expect to see a great game on home ice later this week." Chicken. Shit.

Or too in love to do the right thing.

"Does that mean you'll come to the game?" he asked with a wink.

Oh that simple blink of an eye could get a girl into a whole lot of trouble. She nodded slowly, giving up the fight.

Ben smiled.

And all thoughts of ending things got lost in cyberspace.

CHAPTER 20

❧

*B*en had never been distracted by a woman in the stands, but resisting the urge to glance Olivia's way each time he passed her seat was a challenge. Three nights on the road away from her had been tough, and he was looking forward to getting her back to his place after the game.

Playoff game, he reminded himself. He was the MVP for a reason. He couldn't lose focus on the ice because of unwanted distractions, he couldn't let anything else jeopardize the season. This was game four of the Stanley Cup finals on home ice, with his team losing the series 2–1. The pressure was on—everyone from his teammates to the fans was counting on him to tie it up.

If only Olivia didn't look so freaking gorgeous, her red scarf draped over a white, off-the-shoulder cashmere sweater like a beacon, calling his attention whenever he skated past. In the sea of blue and burgundy jerseys, she stood out…and in a crowd she was the only one he saw.

"Westmore, you're in," his coach yelled, as several players approached the box.

He jumped over the boards and headed straight for the puck.

From the corner of his peripheral vision, he saw Dennis Carson, a Boston left wing skating toward him. Again. What the hell was with this guy tonight? They'd played on the same team two years ago when Carson had spent a season in Colorado, and they'd gotten along fine. Hadn't he even gone to the guy's wedding last summer?

Now he was acting as though they had their own score to settle.

Ben scooped the puck as it sailed toward the boards and dodged several players, including Carson, as he skated toward center ice. He heard some trash talk behind him, but that was standard. The finals brought a lot of emotions to the surface, and the key was to continue playing a smooth, clean game, keeping a clear head.

The Avalanche was winning one to nothing, so the other team was trying to make up for their crap ice skills by irritating the players earning their paychecks. That was fine. Let them try to throw him off his game. That night he had two goals—win on the ice and then score back at his place.

But as he approached the net, Carson skated next to him. "You have impeccable taste in one-night stands."

Ben didn't even tense. Really? The guy thought harassing him about his past was going to get him riled up? He handled the puck with ease as he circled the goalie's net. Carson followed, but didn't make a play for the puck.

"I mean, cheerleaders and clingy puck bunnies are one thing, but Olivia Davis…" He let out a low whistle.

Ben frowned, his shoulders tensing now. This guy knew Olivia? He skated to the front of the net, and dared a glance toward her. Her look of excitement—the anticipation of an upcoming goal—faded as another player stole the puck from him.

Fuck.

Behind him, Carson laughed. "She *is* distracting. If you like ball-busting attorneys with big tits and amazing legs…"

Ben swung around. "Watch yourself."

Carson skated past with a shrug. "I'm just saying, good play, man—seducing the opposing counsel. I'll keep that in mind next time I'm fighting against her in court. You'll be done with her soon, right?"

Something snapped. Skating toward the bigger player, Ben dropped his stick and gloves simultaneously.

Carson's face clouded, then the brawler, known for his on-ice fights, dropped his own gear and raised his hands.

Ben didn't swing. Instead, he grabbed the guys' jersey and pushed him up against the boards. "You don't know what you're talking about, so I advise you to shut it, man."

Carson shrugged him off. "Fuck you, Westmore. We all see what you're doing with her." He grinned. "We think its genius. But you can drop the act now that your divorce is settled, right?"

He clenched his fist. "Another word. I dare you." Ben's calm, clear head had disappeared.

Carson loomed over him, challenge clearly accepted. "Let me ask you, does a woman like her prefer to be on top, or does she ever submit? I always wondered about that…" His dark, threatening gaze lifted past Ben to the stands and a disgusting grin appeared on his face. "Yeah, definitely let me know once you're done with her."

Ben's right hook landed with precision on the taller man's jaw, and he shoved his hip into him, crushing him to the boards once more as he threw a left that failed to connect.

"Well, fuck me—Ben Westmore's got a girlfriend," Carson taunted, seemingly unfazed by the shot.

The ref tried to separate them and the crowd was yelling "Fight!" as Ben delivered another shot.

This one was harder, and it erased any amusement from Carson's face.

The blow to his own left cheek had him reeling from the impact, but instead of retreating, he moved in closer, using his hold on the guy to steady himself.

"Oh, she looks concerned," he said. "Looks like someone might get to play nurse later…"

He moved back and swung again, but the ref grabbed his arm midair, dragging him away.

He struggled against the hold, and once free, the temptation to skate back toward Carson was overwhelming, but the game announcer was already announcing his two-minute penalty. Continue this petty schoolyard fight and he'd get five minutes. He couldn't do that to his team.

He dove for his gloves and stick and removed his helmet as he skated toward the penalty box, ignoring the annoyed look from his coach and teammates, and the questioning one from Olivia. A look that also held a trace of admiration.

He smiled. That look made sitting in the box for two minutes just a little easier.

* * *

"You guys realize you're on ice and not in a boxing ring, right?" Olivia asked, handing him an ice pack for his swollen cheek.

Ben rested his head on the arm of the couch, stretching his legs across the cushions. "Fighting is part of the game." It wasn't usually part of *his* game, but he'd made an exception. Luckily it hadn't cost them the win. Only three possible games between him and the Stanley Cup.

Olivia sat on the edge of the sofa, and he took her hand in his, loving the comfort having her with him provided. He'd take a punch to the face *every* game if she was there afterward to nurse his injuries. The team had been going out after the game to celebrate, but he'd passed on what would normally have been an evening of debauchery to take Olivia back to his place. He'd been desperate to be alone with her since he'd seen her sitting in the stands.

"So, what was the deal with that number sixteen anyway? Carson, right?"

He nodded, but just shrugged. He was embarrassed that he'd let the idiot's words get to him the way they had, and his rare flare of temper wasn't the impression he wanted Olivia to have of him.

"I mean, neither of you even had the puck when the fight started."

He looked away. "Sometimes guys run their mouth, and playoffs are intense. It's harder to keep a cool head."

"So, that was it? Just playoff bullshit?"

"Yup." She had the bullshit part right.

She seemed to be thinking hard as she studied him. Then recognition registered on her face. "Oh, now I remember him—*Dennis* Carson, right?"

Shit. "Probably not the same one you know..." his voice trailed.

She nodded. "Oh, yes, it's the same one, all right. I represented his wife in their divorce three years ago. Asshole," she muttered. "I thought I was imagining the dirty looks he was shooting me when he skated past."

"He's a moron." Ben suspected a strong, independent woman like Olivia wouldn't be impressed by the macho display of his. He would probably get another punch if he came clean.

"That fight was about me, wasn't it?" she asked.

Her expression was unreadable, so he hesitated. "What's the right answer here? The one that will earn me a kiss?" Maybe he could flirt his way out of trouble.

She smiled and leaned toward him. Gently, she placed a soft kiss on his sore cheek, then another one on his lips, then she slapped his shoulder. "That fight got you a penalty, which led to the other team scoring. We almost lost the game."

The pout on her pretty face and the half-hearted scolding was hot as hell. "We?" He pulled her hands, dragging her body toward him. Her hair fell onto his chest and he breathed her in. He'd missed the familiar scent of her hair and neck and body while he'd been away. He'd missed her. Their nightly Skype sessions had only made him want to be with her even more. Talking to her at the end of the day reiterated just how much he wanted her in his life. Needed her in his life. And the idea no longer frightened him. They had to talk. About them. About a future together. About the baby. They'd avoided any real heart-to-heart discussions, but that needed to change. He knew his reputation would make her reluctant to take a chance on them, and he wanted to prove to her that he was in this for the long haul. "Since when are you an official hockey fan?" he whispered against her lips.

"What can I say? Playoff fever is addictive." She slid her arms around his neck.

He smiled. "That's it? The only reason you're attending the games and have an interest in the sport?"

She pretended to think. "Yup. That's it."

"It has nothing to do with how hot I look on the ice?"

He moved his hands up her back, massaging her shoulder blades.

Her body relaxed and she closed her eyes. "Not at all."

"Liar," he said, his hands moving to the back of her neck.

She tossed her hair to one shoulder, giving him better access to her skin. "Okay, maybe seeing you out there is a little bit hot, but then, with these pregnancy hormones going crazy, I find the Chinese delivery guy hot these days."

"That's not nice. I can't compete with a guy bearing food."

"You could try," she whispered, opening her eyes.

Removing the ice pack from his cheek, he set it aside. "How have you been feeling?" he asked.

Her dark eyes met his. "About us?"

He wanted an answer to that, too, but right now, he was wondering about her. "With the pregnancy." He didn't know anything about these things, and he found himself wanting to know.

"I feel great. No morning sickness yet…" She looked away.

"What's wrong?"

She smiled but it seemed forced. "Nothing…just…things are complicated."

Understatement. But he was no longer afraid of complicated, and he wanted her to know that. Unfortunately, words and confessions of feelings weren't something he was good at. Maybe he could show her. Show her how he felt. Give her the reassurance she needed, not through his words, but by his actions. Only time would really prove his intentions anyway.

Shifting their bodies, he laid her on the couch, hovering on his side next to her. He brushed her hair away from her face, tucking several loose strands behind her ear. "You are so amazing," he said, letting his hand trail along the soft skin at her neck, then down across her chest, grazing lightly over the swell of her breasts visible above the cashmere. "Beautifully distracting…" He lowered his lips to her flesh where his hand had just been. "You can't come to the games anymore."

Taking his face in her hands, she lifted it to look at him. "Try to stop me." She pressed her lips to his and he shifted his weight to lie on top of her.

"Is this okay?"

She nodded. "More than okay." She ran her hands through his hair, love undeniable in her dark eyes. "I missed you while you were away."

He swallowed. He'd told her being on the road was one of the reasons he didn't believe in commitments…but while it had been hard being away, not having her to come back to would have been so much harder. "It'll get easier…We can make it work."

Her eyes widened and she opened her mouth to say something, but she kissed him instead.

All of the longing for her he'd felt in the last few days came immediately to the surface, and he returned her kiss—hard, desperate as though he needed her to feel everything he was. All the uncertainty, all the fear, all of the words he needed to say melted away in the passion of the moment.

Her fingers tangling in his hair, she held his mouth to hers. She needn't worry. He was going nowhere.

He couldn't remember the last time he'd made out on his couch. The same excitement and anticipation he'd had as a teenager about to get to second base surged through him, and his dick awakened from its semislumbering state. His tongue teased her bottom lip, and his teeth caught it. He bit gently.

She closed her eyes and moaned, arching her back so that there was no gap between their bodies as she gripped his shoulders.

His hands pressed against her hips, and he separated her legs with his. Settling himself between them, he felt his cock push against the fabric of his jeans. Jesus, he was already close. Kissing a woman was nothing new for him. Touching a woman, caressing her, seducing her had been part of his game for so long…but it was never like this. This time, he was the one getting played.

He knew it. He didn't care. He was too far gone.

He rocked himself against her and she moaned again, holding the back of his head to keep his mouth from leaving hers.

He couldn't drag his lips away even if he wanted to.

He slid his hands beneath her sweater, slowly moving upward until he felt the edge of her bra. God, he wished another wave of the sexual revolution would hit and women would burn these stupid things. All breasts deserved to be free, admired, and cherished. Especially hers. He forced his hands beneath the underwire and cupped the soft mounds, ignoring how the metal bit painfully into his flesh.

She laughed against his lips as she struggled to reach behind her back and unclasp the bra. "Better?"

"Much." He lowered himself further, sliding the sweater and the loose bra upward as he took a nipple in his mouth. The hard little bud was delicious, smelling like honey and tasting as sweet. He sucked gently at first, then more eagerly.

"Ben…Oh my God, Ben…I'm going to come just from you doing that. They weren't kidding about pregnancy sensitivity," she said.

"Trust me, I don't think it's the pregnancy," he murmured, sitting up slightly to display the full, hard erection. "Not unless I'm pregnant, too."

She grabbed his shoulders and pulled him back down on top of her, moving her hips up and down against him.

The friction between their thighs was going to put him

over the edge in no time. He couldn't remember the last time he'd come in his pants.

Her movements grew frantic, and her eyes closed as her head fell back. "Ben, I'm going to come, and I don't want to stop."

Coming in his pants it was.

He pushed his hips against her even more and began his own rhythmic rocking, his hands massaging her breasts as he pressed harder against her…faster…His breath was labored as he lowered his mouth to her ear. "I can't get enough of you, Olivia. You make me crazy for you…for your body…your mind…your heart…" He was spiraling out of control in so many ways. The emotions like a whirlwind through him, making him desperate for release.

Olivia moaned and clung to him. "Ben…Ben…" she whispered his name over and over.

"Come for me, baby," he murmured, biting her neck as he pinched her nipples.

A second later she cried out as her body shook slightly beneath him. She held her breath for a long second as release took over, and then she sighed, content and spent.

Opening her eyes, she smiled at him.

Fuck. Nothing else put him over the edge like that smile. The one she seemed to save just for him. The one he'd come to crave as much as he craved her body. He pushed a final time and shuddered as his own orgasm wiped all coherent thought from his mind and he went limp on top of her. "Damn," he muttered, feeling the wetness seep into the fabric at the front of his jeans.

She cradled his head into her chest and he glanced up at her. "Am I too heavy?"

"No," she whispered, hugging him tighter. "Don't go."

"Never," he said, kissing her gently. He waited for anxiety

to appear after making a promise he'd vowed he'd never make again, but he felt only a silent determination to prove to her that he planned to keep it.

* * *

Lying in his bed hours later watching the sun come up, Olivia rested her head against Ben's shoulder, loving the feel of his arm draped across her waist. In less than two hours, he had to be at the stadium for practice, she had to be in court, and neither of them had gotten a wink of sleep. She didn't care.

Being with him was a feeling unlike any she'd experienced. No other man had ever looked at her the way Ben did. No one else's touch had been both gentle yet passionate, comforting yet desperate. She was in love with him—smart or not, it no longer mattered. His words, or rather one simple word, the night before had sent her heart and hopes soaring. She knew she should keep her walls up, but he was making them come crashing down around her and she let them fall.

She no longer felt the empty, lonely void that had always been inside of her. With Ben, she felt like she had someone she could trust, someone she could count on…family.

She glanced at him to see if he was awake. He was, and he was staring out the window, a relaxed smile on his face. She didn't need an explanation for the look; she felt the exact same way.

Propping herself up on one elbow, she pulled the sheet around her chest and asked, "So, when did you realize that you could make it to the NHL?" She imagined it was the dream of many kids, but there had to be a moment of realization along the way, when a kid knew they either had the potential to make it to the big leagues or not. A moment when they either worked harder to achieve their goal or acknowledged it wasn't in their future.

"When I first picked up a hockey stick."

She shot him a look. "Even you're not *that* cocky."

He laughed, pulling her back toward him. "You're right." Taking her hand in his, he stared at their entwined fingers. "I don't know…I guess I started taking it seriously when I kept making the A list teams, and I felt like it wasn't fair to the other players who had to play against me. And I don't mean that to sound as arrogant as it does. I just mean, I wanted to be challenged, and I never really was."

"A natural-born athlete. Growing up, I hated people with your coordination."

He grinned. "When I made the Major Junior team, I was advised to get an agent, and that's when it hit me that this was real, that things were getting serious."

"Major Juniors—so you were still a teenager?"

He nodded. "Fifteen."

"An agent at fifteen—wow." She knew hockey was a competitive sport for these athletes and that a lot of their lives were devoted to it if they were serious about turning their passion into a career, but she hadn't realized how young it all started.

At fifteen, she was just trying to survive high school.

"Thank God for Peter, who's still my agent today. Being the oldest and the first one to go after a pro athlete career, my parents didn't know what to do to help me prepare for my future, so Peter's been invaluable, as were the Harrison family, who I went to live with."

"You were billeted?" Fifteen seemed so young to move away from home and give up friends and a familiar school, not to mention family. She knew how hard the transition had been on her when her parents died. Choosing it for his career must have been tough in a different way.

He nodded. "I had to decide if I wanted to take the Major Juniors path to the NHL or play college hockey once I graduated high school. Most guys were getting drafted through the Major Juniors, so that's the way I went."

"What did your parents think?" Ben was a success, and his choice had obviously been the right one, but she couldn't imagine how nerve-wracking it must have been for his parents—the gamble he was taking on his future.

"They were supportive. They were nervous. So was I," he said, giving her that rare glimpse into the vulnerable, real side of him, which was even more irresistible than the sexy, arrogant side.

"Are you nervous now?" she asked.

"In bed with you? No. Why? Should I be?" he teased.

She pinched his nipple. "In the playoffs, smartass."

"Ow!" He laughed, grabbing both her hands and holding them to his chest. "Nervous in a different way. This is more like a nervous energy. It comes mostly from the fans once I step out onto the ice. Before then, it just feels like another day doing what I love."

"But during the playoffs, there's more at stake."

"Absolutely."

She hesitated. "Is that why you…" How could she ask without offending him?

"Choke?"

"I heard a rumor," she said, wishing she hadn't brought it up.

He pulled her closer. "It's true. Both times I made it to the playoffs, my game went sideways, I couldn't get it back, and the team ended up out in the first and second rounds." He paused. "The first time was the month after my dad died and the second was the season Janelle left," he said quietly.

"Oh, Ben…"

"I let the stress in my personal life take over."

"And then this season—the divorce case…"

He nodded. "Didn't help." He hugged her tight to his chest, smoothing her hair away from her face. "But if it hadn't been for the case, I wouldn't have you."

She swallowed hard. He was saying all the right things, and her heart begged her to believe him, to not question it, but she was still terrified. She was so afraid of losing him now that she had what she'd always been searching for. "So, what's the big deal anyway?" she asked, changing the subject. "I mean, I get that every team wants to be considered the best in the league, but why is the cup so important anyway? It's just a big silver trophy."

He shot her a look that suggested she'd insulted his mother. "Watch it, lady."

She laughed. "Sorry. I know some people are crazy about it, and I find it odd, that's all." No doubt because she'd never been involved in competitive sports, she didn't quite get the insane dedication and determination some of these athletes possessed. "I had one client who tried to get her soon-to-be-ex-husband's personal day with the cup in her hometown instead of his, should his team win that year."

Ben's eyes widened. "What a bitch."

She laughed. "I talked her out of it," she said, pulling the bedsheet around her chest as she sat up. "Even *I* could see that was just being unreasonable and petty." She looked around the room for her clothes. As much as she hated to, she'd have to leave soon.

"You're a good woman," Ben said, pulling her back toward him.

She resisted. "I have to go."

"Not yet," he said.

She didn't need much convincing. With him was the only place she wanted to be. She rested her head back against his chest. "Okay, tell me more about this cup. Make me understand its power."

He stroked her bare arm as he spoke, and a tingling sensation coursed through her entire body at the simple, gentle caress. "That cup has been all over the world and has its fair share of experiences. It has dozens of superstitions associated with it, and some go as far as saying it could be cursed."

She turned her head to look at him. "Seriously?"

"Not shitting you. When Madison Square Garden's stadium mortgage was paid off years ago, the New York team managers and the building's owners held a mortgage-burning party. Rumor has it they burned the mortgage docs in the cup, and then supposedly several teammates peed in the cup as some weird celebratory gesture."

She wrinkled her nose. "Gross."

"Even worse, the team didn't win again for over forty years."

"Could have been just bad playing."

"Most likely, you're right. A lot of guys won't even touch our division trophy because they think it ruins our chances of winning the real thing. I don't believe in superstition, so I snapped a selfie with it when no one was looking."

She laughed. "A selfie? Really, Ben?"

Reaching across to the bedside table, he retrieved his phone, typed in his password, and flicked through several pics. He turned the phone toward her.

There he was, grinning while holding up the division trophy.

"You're crazy."

"Maybe. Just don't tell the guys."

"That you're crazy? Pretty sure they already know."

He tickled her waist. "About me touching it. If we lose, I'll never hear the end of it."

"Fine," she said, wiggling away from him. "So, will you get to take the cup home, if the team wins?"

"When. *When* the team wins, yes, I get a personal day with it. Jackson and Ash will love it, and my niece Taylor will take a dozen selfies with it. Of course the keeper of the cup will probably be photo-bombing in the background, but he's become part of hundreds of families now." He laughed.

"Keeper of the cup? Like a guy who babysits it?"

Ben nodded. "Twenty-four seven. Same guy now for decades. He keeps it safe."

"Safe? What could possibly happen to it?" she asked.

"Well, let's see—it's been kicked into Rideau Canal in Ottawa, left on the side of the road in a snowbank in Montreal when the team pulled over to change a tire on the way to the victory banquet, been taken to strip clubs…"

She raised an eyebrow.

"Not by me. Peed in…"

She wrinkled her nose again. So far that was still the worst.

"Thrown into Messier's pool, and recently it went to war."

She sat straighter. "It went overseas?"

He nodded. "To Afghanistan for the U.S. and Canadian troops."

"Wow. I didn't know it was such a morale booster."

"It is. The thing is actually pretty impressive up close. It takes the professional engraver over ten hours to put all of the names of the winning team's players on it."

"Wow."

"Maybe I'll even let you hold it once we win," he said with the grin she'd once found arrogant but had come to love.

Still, the urge to bring him down just a fraction of a peg was there. "Confident much?"

He pulled her closer, his intent gaze locked on hers. "We're only a few games away."

"What if you lose?"

"We won't."

"How do you know?" she whispered against his lips.

"I always get what I want."

"What do you want now, Ben?" All thoughts of leaving disappeared the longer she stayed, the tighter he held her, the stronger the connection between them grew. She was in trouble if Ben Westmore had a change of heart and decided he couldn't deliver on his promise of never leaving. So while he was in her arms, she would stay right where she was.

"I thought that was obvious, but if not..." He flipped them over so that his body hovered over hers. "Let me make it clear."

CHAPTER 21

❧

The Avalanche was now leading the series 3–2, but tonight's score hadn't even been close. Most times, fans are happier with close scoring games, back-and-forth leads between teams. The buildup of anticipation with the possibility that their team might lose made the victory all the more sweet. But the home crowd had been wild the entire game.

He removed his gloves, opened his locker, and wondered how much of it had to do with his time with Olivia. He'd never refrained from sex during playoffs, not believing in any of the customary superstitions. The only reason he grew his lame attempt at a playoff beard was to show solidarity with the team and his fans—and not be blamed for a Stanley Cup loss because he'd shaved. But he didn't believe any of it worked. Common sense suggested that every team would win, if that were as magical as it was given credit for. But there was no place for common sense in the hype of playoff hockey.

Either way, he'd never given up the pleasure of a woman's body, and what his teammates didn't know couldn't hurt their pregame psyche. But he knew it wasn't the sex that had put his mind at ease and made his body relax. Spending time with Olivia felt different. He felt different.

He shook his head, thinking about the time they'd spent together, picking out pregnancy books and bribing some kid with a new bike, a skating lesson that had been more of a battle of wills and each trying to outdo the other at a charity event. Not exactly his normal definition of fun, but with her, he'd probably consider watching the paint on his lake house dry to be the most fun he'd ever had on a date.

For the first time since Janelle, he found himself truly relaxed around a woman. Olivia was herself at all times—no pretenses, no bullshit—and it forced him to act the same. He didn't need to be Ben Westmore, the king of the ice, the MVP of the league, the charming playboy of the NHL. Those versions of him didn't impress her. So, with her, he got to be Ben. The guy who loved what he did. The guy who felt blessed to be able to be the best at something. The guy who was humbled by his family's complete failure to be awed by him.

He was in love with her. Didn't just crave her and her touch and those sexy-as-hell legs that had been wrapped around him the night before and into the early hours of morning...but her. His mouth went dry as he removed his sweat-drenched hockey gear and tossed it into the duffel bag.

He could sense her concern about them, and he couldn't wait to see her to continue reassuring her she had nothing to worry about.

"Hey, man, great game. Thanks for showing up," Owen said, coming out of the showers.

Ben averted his eyes quickly from his friend's dick. Another stupid superstition—air-drying after a win, so as not to wipe the winning mojo away. "Always," he said, grabbing a towel and his body wash and shampoo.

"Really though, you're playing better than ever. You were on fire out there tonight. Four goals. I don't know what's going on with you, but whatever or whoever it is, hold on to it."

Hold on to it. Hold on to her.

"Oh, and by the way," he said, pulling on underwear—the same ones he'd superstitiously worn for twelve days. "I want this series over in best of six…the pressure of a seventh game might kill me."

Ben shut the locker and patted his friend on the back as he passed him. "I'll do my best." Funny thing was, he wasn't scared of a game seven. This year that cup was his. This year, the cup and the girl were his.

Leaving the locker room, he took out his phone to text her. She hadn't made it to the game that evening, but he smiled seeing several texts from her, as she'd obviously watched the final period on television. Her newfound excitement for the sport warmed him—a future together would be a lot easier now that she was a converted fan. Opening the last text from her, he sent a reply.

Meet me at my place in twenty?

Already there.

He couldn't get home fast enough. He had a surprise for her. Glancing into his bag, he made sure he hadn't left the miniature-sized jersey he'd bought at the stadium pro shop in his locker. He couldn't believe they made hockey jerseys that small, and he'd had her last name put on the back, along with his number: 77. She was going to love it.

"Oh, Ben, thank God," he heard to his right as he passed the last set of doors before the players' exit.

Turning, he repressed a sigh. "Hey, Brittany. You're here late."

"Late night practice," she said, wincing as she took a tiny step toward him. "I think I sprained something." Her face contorted in pain as she tried to put her weight on the foot again.

"Better get it checked by the team's doctor before next game," he said, reaching into his pocket for his keys.

Brittany nodded, her blond ponytail bobbing. "I will...but...this is embarrassing to ask."

Right. As though the tiny cheerleader with the amazing rack he'd already examined up close would be embarrassed about anything. She hadn't seemed exactly shy the night they'd spent together three months ago. "What's up?" He glanced at the time on his phone. It was after ten, and he didn't want to keep Olivia waiting. He'd be flying to Boston the next day, and he wanted to spend as much time with her as possible.

"Could you possibly carry me to my car?"

Was she serious?

"You know, Derrick Marsh tore a ligament out there tonight and finished the game."

She cocked her head to the side, a look of annoyance on her face. "You're comparing me to you big boys?"

"I thought women had higher pain tolerances." Wasn't that what they were always claiming? Becky spouted it whenever either he or his brothers complained about legit injuries. He was stalling, but the last thing he wanted to do was carry the cheerleader anywhere. Especially this one.

"Come on, Ben. It really hurts." The whiny tone grated on his nerves.

Shit. "Fine." He shrugged his bag higher onto his shoulder, and walked toward her. Better get it over with and quick.

He already felt guilty about it, knowing Olivia was waiting for him.

He bent low and scooped her effortlessly—all one hundred pounds. Odd how he didn't find the tiny frame tempting anymore. Sure, she was in fantastic shape, and the aforementioned rack was doctor-enhanced, but compared to Olivia's soft curves and strong legs…He got hard just thinking about it, and the last thing he needed was for Brittany to mistake his semi-erect state as her doing. "Where are you parked?"

She looked embarrassed for real now. "Okay, so I lied before. I also kinda need a ride. My car's in the shop."

He sighed. "I really have somewhere else to be."

"I live like ten minutes away. East of downtown."

More like twenty minutes farther in the wrong direction. He hesitated. It was innocent enough, but would Olivia see it that way? She was expecting him in fifteen minutes. He was dying to get home to her.

"Ben, you're not honestly thinking about leaving me stranded are you?"

Yes.

"Everyone else has left already. Please, Ben."

"Owen's still here."

She shuddered. "That big furry thing hits on me at least eight times a game."

"Fine." He walked toward the players' exit, and headed out into the rain. Damn. This was not a good idea. He jogged toward the Hummer and handed her the keys.

She unlocked the vehicle and he lifted her into the passenger seat and slammed the door. Climbing behind the wheel, he took his phone from his pocket and, feeling guilty as shit, texted Olivia to say he would be late.

CHAPTER 22

~∞~

$\mathcal{H}$ow are you today?" Dr. Chelsey asked the next morning.

"Hoping to be pregnant," Olivia said with a nervous laugh. Since taking the home pregnancy test two weeks ago, she'd resisted the urge to take another one. Her lack of symptoms so far was starting to worry her, so she'd booked the appointment yesterday. Now, she was nervous. She wished Ben hadn't had to fly to Boston that day.

She brushed the thought away. She could do this on her own. After all, that had been her original plan.

Still, she'd feel better with him there.

The doctor smiled. "Well, we just have a few more minutes to wait."

The nurse had handed her a cup the moment she'd entered the clinic, and she'd been waiting to see Dr. Chelsey in the examination room for almost twenty minutes. "The at-home kits took less than thirty seconds to register. Come on, doc. You've got to have better technology than that," she said with a nervous laugh. She had expected him to have her results by now.

The doctor's face took on a slightly worried look. "You took more than one?"

She nodded. "I took two a couple weeks ago," she admitted, feeling slightly embarrassed by her eagerness. She just needed a real confirmation. Her period was now a week late, so her confidence had increased, but she needed to hear it from him.

"At the same time?"

"Yes. Why?"

"We recommend taking them a day apart for better accuracy, that's all. And results that early in the process are less accurate."

"Oh." Her chest tightened.

"And it was morning when you tested? First pee?"

She shook her head. "Evening. Had to struggle for even a drop." She bit her lip. "I'm starting to feel as though I failed a test I thought I'd aced."

He gave a reassuring pat on her shoulder, which actually just made her feel worse. "Don't worry. We'll know in"—he checked his watch—"twenty seconds. I'll be right back."

She swallowed hard as he left the room. Morning pee, first pee—she'd had no idea there were different types of pee. Maybe she should have read the instructions on the box after all. She forced a deep breath. She wouldn't worry until there was something to worry about. She just needed to be positive.

She reached for her phone and reread the text from Ben—the last one he'd sent before boarding his flight to Boston.

Try not to worry. Everything will be fine. Wish I could be there with you. I'll call as soon as I land.

She clutched the phone in her hand. Ben was right. Everything was going to be fine.

But fifteen minutes and still no doctor later, her attempt at staying positive was fading faster than a summer tan in winter. She reread the charts on the wall—the ones outlining the stages of pregnancy—and she leafed through the parenting magazines on the table. She started to pull up the email app on her phone, but decided the emails would only stress her out and put the phone away.

Feeling faint and slightly nauseous, she lay on the examination table and closed her eyes. Everything would be fine. She pressed a hand to her stomach, hoping that the absence of any physical signs to date—no cravings, no sickness, no breast tenderness—were not indicators. It was just too early maybe…Or maybe she'd be one of those lucky women who didn't experience morning sickness…Or maybe…She stopped. She couldn't keep stressing herself out. If she was pregnant, the stress could affect the baby's brain development. Ben had told her that.

Unexpected tears sprang to her eyes at the thought of him. Thank God his season was almost over. If she missed him this much now and longed for him to be a part of all of this, she could only imagine how tough it would be later in her pregnancy. Anxiety made it harder to breathe as she thought about what he'd said about his career taking a toll on relationships and families. All of the marriages she'd watched dissolve in part because of the pro athlete lifestyle flashed in her mind, making her stress levels rise.

She forced the negative thoughts away. It could be different for them. It would be. She trusted in him. Trusted in what they had.

The door opened and she sat up, blinking away the emotions.

The look on the doctor's face told her the news wasn't what she'd been hoping for.

"I'm not pregnant, am I?"

"I'm sorry, Olivia. We ran the tests three times. The level of hCG was high in your sample, which was what triggered the positive reading on the home tests. I was a little concerned when they read positive so soon in your cycle."

She nodded. Not pregnant. The in vitro attempt had failed.

The doctor handed her a tissue before she felt the wetness on her cheeks. She took it silently and wiped the tears away, then she sat up straighter. "Okay, well, what's next?"

"We have to wait at least two months to try again. Give the body more time on the hormone injections, and then we can use the eggs from the last extraction, so it's one less step in the process."

One less step in the process, but waiting two months seemed like forever. Having her hopes lifted only to have them crash made it difficult to be patient. And the idea that in two months, she'd have to go through this again…She knew for sure she wouldn't be taking a home pregnancy test early next time. Better to wait to hear it from Dr. Chelsey. "What if it doesn't work again?" She hated to let the negative thought slip past her lips, but there was the possibility of another failed attempt.

"We'll cross that bridge if we come to it," the doctor said, touching her hand.

Leaving the clinic twenty minutes later, she wasn't sure how she felt. She'd been nervous, but so excited about the baby, and now she was disappointed and conflicted. But not as much as she would have thought. Being with Ben gave her another option—one she'd given up hope on. He'd wanted to be there for her and the child she'd thought she was carrying. Would he want to have one with her? She released a sigh. It was far too early in the relationship to be thinking about that, but…

Everything will be fine.

Maybe Ben was right. In fact, maybe this was for the best. Things were going great between them, there was no reason to think that she couldn't have the family she wanted—a different way. She'd been ready and willing to do it alone, but that was before Ben. Before she'd fallen in love.

Feeling a little better, she drove to her office, arriving just in time for her first appointment that afternoon. "Hi, Madison. Just give me a minute and then send Mrs. Dawar in, please."

"Okay…" Madison said, looking concerned. "You're coffee is on your desk…along with something I think you should see," she said, a sympathetic expression on her face.

Olivia's heart fell to her stomach as she went inside her office. Next to her coffee sat a copy of that day's *Entertainment Digest*—the daily celebrity gossip rag. Picking it up, her hand trembled slightly as she saw a picture of Ben taken the night before, carrying a beautiful blond woman to his Hummer in the stadium parking lot.

Her stomach turned, and she couldn't blame the urge to throw up on morning sickness.

NHL'S PLAYBOY BACK IN THE GAME.

Inside were several other shots of Ben, images of him with different women—one at a basketball game, another kissing at a night club, and another getting yogurt at a Menchie's. She tried to swallow the lump in her throat, but it refused to budge.

She'd been a fool. She stared at the pictures of Ben and the string of beautiful women, her eyes filling with tears when she glanced back at the one on the cover. This was why he'd been late. He'd lied to her…about everything. And she'd fallen for every word.

* * *

Two days of unanswered calls and texts were driving him crazy. In his gut, Ben knew Olivia had seen that ill-timed paparazzi shot, but she needed to give him a chance to explain. Being in Boston for game six had left him at the mercy of her answering machine, and the stress of not being able to reach her had completely thrown him off his game. The team had lost four to one, but the only thing on his mind was getting back to Colorado. Back to Olivia.

Being the victim of a paparazzi incident herself, he hoped she would understand a picture often told a different story. Though it certainly hadn't been the case for them. That photo had captured what was happening between them perfectly.

Or what *had* been happening.

He needed to talk to her. He had to explain the photo of him and Brittany, but most of all he needed to hear her voice, see her smile, hold her…If he thought his obsession had driven him crazy before, it was nothing compared to the longing and unease not hearing from her had evoked. He knew the feelings he had for her were torturously real, and he feared the walls around his heart had shattered. He'd let her in. And he was terrified, but he was willing to fight for a chance with her, if she'd have him.

Pressing the buzzer on her apartment building ten minutes later, the door clicked immediately.

Was she expecting someone else?

The thought spiraled into an out-of-control mess until his anxiety had him fuming by the time he reached her door.

Was that the reason she was ignoring him? She was seeing someone else?

Being the recipient of his own customary behavior made him nauseous.

He knocked and placed his hands on his hips. Then he folded his arms across his chest. Then let them drop to his sides as he paced in front of the door.

"Coming," she said from the other side.

When she swung it open, her look of surprise was like looking in a mirror.

If she were in fact expecting a date, she hadn't gone out of her way to get ready: Winnie-the-Pooh PJ pants and a yellow tank top, her hair piled high on her head. "Ben?"

"Expecting someone else?" he asked, though the edge in his voice wasn't there.

"Chinese food delivery," she said, blocking his entrance. "What are you doing here?" Her attempt to hide herself behind the door failed, and the sight of her nipples poking through the thin fabric of the shirt made his dick and annoyance rise simultaneously.

"You were going to answer the door to a strange delivery person like that?" He gestured to her chest.

"What? As if Gino cares if I'm in pajamas," she said.

"That's not what I was referring to." She knew the delivery guy by name. A pang of jealousy hit him. "Can I come in?"

"I don't think that's such a great idea."

"You've been avoiding me for days, and we need to talk."

"There's nothing to talk about. The picture in *Entertainment Digest* was pretty loud and clear."

"That picture was bullshit. Nothing happened between Brittany and me." She tried to close the door again, but he held it open. "She hurt her ankle and needed a ride home."

"Adding knight in shining armor to your resume now?"

He released a deep breath. Damn, why hadn't he just called Brittany a cab? Even though the situation was exactly the way he said it was, what credibility did he have when his past was full of paparazzi shots like that one? Olivia had every right not to believe him, and for the first time, he was desperate to prove his innocence. "I just wanted to drop her off and get home to you that night."

"Why didn't you tell me the reason you were running late?"

The hurt in her voice killed him. He ran a hand through his hair. "I should have. You're right. I guess I just didn't think you'd trust me."

"I don't."

The words were a shot to his stomach. "Really? Still? Haven't I proved myself? Proved that I've changed?"

She looked away.

"Olivia, I wouldn't lie to you. She hurt her ankle and needed a ride." He would only say it once more. If she still chose to believe the image in the magazine, it was out of his control. She would always choose to believe the image in the magazine, and a relationship would be doomed from the start.

She sighed. "Okay. Is that all?"

Not even close. "Please, Olivia." He didn't recognize the pleading in his own voice. He needed another chance, and he wasn't about to let his pride get in the way of asking for one.

Her expression was full of hurt and disappointment when her gaze met his. "Ben, we both know this won't work. Your career is practically designed for you to be unfaithful, and I'm not interested in being another woman on the list of women who were dumb enough to think they could be the one to get you to settle down."

"Please, just trust in me. Trust in what we have." She couldn't honestly believe that everything between them had been fake. That it had all just been an act. She knew him better than that. She knew *him*.

Her internal struggle was evident in her eyes. "You should go now," she said, tears in her voice.

The sound broke his heart. "So, that's it for us then?"

Folding her arms across her chest, she nodded. "There was never an *us*, Ben."

He took a step toward her. "I disagree. For the first time in my life I've been terrified. Completely and utterly terrified. Terrified of how I was starting to feel for you, but worse, terrified that those feelings wouldn't fade."

She couldn't mask the hurt that reflected in her eyes. "See, you never intended for this to get serious."

He took her hands. "You're right. I didn't. And I won't lie about that. But it did get serious. And what scares me most is that I feel like I'm losing you, and I'm too far gone to save myself from the heartache waiting outside that door if you push me away right now."

She swallowed hard.

"Olivia, please." Begging was a foreign concept to him. He hadn't even tried to convince Janelle not to walk away, to give their life together a chance. But no one, not even the woman he had believed was the love of his life, had ever come close to being worth the effort, the sacrifice, the setting aside of his pride.

Olivia looked away.

He knew why. Staring into his eyes made it difficult to think, to breathe, to say the word *go*. He knew because he'd never find the strength to walk away while looking into hers.

"I need you to leave, Ben," she whispered.

In that moment, he felt the ground beneath him start to

give way and emotions threatened to tear him apart. He couldn't argue with her anymore even if he wanted to—the pain and disappointment already too much for his once unbreakable heart.

He released her hands and opened her apartment door. "Bye, Olivia," he managed to say before walking out.

CHAPTER 23

*C*arrying what felt like the millionth box of baby clothes from the back of his brother's truck to the shop, Ben's entire body ached. The hit he took in the game the other night resonated everywhere. Tomorrow was game seven in the series—the Stanley Cup finals game—and yet here he was in Glenwood Falls, carrying boxes of new clothing into his sister's store.

"Over there, please." Becky pointed to the far right of the store, where Jackson was hanging shelves on the wall.

"You know you could hire people to do this shit for you, right?" He knew it had been a mistake to let his family know he was at the lake house on his day off—his recovery day. He'd been craving a quiet place to regroup, to mentally prepare for the game of his career. This was not what he'd had in mind.

"Well, once my shop starts bringing in money, I'll consider that option. For now I have my little brother minions," Becky said with a laugh.

"This does not constitute an emergency by the way," Asher grumbled, moving past them into the back room.

Becky rolled her eyes. "Come on! You were finished playing for the season already—quit complaining." She turned to Ben and pointed a finger at him. "And you should be thanking me."

"Do explain." He set the boxes in the back storage room and wiped sweat from his head with his forearm.

"You have a crazy important game to win tomorrow night. The pressure you're feeling must be huge—monumental, even." She reached above her head and grabbed several of the tiniest shoe boxes he'd ever seen.

It reminded him of Olivia and the tiny shoes she'd be needing. Being in the shop was annoying for several reasons—the biggest was the constant reminder that the woman he was falling in love with was having a baby, and she was pushing him away when all he wanted was to be there for her. With her.

"I mean this game could make you a legend around here…"

"Becky!"

"Okay, okay. The point is, I'm helping you relax your mind with physical labor." She shrugged, handing him an armful of baby girl dresses.

"What the hell do you think playing hockey is—meditation?" He followed her to the front of the store. "Where do you want these?" he asked with a sigh. He was there now. There was no getting out of helping her. The faster he could get this done, the faster he could be alone at the lake house…where another reminder of Olivia would haunt and torment his thoughts. God, he hoped the smell of her perfume had faded from his couch cushions faster than she was fading from his heart.

"They need to be hung up on that rolling rack near the window," she said, pointing the way.

She followed him with an armful of hangers—tiny pink ones. He wondered if Olivia knew they made hangers this small. He absently reached for the dress on top, but Becky snatched it away.

"Not that one. I'm holding it for someone," she said.

That look on her face was suspicious. His eyes narrowed. "Who?"

"Baby Chic client confidentiality."

"That's not a thing."

"Yes, it is."

He reached for the dress again. Olivia had mentioned she'd been in Becky's store, and his sister was about as good at keeping things from him as she was at doing her own freaking work. "Olivia wants this dress?" He touched the sunflower in the center of the soft fabric. So tiny. He'd never believe a real human baby could fit inside had he not seen it firsthand with two nieces. In eight months, the woman he loved would have a tiny little human…Alone. And he wouldn't be there for her. Because she didn't want him to be.

He was a complete asshole. It wasn't as though she hadn't warned him. Told him about the process, begged him to stay away, to not hurt her by pretending this was something he could handle, warning him that this was something she intended to do alone…

Damn. He should have listened.

"Ben!" his sister shouted.

"What?"

"I said *you* could give it to her. I mean, if in fact the dress is being held for her," she added quickly.

Could he? He already had the tiny jersey hung in his locker at the stadium—he'd forgotten to give it to her the night he'd bought it, and it was currently serving as another form of torture. He didn't need any more. He shook his head, setting the dress aside. "No. And you really suck at client confidentiality," he said, before abandoning his post and heading out of the store.

He was heartbroken, and he had the game of his career in less than twenty-four hours. His family would have to forgive him just this once.

* * *

The television paused on the hockey game taunted her from the living room as Olivia prepared a salad for dinner. She took a sip of wine and sighed.

Just because she couldn't be with Ben didn't mean she couldn't watch the game. She could be a hockey fan if she wanted to. The series between the two teams had been electric, and it was all down to this final game. She wasn't sure she could watch.

Knowing how much this win meant to Ben made her heart race. She wondered if things between them ending the way they did would affect him? Affect his game? Would she be to blame if he choked a third time in the NHL playoffs?

She could watch it. She could be just an impartial fan hoping for a win, right?

God, she was completely delusional.

Going into the living room, she hit Play on the remote and tucked her legs beneath her as the game started.

Ben Westmore—MVP of the NHL and holder of her heart—had a big job to do. She hoped he could pull off the win.

Tears blurred her vision as she watched. She missed him. Missed the feeling of home he'd given her. Everything she'd always wanted had been within reach. Would she ever have that again?

*   *   *

The puck left the blade of his stick with a purpose, a destination heading straight for its target. Ben held his breath along with all of the Colorado Avalanche fans in the packed stadium now on their feet.

A pin drop could be heard as time stood still. The only person moving on or off the ice was the Boston goalie as his body shifted left and right, trying to determine where the puck would go.

Like watching a slow-motion film, Ben could see every inch the puck traveled through the air, the looks of determination and then the oh-shit expressions forming on the opposing players' faces. His skates pushed forward, following the puck toward the win.

He saw the goalie's body leave the ice as he lunged to block the shot heading straight toward the top left corner of the net.

Three seconds ticked away on the clock, three lifetimes… Ben waited to see if he'd just scored the winning goal for the Stanley Cup in the first overtime shoot-out.

The buzzer sounded and the green light illuminated behind the net. His legs gave way as a deafening roar filled the stadium. His teammates dog-piled him a second later, whooping and hollering, gloves and sticks flying into the air, helmets being tossed onto the ice.

They'd won.

He'd led his team to a victory. Scoring four of the five goals, there was no question in his mind that he'd done what he'd set out to do—dominate and win and make sure he let no one down—especially himself.

He scrambled to his feet within the sea of players and looked toward the stands. His family celebrated in the seats behind the home team's bench. His mother and Asher were hugging. Jackson and Abby were kissing—figures; they'd use any excuse to make out. His niece Taylor and Abby's daughter, Dani, were already dragging Emma, Asher's best friend, through the stands, obviously planning to weasel their way into the locker room for autographs and a close-up glimpse of the cup. Fans were still on their feet cheering—a chant of "Westmore!" filling the sold-out arena—and a small smile formed on his lips as emotion welled in his chest. He was happy he could bring this moment to the fans, to his family, to his teammates and coaches, to himself…but the one empty seat in the crowd was the only thing he saw.

* * *

"Water? Are you serious, man? Of everyone here, you should be celebrating the hardest."

Ben smiled as his buddy sat in the chair next to him the following evening. "You do remember what happened the last time I drank, right?"

Owen loosened his tie and rolled the sleeves of his dress shirt, revealing two full tattoo sleeves. After the game, he'd gone to a tattoo shop to have an image of the cup added to the eclectic group of designs that he swore meant something. He'd tried to convince Ben to join him in the celebratory tat, but he'd declined. The cup meant a lot to him, and three months ago, he might have. Now, suddenly he knew what he was missing in life and the reality that his career—this fast and crazy lifestyle—was going to leave him behind some day made his victory bittersweet.

Wow, he was depressing the hell out of himself with

these thoughts. Maybe he *could* use a drink. Though the star player and MVP drowning his sorrows at a party to celebrate his hard-earned win was one cliché he didn't want a part of.

"You know, it could be argued that, hadn't you gotten completely wasted, gotten married, and gone through this divorce, you'd never have met Olivia," Owen said, taking a swig of his beer.

"And that would have been a bad thing?" he mumbled. Could he just get through one day without someone mentioning her?

He didn't need to hear her name to trigger thoughts of her. What he needed was to get hit so hard, he'd suffer memory loss complete enough to forget her. Even five minutes of not having her on his mind would be a gift. He felt as though he were walking in a haze. He'd surprised the hell out of himself with the game seven win because while his body had played on autopilot, his mind and heart certainly hadn't been there.

"Look, I know the situation with her is complicated."

Ben looked away. Allowing his friend to assume that once again it had been Ben to end things at the first sign of commitment had been the only thing he could do—a self-preservation thing. Admitting he was ready to put his playboy days behind him and get serious with a woman would have been met with disbelief anyway.

Owen leaned forward, resting his elbows on his knees. "So, maybe you don't tell the future grandkids how you met…" He shrugged. "But you will never find someone else better for you."

He knew that. That's why he was dying inside. He'd been willing to put it all on the line for Olivia. It had been worth it. She had been worth it. Ben nodded to the beer in Owen's hand. "How many of those have you had?" The mention of future grandkids was making his jaw clench. *Her* grandkids. Any she had would be hers and a sperm donor's. And he would no longer be there to support her through it. To be a part of the child's life.

The fact that he'd wanted to be had never been so vividly clear as it was now that the opportunity had been taken away.

Looking around the room at the players with their wives, girlfriends, dates, his chest tightened. He wished Olivia was there with him. Celebrating this win. Celebrating them. Every part of him missed everything about her.

"I'm not drunk. I'm your best friend. And I have never seen you so completely torn up. The best night of your career, and you're sitting here realizing none of this shit matters—that's love, my friend," he said, pointing a finger at him.

Love. He'd thought it was love once and it hadn't even been close. Loving Olivia had taught him that there were different levels of love. Some left pain when it ended and, with it, a reluctance to ever put a heart on the line again—like Janelle. Others left an aching longing to feel it again, a desperation to once more feel so alive…that was the kind of damage Olivia left.

Lifting his eyes from his perspiring water glass, Ben's heart nearly stopped. "Oh no." He looked around for an escape, but it was too late. "How did she get in?" Sure, she'd dropped the case and signed the divorce papers, but that didn't make him happy to see Kristina Sullivan walking into the room.

"I invited her," Owen said.

"You what?"

He shrugged. "When Sanders said that she'd signed the papers, I kinda looked her up on Facebook."

His friend really was insane. "And she agreed to go out with you?" Ten minutes after divorcing him?

•

"Not entirely. I just invited her here. She said she was hoping to talk to you, but I'm hoping she'll consider leaving with me." He winked.

Ben shot his friend a look. "Careful with this one, man. She's complicated."

Owen grinned. "What woman isn't?"

His friend had a point.

"Hi, Ben," Kristina said, stopping at their table.

Dressed in a long, green sequined gown, light hair loose around her shoulders, she looked beautiful.

"You look hot," Owen said next to him.

No wonder his buddy had trouble with the ladies.

But Kristina blushed as she smiled and accepted the compliment. "Thank you for inviting me. This is pretty exciting. Congrats on the win, Ben."

She looked nervous, so he extended a hand. "Thank you for allowing me the first win. It may have helped fuel the fire for last night's victory."

"So, I *should* have gone after money in the divorce," she said, but her tone was teasing and her gaze held a hint of nervousness.

"You do look pretty," he said, relaxing.

"Thank you." She toyed with the clasp on her clutch in the awkward silence that followed, made even more awkward by Owen's openly admiring gaze on her. "Can we talk for a second?"

"As long as we don't end up married again, sure." He stood and led the way to a quieter section of the five-star hotel's banquet room.

"I'll be right here," Owen called after them.

She laughed. "Is he always this obvious?"

"I think the word you're looking for is *desperate*." Ben glanced over his shoulder where his buddy was using the reflection of the centerpiece vase to check his hair. "He's a good guy, though. You're in safe hands tonight."

She nodded. "Speaking of good guys, Brandon told me what you did for him, so I wanted to thank you."

"I hope I was able to help." Giving her what she wanted had obviously been what had changed her mind about signing the papers, but it didn't matter anymore.

"You did. The coach was impressed by his letter and his actions. He invited him personally to try out for the team again next year."

"No go for this year, huh?" That was too bad. The kid was a fantastic player.

She shook her head. "But I think it's for the best, you know? A year in the anger management group will help him work through some issues and make him that much better next time."

He nodded. She was right. If the kid could learn to control his emotions, he'd be unstoppable the following year. "He's a great hockey player. A bit of a smartass."

She grinned. "He comes by that honestly." She blushed. "He told me he called you Dad."

"Yes, he did." Ben laughed. It was actually a little funny *now*. "And I'll have you know, I was a pretty damn good one for all of three minutes."

"I'm sure you'll make a great one someday."

This conversation wasn't helping his mood. He'd been ready to be one to Olivia's baby. He'd been ready to be so much for her.

He cleared his throat. "Well, I'm glad it's working out. Don't doubt for a second his abilities on the ice. He can go pro if he can get that temper in check, and if there's anything I can do…"

"Thanks, Ben."

"Thank you for signing those papers." He hugged her quickly in a one arm squeeze that didn't feel as awkward as he thought it would. "They'll be bringing out the cup in a minute. Are you planning to stick around?" He nodded toward Owen. "I think you'll break his heart if you don't."

She nodded. "Yeah, I'll stay for a while."

"Great. Have fun," he said, heading toward the front of the room, where the other players waited to hoist the cup for photos.

"Hey, Ben," she called behind him.

He turned.

"Where's Olivia?"

He shook his head as he tried to shrug nonchalantly. "Wasn't meant to be," he said. "What can I say? Once a player…" He winked, then turned quickly, feeling the lie strangle him.

The cup was carried out—full of the customary Champagne—and the players gathered around. Coach Bencik waved him over. He'd be the one to drink from it first. It was tradition, and no one was breaking tradition.

Joining his teammates, he forced himself to push everything aside and celebrate the win. After all, the only thing he'd thought mattered was the only thing he had left.

CHAPTER 24

The Grumpy Stump was at maximum capacity. Everyone in town had shown up to see him—or rather, the Stanley Cup.

From where he sat in a booth with his family, he could barely see it near the bar, surrounded by Glenwood Falls residents taking the best selfies they could.

"So, that guy over there just follows the cup around?" Emma asked, sitting across from him.

"Hence the title keeper of the cup," Asher told her.

"I thought you were fucking with me when you said the cup had a babysitter."

"Nope. Guy's held the job for years," Jackson said, slipping an arm around Abby.

"Almost three hundred days a year, he travels with it," Asher said.

"Must be difficult to have a life," Becky said, her arms wrapped around Neil, standing next to the booth. His brother-in-law had gotten back from overseas the day before, and the two hadn't taken their eyes or hands off of one another all day.

Did they all have to look so cozy and nauseatingly happy? Ben took a swig of his beer and tried to look anywhere else. Being surrounded by the couples was proving overbearing. Everyone else had someone to celebrate his win with, except him.

"I was thinking, what a great life," Emma said. "I mean, hanging out with hockey players would get old pretty quick, though."

Asher punched her arm. "You've put up with *us* long enough."

She laughed and it turned into a yawn. "Actually, you're right. I should call it a night. I'm opening the clinic early tomorrow morning for a session before the patient goes to work."

Emma had been a professional snowboarder, but now she was a physical therapist in town. Ben didn't know the details, but he knew an injury had put her Olympic dreams on ice. Though compared to most athletes with their futures derailed, she seemed to be adjusting well to her new life path.

He had no idea what the deal was with her and Ash, but even his baby brother seemed to have a constant in his life.

Would he ever have that? Twice in a lifetime suffering through this heartache was probably his limit. He'd taken a risk putting himself out there again. He wouldn't be in any rush to try a third time.

Emma stood and gathered her things. "Congrats again, Ben. Well deserved."

He nodded his thanks.

"Hey! I thought you said I was your favorite player," Asher said as he stood.

Emma shrugged. "I'm a bandwagon jumper," she said with

a grin. "Goodnight everyone." Turning to Asher, she added, "You sure you can be apart from the cup long enough to drive me home?"

"Don't worry. I'll have her all to myself next year, and I'll be spending my day alone with her, not bringing her to some small-town bar to be molested like that," he said, nodding to the group of men posing for a pic, their lips pressed to whatever free spot on the cup they could find.

"You can certainly try, baby brother," Ben said. He'd welcome the challenge of taking on his brother in the Stanley Cup finals. They'd been so close this year. Though watching him walk out of the bar, he frowned. The injury from the World Championship game seemed to still be causing him to limp slightly.

"What's the deal with those two?" Abby asked in a hush. "I've been trying to figure it out all night."

"Deal with Ash and Emma?" Jackson asked, pulling her close.

"No deal," Ben said. "Best friends for as long as I can remember."

Abby shot him a look that suggested he was the dumbest man on the planet. "I'm calling bullshit. You don't see the chemistry between them?"

Jackson laughed. "Just because you've fallen for the Westmore charm doesn't mean everyone has."

Abby raised one eyebrow, and his brother nearly choked on his beer.

"The boys are right this time, Abby," Becky said.

"Yeah, I don't see it either," Neil chimed in.

"You're all wrong," Abby said. "I may have been wrong about Ben and Olivia, but I'm right about those two."

Ben shifted. One night without someone saying her name. That's all he asked for. The problem was Abby *hadn't* been wrong. She'd been painfully right. "I'll be right back. Jackson, make sure someone doesn't knock out the keeper and steal my trophy, okay?" he said, climbing out of the booth.

"I can't promise *I* won't," Jackson said. "It's the closest I'm getting to it." The longing in his voice was so faint only Ben could detect it. But when he moved closer to Abby and she giggled at something he whispered in her ear, he knew his brother would give up a hundred Stanley Cup wins for the woman and the life they had now.

He swallowed hard, jealousy and longing making him irritated.

In the hallway near the bathroom a moment later, he checked his phone. Fifty-six new text messages. He wasn't surprised. He'd heard the phone chime above the noise inside the bar all evening, but the tone had never been the Olivia-assigned one, so he'd ignored them.

She had to know they'd won the cup. In a few short weeks, she'd become as fan crazy as anyone else. She had to have watched the game.

Yet silence? No congrats even? That was just rude.

He should totally call her out on it.

He scrolled through the contact list to her name and picture and hesitated, staring at her smiling face.

God, he missed her.

"Time's up, Westmore," the keeper of the cup said, swinging open the bathroom door.

"Already?" he asked, tucking the phone into his pocket.

"Ten o'clock." The man tapped his watch.

The rules were clear: twelve hours, no more, no less, with each player. His time with the cup had flown by. They'd brought it to the stadium, where all of the Junior leaguers got a chance to see it, then the sports store, where he'd signed autographs and posed for photos with fans, then the bar. "Okay." He looked past him and saw Ash reenter the bar. Thank God. If the cup had left without him saying goodbye, his brother might actually cry. "Let's just let Ash hold it one more time."

"Fine. Two more minutes. I have to be on a plane at six a.m."

"Where you headed next?"

"Florida."

"Jimmy Miller?"

He nodded.

"Doesn't it get old, man? Babysitting this thing?" Becky was right. What kind of life was the guy supposed to have, traveling all over the world, staying in each place for less than forty-eight hours? Three hundred days a year? Even the players got a better break than that.

Before the man could answer, several women approached. Great. "Hey, ladies, we were just…" he started, but they ignored him. Their attention was on the keeper.

That was a first.

He stood back and watched the man flirt and laugh with the gorgeous blondes. After he collected their phone numbers for the "next time he was in town," he turned to look at Ben. "You were asking if it got old?"

"I retract the question."

Ten minutes later, after peeling the cup out of Asher's hands, Ben unlocked the Hummer and climbed in behind the wheel. Once he dropped the keeper off at his hotel, he planned on spending the night and the next few days at the lake house before returning to the city, where he would meet with press and his coaches to discuss the season and make plans for the next. October would be there again before he knew it.

Which was good. He'd been looking forward to the

break, but now, the thought of all that free time on his hands, on his mind…He hit the button to start the engine as the keeper climbed in with the cup.

"This looks a little small for you, and it's not really your color," the guy said, holding up a tiny dress.

Ben's chest tightened. The dress from his sister's shop—the one Olivia wanted. He was going to strangle Becky. "Just a cruel joke," he said, putting the dress on the dash and backing out of the parking space.

"So? How does it feel to have it all?" the keeper asked.

How does it feel to have it all? To anyone on the outside looking in, it must appear that he did. Yet, the big gaping hole in his heart knew better. But he'd tried. He'd put himself out there, risked it all, and she'd denied him.

His gaze fell on the dress. She should at least have it. He glanced at the cup. For many, it was a sign of victory; for others, a sign of hope. Could it be both once more for him? Man, he was reaching, but fuck it. "Hey, do you think we could extend my time just a little bit longer." Hell, if the cup worked for this guy, maybe it could work for him.

It was worth a shot. What did he have to lose by making one more play for the woman he loved?

"Oh, I don't know…" the guy hesitated, checking his watch.

Ben turned the car onto Main Street, heading toward the highway exit. "You wanted to know how it feels to have it all? Do this for me and let me find out."

*   *   *

Was there anything else on television the week after a Stanley Cup victory?

Each station somehow found a way to talk about the Avalanche's win. Had it always been like this, or was she just overly sensitive to it this year in her attempt to avoid seeing Ben's face everywhere?

Including her intercom monitor when her door buzzer rang at almost midnight. "Ben?"

"Hi."

The sight of him had Olivia's heart pounding in her chest and her palms sweaty. What was he doing there? A week without a word from him had felt like an eternity. She'd expected each day to get a little better time healed, right? Apparently not in her case. She just missed him more and more. And now he was here. She swallowed a lump in her throat. "What do you want?"

"Can I come up?"

Yes! "No."

"Look, I won't stay long, I just thought you might like to see…the Stanley Cup," he said, grabbing it from someone standing next to him and holding it up to the monitor.

"Who's with you?" Had he brought the whole Colorado Avalanche team as reinforcements?

"The keeper of the cup," he said, his face reappearing on the screen. "And he's got me on the clock. I have literally four minutes left. Please let me come up."

God, could she really come face-to-face with him and not give in to the urge to climb into his arms and forgive him for hurting her? Could she really say goodbye to him again?

"Olivia, please."

She was so screwed. She sighed as she hit the button.

"Thank you," he said before opening the door and entering the building.

Going to the door, she opened it and leaned against the doorframe to wait. She wouldn't allow him inside. Whatever he wanted to say so badly, he could do it in the hallway. She had nothing more to say. Her heart apparently disagreed as he appeared at the end of the hall and the sight of him buck-led her knees.

Stay strong.

The guy next to him was barely visible behind the Stanley Cup he carried as they made their way toward her, but she wasn't looking at him or the shiny metal trophy anyway.

Dressed in a pair of jeans and dark blue sweater that brought out the color of his eyes, Ben looked far too amazing to resist.

Stay strong.

The pep talk wasn't working. She could feel her resolve melting away.

"Hi," Ben said, stopping at her door.

She cleared her throat. "You're right. It is impressive." She folded her arms across her trembling body, as she kept her gaze locked on the cup. Safer. The only hope she had of surviving this.

His was locked on her. "God, I've missed you."

Tears threatened, and she shook the emotions away. "Should I take a selfie with it or something? Then you'll leave?"

He reached into his bag and pulled out the dress she'd fallen in love with at Becky's shop weeks before. Her mouth gaped.

"Becky gave me this for you." He handed it to her.

She took the dress, unable to speak without tears escaping. How did she tell him that she wasn't sure she'd ever have a little girl to wear it? The stress of the previous weeks made it hard to fight back the overwhelming emotions bubbling up inside of her. "Ben, I…"

"And, just in case it's a boy…" He interrupted, producing the tiniest jersey she'd ever seen. Turning it around, she saw the name Davis and a number 77 on the back. Her name. His number.

She sighed, accepting the jersey. She opened her mouth to speak but closed it again.

"Look, Olivia. I know you don't trust me, but I swear to you, nothing happened that night. I drove her home, and I hurried to be with you."

She wanted so badly to believe him. If she was honest with herself, she already did.

"I want to be there for you. And not just for the pregnancy. For everything. I want to be with you. I love you."

Her head snapped up, his words helping to erase the dull aching in her heart. He loved her? They'd never said it before, but she'd felt it. And she knew she loved him. "But…" She hesitated, glancing at the stranger, holding the cup next to him, looking uncomfortable by their show of emotions. "This is probably not the best time to talk…"

Taking her hands, Ben stepped into her apartment and closed the door. "Please, just hear me out."

Her eyes widened as she pointed to the door. "You just left that guy out there," she said, not ready to talk to him. Terrified that what he had to say might make her forget all of the reasons being together was a bad idea.

He opened the door and tossed the guy the keys to his Hummer. "I'll pick her up from the airport. Thanks, man." Closing the door, he took her shoulders and crouched to look into her eyes. "I was an idiot. And I know I don't deserve a second chance. Hell, the ink isn't even dry on my last disaster. I know you have no reason to believe that I've changed. But I have…because of you. I'm different because of you. I've never felt this way about anyone," he said, emphasizing the last word.

"Ben…"

"Please. Give me a chance to prove that I can be the person you believed I was and a good father to this child, a good husband to you."

She sighed. "Ben, stop." He was trying so hard to convince her of something she already knew: life would suck without him. But, "The in vitro didn't work. I'm not pregnant."

He frowned. "But the pregnancy test?"

"False positive. Dr. Chelsey says it can happen with all of the different hormones in my body."

He pulled her toward him and hugged her tight. "I'm sorry," he said, strain in his voice.

The sincerity of the gesture brought tears to her eyes once more, and while she longed to take comfort in him, in his being there, in his arms, she wasn't sure she could. She handed him the precious baby clothes. "So I'm sorry to say, but the clothes…and all of this was unnecessary."

He stared at her in disbelief. "You think I'm only here because I thought you were pregnant?"

"I'm not sure why you're here, Ben. I mean, I haven't seen or heard from you in a week. Why now?"

"Believe me, I wanted to come to you before now. Every minute, you've been on my mind and in my heart. But I had to stay focused. I had to prove to myself and everyone that I could win that cup, that I wouldn't choke under pressure this time. I won't choke under the pressure of us, either. You have to believe that. Believe in me." He took her face between his hands. "I know I can be a better man for you."

The temptation to give in, to sink into his arms and let the love she had for him ease the tension and pain in her heart was overwhelming, but unlike him, *she* was still terrified. The last few weeks, she'd opened herself up to the possibility of so much hurt and disappointment, like she'd never done before. And he'd hurt her, the way she'd believed he would. "I love you, but I'm not sure I can do this, Ben," she whispered.

He nodded. "Okay, well, tell me—what do I have to do to convince you that I'm not giving up on you, on us?"

"Ben…" Why did he have to make this so hard? What if she let him in again and he changed his mind? "I still want a baby." She knew it was true. She still wanted a family.

He pulled her in close, his eyes intense on hers. "Give me some practice, and I promise I can make that happen."

Her breath caught in her throat. Ben Westmore, confirmed bachelor, was telling her he wanted to have a baby with her? That he wanted a life with her?

"In fact, why don't we start trying right now?" In one swoop, he picked her up and headed toward the bedroom.

"Ben, you're insane," she said, but the smile she felt tugging at her lips brought an immense sense of relief in her chest. "I'm not sure I trust you." She wiggled in his arms, but he held firm.

Kicking open her bedroom door with his foot, he set her onto the bed, then knelt on the floor in front of her. The look in his eyes wasn't one she'd seen before. It wasn't filled with desire or the burning need she'd seen flashing in them before. It was pure, raw emotion—exposed and vulnerable. Ben Westmore was on his knees in front of her. The man she loved was asking for her love and forgiveness.

"Olivia, I love you, and I want to make a life with you. Not just right now, in this moment, but for always," he said softly, touching her cheek. "I promise you, taking another chance on me—on us—will be worth it."

She knew it was true. She'd never felt more loved, needed, cared for as she did with him. Her heart was so full of love for him that it erased all her fears and hesitation.

Moving closer, she wrapped her arms around his neck and stared into his eyes. "Do you always get what you want?" she whispered against his mouth, all her insecurities fading as the expression in his eyes told her everything would be okay. Better than okay.

"You tell me," he said as his lips met hers.

Asher Westmore is taking his hockey career to the next level, until an injury forces him to the sidelines. When he turns to physical therapist—and best friend—Emma Lewis for help, Asher starts to realize that the game of his career might be the game of love...

See the next page for a preview of *Maybe This Christmas*.

$\mathcal{H}$is body was getting used to the injections. The effect of the cortisone seemed to be weakening after months of abuse. Fully dressed in his hockey gear and ready to go, Asher opened his locker and retrieved the last of the prescription painkillers that he'd been resisting the urge to take all afternoon. He shook the three and a half into his hand and popped them into his mouth, chasing them down his throat with a shot of Gatorade from his water bottle.

Hopefully it would be enough to reach the numbing sensation in his limbs to prevent him limping visibly onto the ice, but not too much to throw off his other senses. He still needed his razor-sharp focus and sensory awareness.

He wasn't sure when he'd become an expert on pill-popping, and the dosing effects on his body, but his heavy reliance on the meds was starting to bother him. Before the injury, he barely took anything at all. He rarely needed anything.

But he wasn't addicted to the shit. Not yet.

After Tuesday's game, it all ends.

Luckily, the electric energy in the stadium would be enough to get him through his twenty-six minutes of ice time that evening.

Checking his phone a final time, he read the text from Emma, saying she'd arrived and wishing him luck. An emoji at the end of the text blew him a kiss and he grinned. He looked forward to her pregame text. Counted on it on his off days. He was glad she was there that evening. Having her in the stands somehow put him at ease.

Closing the locker, he reached for his helmet and swayed slightly off-balance, his shoulder falling against his teammate, lacing up on the bench next to him.

"You drunk, Westmore?" Darius joked.

No. Just probably high as a kite. He felt sweat gather on

his low back beneath his jersey as he forced himself steady. "You're not?" he retorted.

Darius laughed. "We will be." He checked the clock on the wall of the locker room. "In two hours and forty-six minutes. Do not let your brother push this game to overtime," the semiretired left wing who was hanging up his skates at the end of that season said.

"Don't sweat it. Ben's got a girlfriend now waiting for him at home. He's not allowed to stay out past eleven," Asher said, only half joking. Since winning the cup for the Avalanche that spring, Ben had visibly relaxed on the ice. Asher didn't doubt for a second that his brother's new, slightly laid back "there's more to life than hockey" attitude had to do with the lawyer he was crazy about. The one who'd almost destroyed his life earlier that year. How easy love made his brothers blind to reality.

Sticks before chicks used to be the bro code between the three brothers…one the other two had forgotten. Not Asher.

But right now, he didn't care what was causing Ben's lack of competitiveness, as long as his brother didn't fuck with him that evening.

Ten minutes later, as he skated out onto the ice, it didn't matter that he wore the opposing team's colors. The fans, his friends and family and neighbors, were all on their feet. There was Emma cheering and smiling at him from the seat always reserved for her behind the players' box. Immediately, the tension in his shoulders eased as he winked at her.

The reception whenever he played in Denver was always positive, but that evening the significance of the game was felt throughout the arena. He swallowed hard, raising a quick hand to acknowledge the love, feeding off the energy of their support, but knowing he needed to temper his own excited nerves to get through this game.

Nine hundred and ninety-nine games weren't enough.

His blades cut across the ice, and he felt the painkillers taking affect. The throbbing sensation in his knee subsided as he made several warm-up laps around the rink. Still slightly off-balance, he shook his head, hoping to knock his equilibrium back into place.

Taking his place in line with his team as the lights dimmed, he barely heard the words of the anthem, desperate to get this game started.

Desperate to get it over with.

The first period, he played six minutes and was relieved to have to sit out a two-minute penalty for the team's goalie. Less time on the ice, less chance of injury. He hated his new chickenshit mentality, but he was too close to a professional career goal to throw it away on overeager cockiness.

He'd spent years proving himself in the sport, they could cut him some slack that evening if he played at less than 110 percent.

Coming back for a second period, the score was still nothing and the pacing of the play was more intense. The Devils' coach could be heard shooting the same sentiments as the Avalanche's: *steal the damn puck, head up, pay fucking attention to the play!* The two teams were neck and neck for points in the league so far that season, and the Devils had a very real shot of stealing the Stanley Cup away from the Avalanche that year. Not that his brother's team was letting the trophy leave Colorado without a good fight.

Asher's legs felt heavy as he pushed through his second shift, and his mind was foggy. Skating through a haze, he climbed back over the boards as the lines changed, grateful for the break.

But when the Avalanche sent Ben out on a double shift, his coach gave him the nod. "Westmore, get back out there."

Shit. He'd been hoping for a few minutes to calm his thundering heart rate and clear his head. Most games, he loved facing off with Ben. He knew his brother's few weaknesses on the ice better than anyone, and it made for exciting hockey for fans to watch the two of them square off, but that evening, he lacked enthusiasm…and energy. Damn, he was feeling drained, zapped of the adrenaline induced drive he usually thrived on.

But grabbing his stick, he was back on the ice in seconds, skating toward the puck. A Colorado right wing took a shot and he stole the biscuit, skating back toward the blue line with it. The ice beneath his skates felt far away, and he shifted his gaze to the sidelines, but the advertisements blurred in a colorful psychedelic pattern that made him blink furiously. He struggled to focus and shifted his weight as his balance swayed left.

The puck left his stick and he switched directions, moving on instinct more than anything else, as he followed the player in burgundy and steel blue back toward his net. When the offensive player passed, he intercepted and skated along the back of the net with the puck, looking for someone to pass it off to. A defensive player who longed to play offense, he was usually eager to score any chance he had, but not that evening. Right now, he wanted nothing to do with the puck. He was a liability with it.

He glanced at the time clock, desperate to hear a line change. His shift had to be coming to an end, and as soon as his ass was on the bench, he was heading into the locker rooms.

Something wasn't right. Dizziness was making him nauseous, and he could hear his heart beating in his ears, felt it pounding in his chest.

He scanned the ice. Where the hell was Ericksen? Or

Taylor? Or any other fucking teammate? He was going to black out, and there was no one to safely take this puck.

The only person he did see was his brother skating at full speed toward him, where Asher still lingered too close to the boards.

Fuck.

The hit took him clean off his feet, and the pain in his knee almost stole his consciousness. The arena lights blinded him from above as the ice below his body spun uncontrollably before his eyes shut.

The last thing he saw was his brother's cocky grin replaced with a look of concern.

Asshole took me out.

Want a sneak peek of Owen's love story?
See the next page for a preview of *Maybe This
Summer*!

*P*aige glanced at the old jukebox between the booths. "Does that still work?"

"Yes ma'am…" He reached into his pocket for several coins. Quite an inflation in price from the quarter price listed on the machine, covered by the new sticker. "It has everything from the classics of its day to modern noise from twelve-year-old YouTube sensations. What song can I play you?"

"Oh no. I'm good. I was just curious."

"Come on. If I choose the song, it's going to be a sappy country ballad that will make your ears bleed."

She raised an eyebrow. "Country? Really?"

"What? I'm a sensitive, truck-driving, momma-lovin' kind of guy." He winked as he stood. "So…what's it going to be?"

She sighed as she stood and followed him to the jukebox. "Okay, let's see." Leaning over, she peered inside to read the selections.

And damn, if he didn't try so very hard not to let his eyes wander to her ass, but he was only a man. One completely taken by this woman whose hard exterior of a shell seemed to be chipping away faster than he'd expected, as the time passed.

His eyes widened. Shit. Time. He checked his watch. Ben and Olivia and his blind date for the evening would be there soon. "Hey, why don't we go somewhere else? Are you hungry?"

She shrugged. "I'm sure they have food here," she said.

Damn. She was agreeing to stick around even longer. He would be leaping over the freaking moon if shit wasn't about to hit the fan any minute. He needed to text Ben…try to reroute them away from here.

"Okay, I've got one," Paige said, pointing to Bob Marley's "Stir It Up."

If anyone could help him seduce a woman, it was Bob Marley. Sliding the coin into the machine, he kept one eye on the door as she made her selection.

As the soft beat started, she smiled. "I love this song."

He was in love with her smile. As she headed back toward the booth, he grabbed her hand and pulled her into him.

A slight look of intrigued panic flickered across her features. "What are you doing?" she asked as he drew her into him, wrapping his arms around her waist.

"Dancing with you. I knew if I asked, you'd say no," he said, swaying slowly to the beat.

She glanced around the bar that had gotten busier while he'd been caught up completely in her. "No one else is dancing."

"That's okay. I don't want to dance with anyone else."

She sighed, as she glanced at their feet. "This isn't exactly a dance floor."

"Any floor can be a dance floor," he said, drawing her even closer, as his hands slid a fraction lower.

She shot him a warning look as she readjusted his hands higher on her back.

But she *didn't* remove them completely. "Sorry, I felt a vibe and went for it."

She laughed. "Maybe not the right choice in songs," she said, though finally swaying in sync with him.

His gaze fell to her hips in her tight-fitting jeans and he had to force a breath. "I think it's the perfect choice in song. Now, it's our song."

"Our song?"

"Yeah. Whenever we go to a wedding and they play it, we can say 'hey, it's our song,' or when we're driving through the mountains in the winter on the way to the cabin with the kids asleep in the back and it comes on the radio, we can crank it higher and sing along to…"

"Our song?" she finished shaking her head. "You really get ahead of yourself, don't you?"

"You have no idea," he said, his gaze locked on hers. The drinks, the beat of the music, the dim lighting in that corner of the bar, her soft, sweet smile made it impossible not to want to kiss her…but he held back. Too soon too fast was not the way with this one, and that was the only speed he really knew. Not this time. This time it was her speed, her timing, he had no other choice—he was completely hooked on her.

But that didn't stop him from taking her hand and kissing it.

A conflicted look appeared on her face for just a brief second before she was leaning toward him. When her lips brushed his, his eyes widened. His grip tightened at her waist as her arms went around his neck. Her height made her perfect to kiss. He didn't need to bend at the knees or crane his neck. Her lips were soft, and she tasted like a mixture of gin and watermelon. Her hands crept up his neck and she pressed her lips to his quickly before pulling away.

Embarrassment flushed her cheeks as she touched her lips.

He was still in shock but enjoying it far too much not to take the opportunity to tease her. "That was a little forward, don't you think?"

"Well, since you'd already planned family vacations in your mind, I took a chance that you wouldn't mind," she murmured against his lips as she moved in closer again. "And maybe the alcohol and the music went to my head a little."

He touched her cheek, as they continued to sway. Never

in a million years had he expected this evening to turn out the way it was.

But a second later he knew he was screwed as her gaze wandered past him to the door. "Hey, isn't that your friend, Ben Westmore?"

ABOUT THE AUTHOR

Jennifer Snow lives in Edmonton, Alberta, with her husband and son. She writes sweet and sexy contemporary romance stories set everywhere from small towns to big cities. After stating in her high school yearbook bio that she wanted to be an author, she set off on the winding, twisting road to make her dream a reality. She is a member of RWA, the Writers' Guild of Alberta, the Canadian Authors Association, and the Film and Visual Arts Association in Edmonton. She has published more than twelve novels and novellas with many more on the way.

You can learn more at:
  JenniferSnowAuthor.com
  Twitter @jennifersnow18
  Facebook.com/JenniferSnowBooks

Fall in Love with Forever Romance

TOUGHEST COWBOY IN TEXAS
By Carolyn Brown

New York Times bestselling author Carolyn Brown welcomes you to Happy, Texas! Last time Lila Harris was home, she was actively earning her reputation as the resident wild child. Back for the summer, she's a little older and wiser...But something about this town has her itching to get a little reckless and rowdy, especially when she sees her old partner-in-crime, Brody Dawson. Their chemistry is just as hot as ever. But he's still the town's golden boy—and she's still the wrong kind of girl.

Fall in Love with Forever Romance

UNTIL YOU
By Denise Grover Swank

Tyler has always been a little too popular with women for his own
good. Ever since he and his buddies vowed to remain bachelors, Tyler
figured he was safe from temptation. Lanie and her gorgeous brown
eyes are about to prove him so, *so* wrong. Don't miss the next book
in the bestselling Bachelor Brotherhood series from Denise Grover
Swank!

Fall in Love with Forever Romance

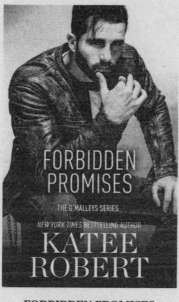

FORBIDDEN PROMISES
By Katee Robert

New York Times and *USA Today* bestselling author Katee Robert continues her smoking-hot O'Malleys series. Sloan O'Malley has left her entire world behind and is finally living a life without fear. But there's nothing safe about her intensely sexy next-door neighbor. Jude MacNamara has only ever cared about revenge, but something about Sloan tempts him . . . until claiming her puts them both in the crosshairs of a danger they never saw coming.

Fall in Love with Forever Romance

MAYBE THIS LOVE
By Jennifer Snow

Hockey player Ben Westmore has some serious skills—on and off the ice—and he's not above indulging in the many perks of NHL stardom. When a night in Vegas ends in disaster, he realizes two things: 1) it's time to lie low for a while, and 2) he needs a lawyer—fast. But the gorgeous woman who walks into his office immediately tests *all* his good intentions. Jennifer Snow's Colorado Ice series is perfect for fans of Lori Wilde and Debbie Mason!